超好學

# 用**365**個單字
## 讓英文會話變簡單

全書MP3
壓縮檔下載

（請參照下一頁的說明）

**如果您沒有可掃描 QR 碼的行動設備，請輸入以下網址下載全書音檔：**

https://drive.google.com/file/d/<u>1</u>Ba6H-eduSH<u>l</u>vyP36VNQT44<u>l</u>Vr4domzsr/
　　　　　　　　　（數字 1）　　　（小寫 L）　　　　（小寫 L）

**iPhone、iPad 使用者注意事項：**

1. 需升級至 iOS 13 以上，方可正常下載全書 mp3 壓縮檔並進行解壓縮。
　較舊版本 iOS 的使用者僅可使用個別單元的 QR 碼分別聆聽。

2. 掃描個別單元 QR 碼時，如網頁播放器無法正常運作，可使用以下方法解決：

**方法1**

1. 點擊網址列左邊的顯示方式切換鈕。

2. 點擊「切換為電腦版網站」後，即可使用網頁上的播放器聆聽音檔。

**方法2**

1. 點擊網頁上方的下載圖示。

2. 選擇「檢視」，即可播放音檔；選擇「下載」則會儲存檔案。

# PART 1 基礎篇
## 簡單好用的會話規則！

| 29 push | 30 put |
|---|---|
| 31 run | 32 send |
| 33 show | 34 shut |
| 35 sit | 36 start |
| 37 stop | 38 take |
| 39 talk | 40 think |
| 41 throw | 42 walk |
| 43 wear | 44 work |
| 45 write | |

## CHAPTER 3　用 56 個核心句型，勇敢面對老外

1　Coffee, please.　請來杯咖啡。

2　Please help me.　請幫幫我。

3　Let's go.　我們走吧。

4　Let's go for it.　我們放手一搏吧。

5　Let me help you.　讓我來幫你。

6　Let me explain it.　讓我來說明。

7　Do you think he's smart?　你認為他聰明嗎？

8　Do you know the time?　你知道現在幾點嗎？

9　Do you mean you hate me?　你是說，你討厭我嗎？

10　What do you mean by that?　你說的話是什麼意思？

11　Do we have to work?　我們必須去工作嗎？

12　We don't have to go.　我們可以不用去。

13　Do you have anything to do?　你有什麼事要做嗎？

14　Do you have anything to open this lock?
　　你有什麼工具可以開這把鎖嗎？

15　Do you want to go to the movies?　你想去看電影嗎？

16　Do you want me to help you?　你要我幫你嗎？

17　How come you don't like me?　你怎麼會不喜歡我？

18　How come?　怎麼會這樣？

⑲ How about her?　她看起來怎麼樣？

⑳ Why don't you eat some food?　你何不吃一點東西呢？

㉑ What kind of food do you like?　你喜歡吃什麼樣的食物？

㉒ What makes you so afraid?　什麼讓你這麼害怕？

㉓ What do you think of that girl?　你覺得那個女孩怎麼樣？

㉔ How do you like my clothes?　我的穿著怎麼樣？

㉕ I can't believe you said that.　我不敢相信你會這麼說。

㉖ What time do you have to go?　你什麼時候必須走呢？

㉗ Can you help me?　你能幫我一下嗎？

㉘ Can you tell me what color this is?　你能告訴我這是什麼顏色嗎？

㉙ How long is the song?　這首歌有多長？

㉚ How far is the airport?　機場有多遠？

㉛ How soon will I see you again?　我何時才會再見到你？

㉜ How often do you go shopping?　你多久去購物一次？

㉝ How much is this candy?　這個糖果多少錢？

㉞ How many friends do you have?　你有多少朋友？

㉟ How long have you been married?　你結婚多久了？

㊳ How long does it take to drive to school?　開車到學校要多久？

㊲ How do you say dog in your language?　用你的語言怎麼說「狗」？

㊳ How do you spell your name?　你的名字怎麼拼？

㊴ How do I do this?　我該怎麼做？

㊵ How can I get a good job?　怎麼做才能找到好工作呢？

㊶ Would you mind if I sit down?　你介意我坐下來嗎？

㊷ Do you mind if I borrow your car?　你介意我向你借車嗎？

㊸ Would you like some tea?　你想喝杯茶嗎？

㊹ Do you like to work for me?　你想跟著我做事嗎？

㊺ We'd better see what's up.　我們最好小心點。

㊻ You'd better hurry.　你最好快一點。

㊼ I'd like to see you.　我想見你。

㊽ I want to go home.　我要回家。

㊾ I'm not going to trust you.　我不打算相信你。

- ⑤⓪ I was just going to go for a walk. 我正要去散步。
- ⑤① I've heard about you. 我聽說過關於你的事。
- ⑤② Have you ever been to Hawaii? 你曾經去過夏威夷嗎？
- ⑤③ I've got to do something. 我應該做些事情。
- ⑤④ We've got to warn people! 我們得提醒大家！
- ⑤⑤ I don't know where to go. 我不知道該往哪裡走。
- ⑤⑥ I don't know what to do. 我不知道該做些什麼。

# PART 2 實用篇
## 用 365 個單字說盡英語會話！

 **CHAPTER 4** 不管遇見誰，招呼用語讓你自信滿滿

- ❶ How are you doing? 近來好嗎？
- ❷ What's up? 過得怎麼樣？
- ❸ Long time no see. 好久不見。
- ❹ It's been a long time. 好久不見。
- ❺ Great! 很好！
- ❻ Just fine. 還可以。
- ❼ OK. 還好。
- ❽ Not so good! 不太妙！
- ❾ This is my friend Tom. 這是我的朋友湯姆。
- ❿ I've heard so much about you. 久仰您的大名。
- ⓫ I didn't catch your name. 我沒聽清楚你的名字。
- ⓬ Bye. 再見。
- ⓭ Take care. 保重。
- ⓮ Let's keep in touch. 保持聯絡。

**CHAPTER 5** 言之有禮！贊同、反對用語說得大方  p132

❶ Can I talk to you?　我可以和你說句話嗎？

❷ Let's talk.　我們來談一談。

❸ Guess what?　你知道嗎？

❹ As you know...　你知道的…

❺ Hey, are you listening?　嘿，你有在聽嗎？

❻ Can you keep a secret?　你能保守祕密嗎？

❼ Let me repeat myself.　我再說一遍。

❽ Excuse me?　你剛才說什麼？

❾ What do you mean?　你指的是什麼？

❿ Do you know what I mean?　你懂我的意思嗎？

⓫ I don't think so.　我不這麼認為。

⓬ Uh-huh.　嗯。

⓭ Oh, look at the time!　噢，時間已經差不多了呀！

## CHAPTER 6　無論去哪裡，交通用語無敵方便

❶ Excuse me, where's the bus stop?　不好意思，請問公車站牌怎麼走？

❷ Which bus goes to Grand Park?　請問哪一路公車會到格蘭公園？

❸ What stop is next?　請問下一站是哪裡？

❹ How much?　多少錢？

❺ Is this seat taken?　這個座位有人坐嗎？

❻ After you.　你先。

❼ Airport, please.　到機場，謝謝。

❽ How much will it cost to the airport?　到機場要多少錢？

❾ Could you please send a cab over right away?
你能馬上派輛車來嗎？

❿ I'm late, please hurry.　我遲到了，請快一點。

⓫ Slow down, please.　請開慢一點。

⓬ Could you turn on the air conditioner?　請你把冷氣打開好嗎？

⓭ Can you pull over there?　可以請你在那裡停車嗎？

⓮ Fill her up, please.　請把油加滿。

⓯ Would you check my tires?　你能幫我檢查一下輪胎嗎？

⓰ Can I park here?　我可以把車子停在這裡嗎？

⓱ I need a jump　我的車子需要充電。

⓲ I'm locked out of my car.　我把車鑰匙鎖在車子裡了。

# CHAPTER 7  大快朵頤！飲食用語盡情享用

p182

1. Would you like to go out for lunch with me?
   你想和我一起出去吃午餐嗎？
2. Do you want to eat something?　要不要去吃東西？
3. Did you bring your lunch?　你帶午餐了嗎？
4. I'd like to make a dinner reservation.　我想訂晚餐的座位。
5. I have a reservation for this evening　我訂了今晚的座位。
6. Could we have a booth?　有包廂嗎？
7. How long do we have to wait?　我們得等多久？
8. I haven't decided yet.　到機場要多少錢？
9. I'd like the New York Steak.　我要一客紐約排餐。
10. Do you have any veggie plates?　有沒有素食餐點？
11. More coffee, please.　我想再多些咖啡，謝謝。
12. Doggie bag, please.　請幫我打包，謝謝。
13. Look! This meat is still pink.　你看！這肉根本沒熟。
14. Could I buy you a drink?.　我請你喝一杯如何？
15. Give me a beer.　給我一杯啤酒。
16. Here's to you!　為你乾杯！
17. Is it strong?　這酒是不是很烈？
18. Check, please.　買單，謝謝。

⑧ Mr. Shelley, please. 請找薛利先生聽電話,謝謝。

⑨ Could you tell him Sarah called? 可否轉告他莎拉來過電話?

⑩ When will he be back? 他何時會回來?

⑪ I'm sorry to call you so late. 很抱歉這麼晚打電話給你。

⑫ I think I have the wrong number. 我想我打錯電話了。

⑬ I guess I've got to go. 我想我該掛電話了。

⑭ I will call back later. 稍後再打給你。

⑮ I need the number for Pizza Hut. 請幫我查必勝客的電話號碼。

⑯ Call me at 333-3131. 打 333-3131 這個號碼聯絡我。

## WORD BOX

♥ CHAPTER 10 旅行靠自已,旅遊用語讓你信心倍增 p250

① I need a ticket to Chicago. 請給我一張往芝加哥的機票。

② I need to leave early in the morning. 我必須一早就出發。

③ How much is coach? 經濟艙的價位是多少?

④ Can I put it on reserve? 我可以預約嗎?

⑤ I need to cancel my flight. 我必須取消班機預約。

⑥ Can I get an aisle seat? 可以給我靠走道的座位嗎?

⑦ Just coffee is fine. 我只要咖啡就好。

⑧ My luggage is missing. 我的行李遺失了。

⑨ I'm here to rent a car. 我要去租一輛車。

⑩ Do you have any convertibles? 你這裡有敞篷車嗎?

⑪ I want a compact car. 我要租一輛小型車。

⑫ I'd like to check in.　我要登記住房。

⑬ I need a room for two.　我需要一間雙人房。

⑭ Give me a wake-up call at 6 o'clock.　請在六點叫我起床。

⑮ I need to check out.　我要退房。

## WORD BOX

## COOL ENGLISH

## TEST

## CHAPTER 11　禮尚往來！居家、拜訪用語最感心

❶ Dinner's ready.　晚飯做好了。

❷ What's on TV?　電視在播什麼節目？

❸ Would you stop that, please?　可以請你住手嗎？

❹ Are you gonna be home?　待會兒你會在家嗎？

❺ Can I bring anything?　要不要我帶些東西過去？

❻ I was stuck in traffic.　路上塞車。

❼ Come on in.　快進來坐。

❽ Can I take your coat?　把外套給我吧？

❾ Would you like something to drink?　喝一點飲料嗎？

❿ Well, it's getting late.　嗯，時間已經這麼晚了呀。

⓫ Would you like to stay for dinner?　要不要留下來吃晚餐？

⓬ Thank you for inviting us.　謝謝你邀請我們。

⓭ Are you all right?　你還好嗎？

⓮ You look tired.　你看起來很累。

⓯ I don't feel good.　我不太舒服。

⓰ She's pregnant.　她懷孕了。

⓱ Oh, isn't she cute?　噢，她是不是很可愛呀？

# PART 3 進階篇
## 用 1、2 個單字就能說出好英語！

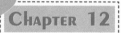 CHAPTER 12　絕對讓老外大吃一驚的 22 種最 in 英語  p298

❶　Almost.　幾乎。
❷　It's you!　原來是你呢！
❸　So what?　那又怎麼樣呢？
❹　What?　什麼？
❺　Yourself?　你呢？
❻　Relax.　別激動。
❼　No way.　不行。
❽　Forget it.　休想。
❾　Got that.　知道了。
❿　Deal?　可以了嗎？
⓫　Hold on.　等一下。
⓬　Take care.　保重。
⓭　Like what?　比如說？
⓮　Guess what?　猜猜看？

⑮ How come? 為什麼呢？

⑯ Just checking. 只是問問罷了。

⑰ It's up to you. 隨你囉。

⑱ You're kidding. 你在開玩笑吧。

⑲ Give me a break. 你得了吧。

⑳ Try some. 嚐一些看看。

㉑ I don't care. 我無所謂。

㉒ And stuff like that. 類似那些東西。

## CHAPTER 13 住過美國才知道的 22 種道地說法  p307

❶ Whatever. 什麼都可以。

❷ Ditto. 我也是。

❸ Exactly. 的確。

❹ Well. 這個嘛。

❺ Incredible! 真不可思議！

❻ Awesome! 真有趣！（了不起！）

❼ Time's up. 時間到了。

❽ Why not? 為什麼不行？

❾ Can't complain. 好得沒話說。

❿ Kind of. 有一點。

⓫ Not really. 並不全然是。

⓬ Good job. 做得好。

⓭ Same here. 我也是。

⓮ That's it. 就是那樣。

⓯ You doing okay? 你還好吧？

⓰ Who cares? 誰在乎？

⓱ It's about time. 該是時候了。

⓲ Is that clear? （我的意思）懂了嗎？

⓳ Listen up! 聽好！

⓴ No kidding. 是真的。

㉑ I appreciate it. 感謝你。

㉒ I swear. 我發誓。

## CHAPTER 14 每天一定會說到的 25 種原味英語 p316

❶ Fine. 好。

❷ Okay. 好的。

❸ Nothing. 沒什麼。

❹ Never? 從來都沒有？

❺ Great! 太好了！

❻ Sure. 好啊。

❼ Anytime. 任何時候。

❽ Thanks. 謝謝。

❾ Please. 拜託。

❿ Say again? 你說什麼？（再說一次？）

⓫ Right? 對嗎？

⓬ That's right. 是的。

⓭ No problem. 沒問題。

⓮ Not bad. 還不錯。

⓯ Of course. 當然。

⓰ Me too. 我也是。

⓱ Come on. 走吧。

⓲ Any questions? 有任何問題嗎？

⓳ Are you sure? 你確定？

⓴ I don't think so. 我不認為。

㉑ Let's go. 走吧。

㉒ I'm sorry. 我很抱歉。

㉓ Don't worry. 別擔心。

㉔ I didn't mean it. 我不是那個意思。

㉕ Really? 真的嗎？

❶ So-so. 還可以。

❷ Terrible. 糟糕透了。

❸ So? 所以呢？

❹ That's impossible. 難以置信。（那是不可能的。）

❺ That's true. 那是真的。

❻ What else? 還有其他的嗎？

❼ Not me. 不是我。

❽ Nothing much. 還不是老樣子。

❾ Got it. 知道了。

❿ After you. 你先。

⓫ Think twice. 再考慮一下。

⓬ What for? 為什麼？

⓭ Anything new? 有什麼新鮮事嗎？

⓮ What's up? 過得好嗎？

⓯ It takes time. 需要一點時間。

⓰ Ready to go? 準備好要走了嗎？

⓱ Got a minute? 有空嗎？

⓲ My mistake. 是我弄錯了。

⓳ It's okay. 沒有關係。

⓴ Bingo! 正確！

㉑ Time to go. 該走了。

㉒ Trust me. 相信我。

## COOL ENGLISH

時下美國年輕人常用的口語英文

# 簡單好用的
# 會話規則！

本書第 1 部分包括 15 種「基礎文法」，以新穎的解說方式為讀者分析英文時態的表現。45 個「基本動詞」，幫助讀者開啟英語會話之門。56 種「核心句型」，幫助讀者勇敢挑戰英文會話。文法、動詞、句型是英文會話最重要的三大支柱，想把英文會話學好，一定要用心閱讀這些單元唷！

CH 1　用 15 個基礎文法，重新打造英語實力

CH 2　用 45 個基本動詞，輕鬆學會英語會話

CH 3　用 56 個核心句型，勇敢面對老外

# Chapter 1

# 用 15 個基礎文法，
# 重新打造英語實力

　　一開始要介紹給各位的，是即便第一次接觸英文的入門讀者也能輕易融會貫通的基礎文法。可是，能確實做到這點的人卻少之又少。

　　會話，其實就是「說話」，「說話」本身的原理並不難，可是很多人在辛苦學習英文之後卻沒有真正學會「說英文的方法」。就從這裡開始，讓我們重頭來過，回顧初學英文時所看過的、聽過的，然後以「說話的原理」重新理解英文的基礎，相信各位讀者自然就能豁然開朗：「喔，原來這就是說話的原理啊！」

　　即便是英文考試得高分的讀者，若不知道如何開口說英文，很抱歉，你還是得被歸類於「初學者」。所有還處於英文入門階段的各位讀者，現在，讓我們從基礎開始扎根吧！

# ❶ I am / I'm not

## 基礎的根本，從 be 動詞出發

I am 的 am、She is 的 is、They are 的 are，和 It is 的 is，我們統稱為「be 動詞」。如下文所示，不同的主詞要搭配使用不同的 be 動詞。

I 要和 am 一起使用，例如：I am a student.（我是學生。）
He 要和 is 一起使用，例如：He is handsome.（他很帥。）
She 要和 is 一起使用，例如：She is nice.（她人很好。）
You 要和 are 一起使用，例如：You are a good teacher.（你是位好老師。）
They 要和 are 一起使用，例如：They are in the kitchen.（他們在廚房裡。）
It 要和 is 一起使用，例如：It is hot.（天氣很熱。）

## 縮寫及否定的造句方法

英文的縮寫形態如下：I am 是 I'm、He is / She is / It is 是 He's / She's / It's，You are / They are 是 You're / They're。此外，若想表達「不」或「不是」這類的否定意義，在後面加上 not 就可以了，很簡單吧！

I'm not a student.
He's not handsome.
She's not nice.
You're not a good teacher.
They're not in the kitchen.
It's not hot.

## 牛刀小試

我們已經學過 be 動詞的用法了，那麼，現在就現學現賣，一起來練習造句吧！

「天氣冷」怎麼說？ It is cold.（= It's cold.）
「我很累」怎麼說？ I am tired.（= I'm tired.）
「他現在不在家」怎麼說？ He is not home now.（= He's not home now.）
「他們是美國人」怎麼說？ They are American.（= They're American.）
「她個子高」怎麼說？ She is tall.（= She's tall.）

# ❷ I'm doing

## 只要熟悉 be 動詞，「進行式」就能朗朗上口

讓我們來看看以下句子的共同點。「我在吃飯」、「我在運動」、「我正要出門」。

你發現了沒？這裡的三個句子都是指「現在…」、「正在…」的意思。想要表達「現在正在進行某個動作」，中文有各種不同的說法，但是英文只有一種形態，即 "I'm doing" 的句型，這就是「現在進行式」。

I am eating pizza.（我正在吃比薩。）
They are fighting.（他們正在吵架。）
It is raining.（正在下雨。）

## 「做…」或「正在…」的說法

誠如讀者所見，現在進行式的基本形式是「我正在做（I'm doing）」，也就是 be 動詞（am / are / is）＋原形動詞＋ -ing。日常生活中有很多情形需要去說明某個人正在吃飯，或是正在看電視。遇到需要說明的情況，先以我在（I'm）/ 他在（He's）/ 他們在（They're）開頭，然後在原形動詞字尾（eat / watch / cook 等）加 -ing 即可。OK，我們來牛刀小試一番。

「我正在吃東西」要怎麼說？ I'm eating.
「她正在看電視」要怎麼說？ She's watching TV.
「他正在做菜」要怎麼說？ He's cooking.

## 現在進行式的否定句型是 I'm not doing

接著，我們來看看「沒在做…」的句型，也就是現在進行式的否定句。還記得嗎？稍早在前面提到過，be 動詞的否定句要在 be 動詞後面加上 not。這裡的作法也是一樣。馬上就來試試看吧！

「我沒有在吃東西」要怎麼說？ I'm not eating.
「她沒有在看電視」要怎麼說？ She's not watching TV.
「他沒有在做菜」要怎麼說？ He's not cooking.

# ③ **Are you / Are you V-ing?**

## 接下來看看如何詢問他人

我們已經學過 "I am / You are / He is / She is / They are / It is" 開頭的句子，以及 "I'm eating. / He's cooking. / She's watching TV. / They're fighting." 這些「正在進行某個動作」的現在進行式句型。接著，我們要來看看如何將這些句子換成疑問形態，也就是要來了解一下如何完成疑問句型。

疑問句是指「你在吃飯嗎」、「你的英語說得好不好」這類詢問的句型。其實作法相當簡單，我們只要把原來的句型反過來，I am 變成 Am I，He is 變成 Is he，然後在句尾加上一個問號就大功告成囉！請看看例句。

Are you tired ？（你累了嗎？）
Am I late ？（我遲到了嗎？）
Is he Japanese ？（他是日本人嗎？）
Are these your shoes ？（這雙是你的鞋嗎？）
Is it hot ？（熱嗎？）

## 現在進行式的疑問造句也一樣

跟前面一樣，現在進行式同樣可以改成疑問句，現在就請各位讀者注意看下面的例句。

Are you working ？（你在工作嗎？）
Is it raining ？（在下雨嗎？）
Is Mary crying ？（瑪麗在哭嗎？）
Are they running ？（他們在跑步嗎？）

# ④ I work / I read

## 大同小異的動詞造句法

剛才我們學過 am / are / is，這些叫做 be 動詞。不過，除了 be 動詞之外，還有很多其他的單字也叫做「動詞」，像是：喜歡、工作、唸書、吃、穿、喝、玩…等。這些動詞的造句方法其實和 be 動詞大同小異。我們來看一下這些動詞的造句方法。

I work.（我工作。）

You work very hard.（你很努力工作。）

They have a lot of books.（他們有很多書。）

She reads a book.（她看書。）

He speaks four languages.（他能說 4 種語言。）

## 一般動詞有明確的意義

上面例句當中的 work、have、read、speak 等動詞都稱為「一般動詞」，一般動詞和 be 動詞在本質上有很明顯的差異，一般動詞本身就具有明確的含義，但 be 動詞本身沒有明確的意義。想要表達「工作」、「看書」這樣具體而明確的含義時，只需要單獨使用一般動詞就可以了。

be 動詞：我是學生＝我（I）＋ 是（am）＋ 學生（a student）

一般動詞：我工作＝我（I）＋ 工作（work）

　　　　　我看書＝我（I）＋ 看書（read）

## he 和 she 後面接的一般動詞要加 -s

請注意這兩個例句："She reads a book." 和 "He speaks four languages."。這兩個句子的動詞 reads 和 speaks 都有一個 "-s"。為什麼字尾要加 -s 呢？

請各位讀者記住這些都屬於特例。he 或 she 後面應該接 reads 和 speaks 而不是 read 和 speak，至於是什麼原因我們就不用太在意了，這只不過是老外慣用的語法，我們只要會講就行了。

我工作。＝ I work.

他工作。＝ He works.

我喜歡動物。＝ I like animals.

她喜歡動物。＝ She likes animals.

# ⑤ I don't

## 我工作 / 我不工作

上一頁已經提過「我工作」這類的說法。現在，我們就來瞧瞧怎樣改成否定說法的「我不工作」。其實很簡單，讓我們回想一下，在 be 動詞的情況下我們學過 I'm / I'm not，在後面加一個表示否定的 not 就行了。那麼，一般動詞該怎麼處理呢？我們先回頭看看稍早的例句。

I like animals.（我喜歡動物。）

You work very hard.（你很努力工作。）

They have a lot of books.（他們有很多書。）

She reads a book.（她看書。）

He speaks four languages.（他能說 4 種語言。）

## 用 don't / doesn't 完成否定句

接著為各位示範將以上例句改成否定句。

I don't like animals.（我不喜歡動物。）

You don't work very hard.（你沒有很努力工作。）

They don't have a lot of books.（他們沒有很多書。）

注意！接下來就有些變化囉。

She doesn't read a book.（她沒有看書。）

He doesn't speak four languages.（他不會說 4 種語言。）

你們看出這些例句的共通性，以及它們之間的差異了嗎？

## don't / doesn't 後面接原形動詞

現在要為各位讀者整理否定句的造句方法。以上例句的共同點就是動詞前面都有 don't 或 doesn't，以及在 don't 或 doesn't 後面接的動詞都是原來的面貌（即「原形動詞」）。差異點在於 I / You / They 開頭的句子要用 don't，He / She 則是用 doesn't。這就是一般動詞的否定句型，是不是比想像中的簡單多了？讓我們小小複習一下前面學過的內容，然後再繼續新的進度。

請試著將以下的例句改成否定句。

I smoke. → _____

答 I don't smoke.

He drinks coffee. → _____

答 He doesn't drink coffee.

# ❻ Do you ...?

## 你喜歡動物嗎？

接下來，我們來試試看把一般動詞的句子改成疑問形式。各位應該還記得吧，我們在前面提到過詢問的語句稱為疑問句，若是 be 動詞語句，則 I'm 倒裝為 Am I，You're 倒裝為 Are you。這個世界上，所有的動詞幾乎都屬於一般動詞，那麼，一般動詞所形成的語句又該如何改成疑問句呢？在這裡，請重新回想一下前面看過的這 5 個例句。

I like animals.（我喜歡動物。）

You work very hard.（你很努力工作。）

They have a lot of books.（他們有很多書。）

She reads a book.（她看書。）

He speaks four languages.（他能說 4 種語言。）

## 用一般動詞造疑問句

我們把上面 5 個例句換成疑問句，試著找出共同點和差異點。

I like animals. → Do you like animals?

I work very hard. → Do you work very hard?

They have a lot of books. → Do they have a lot of books?

She reads a lot. → Does she read a lot?

He speaks four languages. → Does he speak four languages?

各位眼尖的讀者是否已經看出端倪了呢？只要很自然地用 Do 開頭，然後把 you, they, she, he 等帶入句子裡就行了。當 he 或 she 出現在語句裡時，Do 就會搖身一變成了 Does，各位明白了嗎？

## "Do you" 開頭的疑問句，是會話的必備句型

我希望各位讀者別只是一味點頭稱是，應該大聲地把前面看過的所有例句唸一次。"Do you" 開頭的疑問句型是英文會話中最基礎的必備句型，我們再多練習一下：

Do you like me?（你喜歡我嗎？）

Do you eat pie?（你吃派嗎？）

Do you play football?（你玩美式足球嗎？）

Do you have a family?（你有家人嗎？）

Do you play computer games?（你玩電腦遊戲嗎？）

# ⑦ I can

用15個基礎文法，重新打造英語實力

## 我能夠！

「我做某件事」的英文是 I do something，那麼，「我能夠做某件事」的英文要怎麼說？有沒有可以表達「能夠辦到」的動詞？沒有那種動詞。但是，有一個單字能夠幫助其他的動詞發揮這種功能，像是把「游泳」變成「能夠游泳」，「愛」變成「能夠愛」。這個了不起的單字就是 "can"，請看以下的例句。

I do it.（我做這件事。）

→ I can do it.（我能夠做這件事。）

I swim.（我游泳。）

→ I can swim.（我能夠游泳。）

## 無法單獨使用，卻能幫助其他動詞發光發亮的配角──「助動詞」

像 can 這樣協助其他動詞表達詞意的詞，我們稱為「助動詞」。換句話說，語句裡的助動詞，一定都會有一個動詞跟隨其後。助動詞包括：can（能夠）、may（可以）、must（必須）、will（將要）、should（應該）…等，我們先以 can 為重點深入探討。

You can play the piano.（你會彈鋼琴。）

You can speak English.（你會說英語。）

## Can I / Could I

從以上例句中，我們可以看到 can 後面緊接著出現動詞 play 和 speak。如果想用 can 這個句型詢問他人，應該怎麼做？還記得疑問句的造句方法嗎？沒錯，就是這樣，反過來就行了。我們來試著將上面的例句反過來看看。

Can you play the piano?（你會彈鋼琴嗎？）

Can you speak English?（你會說英語嗎？）

另外，can 的過去式是 could，可以表示「過去能夠」。用 could 造疑問句時，也經常表示禮貌的請求。

Could you play the piano?（可以請你彈鋼琴嗎？）

Could you open the door?（可以請你開門嗎？）

Could you tell me the time?（可以請你告訴我現在時間嗎？）

# ⑧ I was / I wasn't

## 現在，該是學「過去式」造句的時候了

到目前為止，我們探討了以be動詞和一般動詞完成「我是學生」、「你會彈鋼琴」等基本語法以及疑問句型。「是學生」和「彈鋼琴」這類的句子，依時間的觀點來看，說的是「當下」的情形。到現在為止，我們學的是be動詞與一般動詞的「現在式」。如果現在的我是上班族，那麼幾年前我應該是個「學生」。「我以前是個學生」的英語要怎麼說？英語的「過去式」應該怎麼表達呢？

## 用 be 動詞表達過去式

好的，我們馬上來實際挑戰看看。下面的例句要怎麼做才能夠表達出右邊的意思呢？

I am tired.（我累了。）→ 昨晚我累了。
She is 22.（她 22 歲。）→ 去年她 22 歲。
The weather is nice.（天氣不錯。）→ 昨天的天氣不錯。
You are late.（你遲到了。）→ 你昨天遲到了。

仔細看看右邊的句子，可以看出都提示著過去的狀態（昨晚 / 去年 / 昨天），所以要把句子改成過去式。

I was tired last night.（昨晚我累了。）
She was 22 last year.（去年她 22 歲。）
The weather was nice yesterday.（昨天的天氣不錯。）
You were late yesterday.（昨天你遲到了。）

## 用 be 動詞的過去式造疑問句

am 和 is 的過去式是 was，are 的過去式是 were，所以，be動詞描述過去狀態時要改成 was 或 were。那麼，我們要如何使用 was 和 were 造出疑問句？是不是和前面一樣倒裝就行了？請看以下的例句。

Were you late?（你遲到了嗎？）
→ No, I wasn't.（不，我沒有遲到。）
Were they students?（他們當時是學生嗎？）
→ No, they weren't.（不，他們並不是。）

從例句中可看出，was 的否定形態是 wasn't（ ＝ was not 的縮寫），were 的否定形態是 weren't（ ＝ were not 的縮寫），請各位記住。

# ⑨ I watched / I didn't

　　接下來，我們要看看使用一般動詞來表達過去式的方法。原理相當簡單，發生在昨天或前天、去年的事情，一律使用過去式。接下來我們把「過去時態」的一些規則做個整理歸納。

## 1. 與表示過去時間的詞語一起使用

　　表示「過去時間」的詞語，包括 yesterday（昨天）、last night（昨晚）…等，句子中如果有這些詞語出現，就必須使用過去式動詞。

I stayed home yesterday.（昨天我待在家。）

I watched TV last night.（昨晚我在看電視。）

## 2. 原形動詞字尾加 -ed

　　將動詞加以變化，就可以變成過去式。一般的作法是在原形動詞的字尾加上 "-ed"。例如：work 加 -ed 之後變成 worked，stay 加 -ed 之後變成 stayed。請看以下例句：

I worked in a bank last year.（去年我在銀行上班。）

I stayed home yesterday.（昨天我待在家。）

## 3. 非加上 -ed 的動詞，必須參考動詞表

　　上面提供的規則是在動詞字尾加上 -ed，可是有些動詞的過去式不能規律地加上 -ed，這些動詞我們稱之為「不規則動詞」。在此我就為各位舉幾個簡單的例子，例如：get 變成 got，meet 變成 met，take 變成 took…等。所有的英文字典後面都有附錄「不規則動詞表」，有需要時可以利用。以下提供簡單的例句給讀者參考：

I got up at 9:30 this morning.（今天早上我 9 點半起床。）

I took a taxi to the airport.（我搭計程車到機場。）

## 4. 過去式的否定句加 didn't

　　那麼，過去式的否定構句呢？很簡單，don't 和 doesn't 的過去式都是 didn't。來，試著把上面的例句改成否定句吧！

I didn't get up at 9:30 this morning.（今天早上，我沒有在 9 點半起床。）

I didn't take a taxi to the airport.（我沒有搭計程車去機場。）

# ⑩ I was doing

　　相信各位讀者都還記得表示「進行當中」的句型是 be ＋ V-ing，而它在文法上的名稱是「現在進行式」。在這裡，我們要對「過去正在進行」的事情，也就是「過去進行式」作一番了解。不用記太多，只要記得過去進行式只有下列兩種：

## 1. 過去進行式是 was / were ＋ V-ing

　　過去進行式的句型，是 be 動詞的過去式 was / were ＋ V-ing。

## 2. 「當⋯的時候，正在⋯」的句子使用過去進行式來表達

　　過去進行式的句型，其實只要記得「當⋯的時候，正在⋯」這個句型就足夠了。我要先提醒各位讀者，「當⋯的時候」的句型是用 "when" 來開頭。請仔細看以下兩個例句：

I was eating dinner when my friend came.
（當朋友來我家的時候，我正在吃晚餐。）
I was sleeping when the phone rang.
（當電話鈴響的時候，我正在睡覺。）

　　想要表達「當時正在」吃晚餐，要說 was eating；表達「當時正在睡覺」則是說 was sleeping。理解了之後，是不是覺得很簡單呢？

## 「過去式」和「過去進行式」的句子裡，一定會出現表達「過去時間」的詞語

　　過去進行式的考題不但會出現在各種口試項目中，在檢定考試或托福考試中也是經常出現的座上客。即便無關乎考試，我們最好還是了解這個句型才不至於臨場詞窮。另外，過去進行式跟過去時態一樣，在句子裡一定會出現表示過去時間的詞語，希望各位讀者能夠謹記在心。最後，我們來練習一下過去進行式的句型：

1. 昨天 11 點 30 分時，你正在看電視。

_____

2. 當我們出門時，外面正在下雨。

_____

答　1）You were watching TV at 11:30 yesterday.
　　2）It was raining when we went out.

28

# ⑪ I have done

## 「完成式」只不過是老外的習慣性説法

　　英文「完成式」的用法，是所有英文時態中公認最難懂的部分。不過，完成式的用法其實只是老外一種習慣的說法。想要學好另一個國家的語言，只要把該國人說話時的「口頭禪」學起來就對了。沒完沒了地追究這樣說的理由，也不一定有幫助。接下來，我們要針對「完成式」這個老外的口頭禪，具體研究一下到底怎麼用、什麼時機用，透過例句直接看個明白。請各位專心閱讀以下的說明。

## 現在完成式的句型是「have ＋動詞的過去分詞」

　　現在完成式的句型是「have ＋動詞的過去分詞」，大多數動詞的過去分詞和過去式都是一樣的，只要在字尾加 "-ed" 就可以了。不能加 -ed 的不規則動詞，請參照字典的「不規則動詞列表」，看看過去分詞長什麼樣子。現在，請各位看一下以下的例句。

I have lost my passport.（我已經把護照弄丟了。）

She has gone to bed.（她已經就寢了。）

I have bought a new car.（我已經買了一輛新車。）

## 「過去式」和「現在完成式」有什麼不同

　　從以上的例句可以看出，現在完成式所表達的含義與過去時態並沒有明顯的不同。若真要打破沙鍋問到底的話，I have lost my passport.（現在完成式）的意思是指「護照已經不見了，到現在都還沒有找到」；而 I lost my passport.（過去式）則是指「護照不見了」，但是從句子中，看不出有沒有找回來，所以在語意上有些許的差別。

　　還是搞不懂嗎？你覺得這不算是重要的差異，也認為沒必要過度在意這一點嗎？我也這麼想！因為，這都只是老外的習慣說法。既然他們都這麼用，我們只需要如法炮製就行了。

　　關於「完成式」就不要追究太多了。偷偷告訴大家一個小祕訣：只要熟練完成式幾種固定常用的說法，你就會覺得完成式變得很簡單喔。（往後的章節中，也會陸續探討這類句子。）

## ⑫ Have you ever ...?

### 最具代表性的「完成式」句型：Have you ever ...?

　　想要學會完成式的用法，不妨先征服「最具代表性的完成式句型」，再繼續了解其他的部分。需要向某人問起「你曾經…過嗎」的時候，我們可以使用 "Have you ever ...?" 這個現在完成式句型。不多說，直接透過例句讓各位讀者看個明白。

Have you ever been to Japan?（你曾經到過日本嗎？）
Have you ever played golf?（你曾經打過高爾夫球嗎？）
Have you ever read this book?（你曾經讀過這本書嗎？）

### 用「現在完成式」句型詢問他人

　　接下來，我們試著從上面三個例句中找出共同點。首先，每一句都有「你曾經…過嗎」的含義。然後，Have you ever 後面接的動詞都是過去分詞（been / played / read）。因此，若想用英語問別人「你曾經…過嗎」，只要記得 Have you ever ...? 或是 Have you ...? 這兩個句型就可以了。記得動詞一定要用過去分詞的形態唷。

### 用「現在完成式」回答

　　如果有人用上面例句的形式問我們，應該怎麼回應呢？

Yes, I have. / No, I haven't.（是的，我去過。/ 沒有，沒去過。）
I have been to Japan many times.（我去過日本許多次。）
I've read it twice.（我讀過兩次。）

　　像這樣用現在完成式句型回答就行了。你說太難了啊？什麼也別管了，只要大聲唸 100 遍，把它背起來就行了。有哪一個英語句型是不用背的？那麼，我們就來複習一下吧！

1. 你到過佛羅里達嗎？

_____

2. 我沒有去過美國。

_____

答　1）Have you ever been to Florida?
　　2）I've never been to America.

# ⑬ I have done / I did

## 讓我們明確分辨「現在完成式」與「過去式」的方法

到目前為止，我們學過「現在完成式」這個老外的習慣語法，以及「曾經⋯過嗎？」、「曾經⋯過」等實際可以運用的問答說法。在結束這個章節之前，我們最後再針對容易讓人混淆的「現在完成式」與「過去式」，介紹一個可以明確分辨的方法。請各位讀者仔細觀察以下兩組例句，比較句子的內容。

## 「現在完成式」有這些説法

下面的例句是現在完成式的用法。不管換成怎麼樣的說法，只會稍微變化含義，但仍舊是完整的完成式。

I have been to Europe
- many times.（我去過歐洲許多次。）
- several times.（幾次）
- a couple of times.（兩次）
- once.（一次）
- once in my life.（這輩子一次）

I have never been to Europe.（我從來沒去過歐洲。）

## 「過去式」有這些説法

接下來是過去式，同樣是怎麼變化都保有完整的過去式含義。

I was in Europe
- last year.（我去年在歐洲。）
- three years ago.（三年前）
- in 1998.（在 1998 年）
- when I was ten years old.（在我十歲時）

## 曾經做過幾次 vs 過去某個時間點做過

想分清楚這兩個時態其實很簡單，現在完成式表示「曾經做過⋯」的句型通常都會附帶有「幾次」含義的用詞；而過去式表示「做過⋯」的句型則會附帶有「過去時間」含義的用詞。換句話說，如果句子裡面有表示「幾次」或是「過去時間」等的用詞，我們就可以很輕易地分辨出句子的時態。下面兩個例句是錯誤的說法，若各位讀者能夠明辨這兩個時態的用法錯在哪裡，就表示你真的已經學會過去式和現在完成式的重要分別了。

I have been to Europe last year.（x）

I was in Europe many times.（x）

# ⑭ Be V-ing tomorrow

## 「現在進行式」也可能表示未來含義

我們在前面的章節學過如何使用現在進行式的句型來表達「現在正在…」的含義，例如：They're playing tennis in the park.（他們正在公園裡打網球。）可是，有時候老外會使用 "Ann is playing tennis tomorrow." 這樣的句子，但現在進行式的句子怎麼會加上「明天」這樣表示未來的字呢？這樣的用法的確會讓人一頭霧水，如果直接把句子翻譯成「明天安正在打網球」，聽起來實在很怪…

不管是拿我們學過的文法來看，或是從語言的一般分析來判斷，這句話都是不通順的。但是，老外卻習慣這種說法，會不會其中隱藏著某種規則呢？讓我們看看以下的例句，仔細找出端倪。

## 「現在進行式」＋「未來的時間」＝「未來含義的語句」

I'm not working next week.（下週我不工作。）
Are you meeting Bill this evening?（今晚你要去見比爾嗎？）
What are you doing this weekend?（這個週末你打算做什麼呢？）
I'm not going out tonight.（今晚我不會外出。）

以上例句都是老外經常使用的日常生活用語。這些例句中的 next week、this evening、this weekend、tonight 都是表示未來時間的詞語，因此，句子就變得有未來含義了。

換句話說，現在進行式的句子中，如果加上表示「未來（明天、下週、明年）」的詞語，就可以用來表示「將來打算做哪些事」的含義。各位也可以自己練習看看。

1. 明天你打算做什麼呢？

_____

2. 今晚我要待在家裡。

_____

3. 琳達星期五要打網球。

_____

答　1）What are you doing tomorrow?
　　2）I'm staying at home tonight.
　　3）Linda is playing tennis on Friday.

# ⑮ I'm going to / I will

## 用「be going to」表達未來語氣

在英語中，想要表達「將要…」或「打算…」的說法時，用的是 "be going to ..." 的句型。也就是說，"be going to ..." 的句型可用來表達未來將要做或將要發生的事。先別管拖泥帶水的說明了，讓我們直接透過以下的例句稍微練習一下，你就會懂了。

Pam is going to sell her car. （潘打算賣掉她的車。）

It's going to rain. （將要下雨了。）

I'm going to buy some books tomorrow. （明天我打算去買一些書。）

## 「不打算…」的句型是 "be not going to"

"I'm going to" 的否定說法是 "I'm not going to"，而且是老外常用的日常生活用語，既然講到了我們就多唸幾次來熟悉這種句型，請仔細看以下例句。

I'm not going to help you. （我不打算幫你。）

I'm not going to lie to you. （我不打算騙你。）

I'm not going to fight. （我不打算打架。）

I'm not going to trust you. （我不打算相信你。）

I'm not going to hurt you. （我不打算傷害你。）

## "be going to" 和 "will"，任君取用

原則上，"be going to" 和 "will" 都可以用來表達未來式，will 的用法類似助動詞 can 的用法，所以，在後面加上原形動詞就可以表達未來的含義了。

"be going to" 和 "will" 幾乎沒什麼差別，有些人堅持一定要分清楚兩者之間的差異，但這在「口語英語」裡並不是絕對必要的。因為，就算用 "will" 替代 "be going to" 也不會妨礙語句的通順。

看看下面的兩個句子吧，"I'm going to buy some books tomorrow." 與 "I will buy some books tomorrow."，對一般人來說，誰有辦法真的很明確地說明這兩句的差異呢？這個艱難的部分就留給語言學家去傷腦筋吧，我們只要挑自己認為方便的句型來盡情發揮就行了。

# Chapter 2

# 用 45 個基本動詞，輕鬆學會英語會話

　　只要認識了基本動詞，會話就難不倒你了！這是為什麼呢？嘿嘿…會話的基礎就是動詞呀！因此，即便只知道基本動詞的用法，能運用在簡單的溝通上也已經足夠了。

　　接下來為各位整理英語會話必備的 45 個動詞。只要了解這 45 個動詞正確的用法，各位就能說得一口簡單的英語會話。打好會話的基礎之後，要再學習進階的會話就不再是難事了。

　　不厭其煩地向各位再強調一次，請停止背誦或鑽研那些會讓人一個頭兩個大的複雜單字，先以簡單的、能夠現學現賣的簡單動詞為主。在學習一個動詞時，請務必多熟練一、兩個跟該動詞有關的基本句型。相信很快地，各位就會深深體會到自己的英文從「基礎」開始蛻變的驚喜。

# ①ask

02-01.mp3

說到動詞 ask，大家就會聯想到 question 這個單字。「問我吧」的英文說法是 "ask me"，「問某件事」可以說 "ask something"。如果要表達有想問的問題，則可以說 have a question。

## Ask me.
**問我吧。**

A: Hey, John. I have a question. 約翰，我有個問題想問你。
B: Okay, ask me. 好的，問吧。

## Can I ask you something?
**我可以問你一個問題嗎？**

這是大家普遍使用的疑問句型，若想背誦與 ask 有關的句型，一開始知道這個句型的用法也就足夠了。"May I ask you something?" 也是常用的句型，最好熟記。

A: Can I ask you something? 我可以問你一個問題嗎？
B: Yes, what is it? 好的，想問什麼呢？
A: Do you love me? 你愛我嗎？
B: Of course, I love you. 那還用說，我愛妳。

---

### 還有這種說法唷！

What did you want to ask me? 你想問我什麼呢？

I wanted to ask you about that. 我想問你關於那件事的問題。

＊想問「有關」某件事情的問題要用 about。

Ask your doctor for some pain pills. 向你的醫生要一些止痛劑。

＊這裡提到的 ask 是指「要求」的意思。請各位務必記住，「要求某事物」時一定要用 for。pain pill 指的是「止痛劑」。

# ² be

在這裡,我們要學習 be 這個字。首先,大家所稱的助動詞 can、will 和 may 的後面都可以接原形動詞 be。不懂嗎?先別急著打破沙鍋問到底,我們只需要知道 will be、can be、may be 這三種用法,分別表達「將是、可能是、也許是」的意思。

## Be nice.
**友善一點吧。**

A: Be nice to your brother.  對妳的哥哥友善一些吧。

B: I'm being nice.  我對他很好了。

A: You're calling him names.  妳在辱罵他耶。

＊ call someone names" 意思是「辱罵某人」。

## I want to be a doctor.
**我想要成為一名醫生。**

若將來的志願是當個醫生,英文可以說 "I want to be a doctor."。若想當老師,則要說 "I want to be a teacher."。有關 "I want to ..." 這個句型,我們會在稍後詳加討論。這裡我們只要對「成為某個人物時用 be」這件事有概念就可以了。

A: I want to be a doctor. 我想要成為一名醫生。

B: You dropped out of school. 妳退學了啊。

A: Maybe I'll get back to school. 也許我會重回學校唸書。

＊退學,特別是進入大學就讀之後,由於成績不好被學校退學的情況稱為 drop out of school。此外,我們通常把大學叫做 university 或 college,但是也可以很簡單地稱之為 school。

### 還有這種說法唷!

Don't be silly. 別傻了。＊這裡的 be 在發音前會有稍稍停頓的感覺。

I can be up early. 我能早起。

＊除了上面例句的這種說法,也可以說 "I can get up early.",不過,大部分的美國人都是說 "I can be up early. ",請各位牢記。

# ❸ bring

02-03.mp3

　　英語的說法裡，不管是用說的、用聽的、用寫的，只要用到 bring 這個字，一律就是指「帶來、拿來」的意思。字典裡對這個字的解釋都太過繁雜了，所以建議各位不需要太在意字典上所看到的內容，只需要記得此一簡單的意思就夠了。因為，這已足夠用來應付一般英語會話。

## Bring me a cup of coffee.
**給我一杯咖啡。**

A: Can I get you anything? 我可以給你些什麼嗎？
B: Bring me a cup of coffee. 給我一杯咖啡。
A: I'll bring it right out. 馬上來。

## Can I bring you anything?
**我能為你準備些什麼嗎？**

　　當然，讀者也可以用 shall 替代 can 說 "Shall I bring you anything?"。各位加油！

A: Can I bring you anything? 我能為你準備些什麼嗎？
B: I'm fine, thanks. 不用了，（我很好，）謝謝。
A: Are you sure? 你確定嗎？
B: Yes, I'm sure. 是的，我確定。

### 還有這種說法喔！

Don't bring your brother with you. 別帶你哥哥一起來。
＊想要表達「和某人一起」就使用 "with" 來表示。
Bring over some beer. 帶些啤酒來。
＊通常，若是被交代要帶來「某些東西」可以只用 bring，再加上 over 則有強調的意味。

37

# ⁴ call

02-04.mp3

　　如果出現 call 這個字，有十之八九是指「打電話」的意思。那麼，其餘的十之一二是什麼呢？是指「叫喚姓名」、「呼叫某人」的意思。換句話說，只要說到「打電話給某人」，一律用 "call" 來表示就可以了。

## Call me tonight.
**今晚打電話給我。**

A: Call me tonight. 今晚打電話給我。
B: What time is good for you? 幾點打好呢？
A: Call me around 7 o'clock. 大概 7 點鐘。

## Can I call you?
**我可以打電話給你嗎？**

　　當然，也可以用 may 替代 can 說 "May I call you?"，不過，想跟老外約會，如果用這麼直接的說法，可能要吃一大碗閉門羹喔。

A: Can I call you? 我可以打電話給你嗎？
B: Why? 為什麼？
A: I like you, and I would like to call you. 因為我喜歡你，我想和你通電話。

＊假設一對男女，有人開口向對方說了 "Can I call you?"，但是落花有意流水無情，對此沒什麼興趣的話，反問 "Why?" 會是比較好的回應。不過，要是我們聽到心儀的對象這麼說，應該會點頭如搗蒜地馬上答應對方吧！這時我們可以回答 "Sure."、"Okay."、"What time?"。

### 還有這種說法唷！

Call up Brian. 打電話給布萊恩。

＊在英語會話中，打電話給某人的說法是 call 後面接 up。

Call Joe. It's time for dinner. 叫一下喬吧，晚餐時間到了。

＊這裡所提及的 call 就是屬於十之八九之外的那一、二，是「叫喚」的意思。

# ⑤ **catch**

02-05.mp3

　　一說到 catch，許多人都以為它只有「抓住或接住」的意思，其實，catch 還有另一個含義，「趕上」延後的工作或「追上」課業進度時也都會用 catch 這個字。另外，相信大家經常遇到，有人得了感冒時會說 "catch a cold"。

## Catch the ball!
### 接球！

A: Hey, catch the ball! 嘿，接球囉！
B: Where is it? 球在哪裡？
A: Over there. Can't you see that? 那裡啊，妳沒看見嗎？
B: No, I can't. 我沒看見耶。

## Let me catch up!
### 等等我呀！

　　除了趕工作和趕課業以外，跟上某人的步伐時也用 catch。

A: Let me catch up! 等等我呀！
B: We won't slow down. 我們不可以慢下來。
A: Then how am I going to catch up? 那我要怎麼趕上呢？

＊番茄醬媽媽和番茄醬小孩正在努力趕路，眼見番茄醬小孩愈走愈落後，番茄醬媽媽就對番茄醬小孩說 "Hey, catch up!"，意思是「快點趕上來」。看到這裡，若有讀者會心一笑，那就表示這位讀者懂得這種美式幽默，就快變成半個「美國人」了。

### 還有這種說法唷！

Catch me if you can! 如果你有本事就來抓我啊！

I need to catch up on my work. 我必須趕上我的工作進度。

I heard you caught a cold. 我聽說你感冒了。

39

# ⁶check

02-06.mp3

　　檢查某件事或某種物品都可以用 "check" 這個字。醫生會 check 病患的狀況，我們會開信箱 check 郵件，查看電視節目表也是 check。

## I'll check.
**我來檢查一下。**

A: Is Pete home? 彼特在家嗎？
B: Just a second. I'll check. 等一等，我去看看。
A: Thanks. 謝謝。

＊若想要詢問「某人在不在家」，只要簡單地用「Is ＋人名＋ home?」就可以了。

## Check out that girl.
**看那個女孩。**

　　要表示在酒吧或某個派對上打量美女或帥哥的舉動，可以把 out 放在 check 後面，用 "check out" 來表達。

A: Check out that girl. 看那個女孩。
B: She's married. 她已經結婚了呀。
A: That's okay. I don't mind! 那有什麼關係，我不介意啊！
B: Her husband might. 她的丈夫可能會介意。

### 還有這種說法唷！

Check channel four. 看第 4 頻道播什麼節目。

Check up on your patient. 巡視一下你的病人。

Check out, please. 退房，謝謝。

＊這句話在 hotel 使用率非常高唷。

# ⑦ close

02-07.mp3

通常「關上」門窗或是法院將申請案件「結案」時會用到這個字。用不著記一大堆繁雜的含義，只要記得 close 簡單的意思是「關上」，就不怕在說英語時出洋相，應付簡單的會話也不會有問題了。

## Close the door.

把門關上。

A: Close the door for me. 幫我把門關上。

B: I'm not your servant. 我不是你的傭人。

A: It's a simple request. 又不是什麼大不了的事。

＊ "simple request" 是指向對方提出微不足道的「請求」。

## The case is closed.

那件訴訟案已經結案了。

close 可以用來表示一件訴訟案或是會談「關上」了，也就是「結束」的意思。

A: Your Honor, may I ask you something? 法官，我可以問妳一件事嗎？

B: Sorry, the case is closed. 對不起，這件訴訟案已經結案了。

A: What?! 怎麼會呢？

### 還有這種說法唷！

I closed the window. 我把窗戶關上了。

Close your mouth when you chew. 咀嚼的時候嘴巴閉起來。

This conversation is closed. 這個會談結束了。

# <sup>8</sup>come

02-08.mp3

come 加 out 或 down，就能呈現稍微不同的含義，不過，根本不需要去顧慮那麼多，只要了解基本含義就夠了。這個字可以用來使喚看起來好欺負的軟腳蝦，用手指著那人的鼻子很不屑地說 "Come!"。可是，這麼做的話，很可能會被打吧？呵呵。

## Come here.
**過來。**

A: Come here. 到這裡來。
B: Why should I? 為什麼？
A: I need to talk to you. 我有話跟妳說。

## Are you coming to my apartment?
**你要不要到我的公寓來玩？**

一般來說，大家都以為像 "Are you coming ..." 這種句型在文法上屬於現在進行式，其實偶爾會有例外的用法。就像上面開頭的例句，這個句型也可以用來表示未來。

A: Are you coming to my apartment? 你要不要到我的公寓來玩？
B: Yes, I'll be there later. 好啊，我等一會兒過去。
A: Okay, I'll be waiting. 好的，我等你。

---

### 還有這種說法唷！

Come over sometime! 有空來坐坐吧！

Come over here sometime! 有空就到這兒來吧！

* over 有「越過」的意思，come over 是「過來」的意思，更廣義的含義可以用來表示「拜訪」的意思。

# ⑨ **cover**

02-09.mp3

　　即使是三歲小孩，如果學過一點英文，應該也知道這個單字。這個字有「蓋住」的意思，替孩子蓋棉被時，或是打哈欠時以手摀住嘴巴的動作，都可以使用 "cover" 這個動詞來表達。

## Cover the window with paper.

**用紙蓋住窗戶。**

A: Cover the window with paper. 用紙蓋住窗戶。
B: Is that so the paint doesn't get on it? 是為了不要沾到油漆嗎？
A: You got it. 妳答對了。

## What are you trying to cover up?

**你試著在隱瞞什麼？**

　　看警匪動作片時一定會出現 "cover" 這個字，此時的 "cover" 可以有兩種含義。其一是「隱瞞」事實，另一個是「掩護」的意思。在本例句中是用來表示「隱瞞」的意思。

A: What are you trying to cover up? 你試著在隱瞞什麼？
B: I have nothing to hide. 我沒什麼好隱藏的。
A: I don't believe you. 我不相信你。

### 還有這種說法唷！

Cover me. 掩護我。

Cover the baby with a blanket. 幫寶寶蓋件毯子。

We'll need to cover up our mistake. 我們必須掩飾所犯的錯誤。

# 10 cut

02-10.mp3

漢堡太大了一個人吃不完，要求切成一半的時候可以說 "Would you cut in half?"。不論是將某樣物品切成一半或切成塊狀，都可以用 cut 來表示。當然，cut 也有當俗語用，表示「吵死了」、「閉嘴」的意思。

## Cut this for me.
**請幫我切。**

A: Cut the carrots for me, please. 請幫我切這些紅蘿蔔。
B: What should I use? 該用什麼切呢？
A: A knife, of course. 當然是用菜刀。

## Cut it out.
**閉嘴。**

美國的年輕人常用 cut 這個字來表示「閉嘴」。這時候通常要加 out。這個用法必須考慮場合與對象才不會落得用字不當的後果。

A: I heard your girlfriend is a dog! 我聽說你的女朋友是個恐龍！
B: Cut it out! 閉嘴！
A: I'm just kidding. 我只是開玩笑而已。

＊在美國，成績不好的學生和相貌醜陋的女人都被稱為「dog」。此外，若是因為說錯話惹得對方生氣時，可以說 "I'm just kidding." 或是 "I'm just joking." 來化解尷尬。

### 還有這種說法唷！

I cut myself with the knife. 我用刀割傷了自己。

Cut this piece of paper in half. 把這張紙裁成兩半。

Cut it out. You're bothering me. 閉嘴，你把我煩死了。

# ⑪do

02-11.mp3

　　do 這個傢伙，有許多人因為害怕它而學不會怎麼用。其實，用不著把它想得很難，只要很有自信地用 do 完成疑問句就 OK 啦。do 開頭的疑問句後面遇到主詞 he 或 she，則必須用 does，各位讀者明白了嗎？

## Do you like me?
你喜歡我嗎？

A: Do you like me? 你喜歡我嗎？

B: As a friend. 像朋友一樣的喜歡。

A: Not more than that? I like you a lot. 沒有更多的喜歡嗎？我很喜歡你。

## Do you take this man to be your husband?
妳願意接受這個男人成為妳的丈夫嗎？

　　這是在婚禮上牧師為了證婚而向新娘提出的問題，先知道一下，或許將來的異國婚禮會用得上呢。哈哈哈。

A: Do you take this man to be your husband?

　　妳願意接受這個男人成為妳的丈夫嗎？

B: I do. 我願意。

A: I now pronounce you husband and wife. 我現在宣佈你們成為夫妻。

＊就算是國際婚禮，若不是在美國就可能沒機會用到這個例句，可是，誰知道呢？先記下來，搞不好真的有機會舉行一場異國婚禮呢！另外，pronounce 是「宣佈、公佈」的意思。

### 還有這種說法唷！

Do you play basketball? 你玩籃球嗎？

Does your girlfriend go to our school? 你的女朋友是我們學校的學生嗎？

Do you eat meat? 你吃肉嗎？

# <sup>12</sup> drive

02-12.mp3

駕駛所有能夠移動的物體，這個動作就叫 drive，但僅限有 4 個輪子的物體。如果要表達正在開車，英文可以說 "I'm driving."。我會開車就說 "I know how to drive." 或是 "I can drive."。除了開車，讓他人「搭便車」也可以用 drive 這個動詞。

## Can you drive?
### 你會開車嗎？

A: Can you drive? 妳會開車嗎？
B: Yes, but I don't have a license. 會啊，不過我沒有駕照。
A: Then you cannot drive. 那麼妳就不能開車。

＊原則上駕駛執照稱為 driver's license，但是也可以像前面的例句簡短地說 license.

## You're a fast driver.
### 你開車速度很快。

fast driver 還不到飆車族的程度，但指的就是開車開得非常快的人。各位讀者，你是 slow driver 嗎？還是 fast driver 呢？

A: You're a fast driver. 你開車速度很快。
B: Does the speed bother you? 速度讓妳不安了嗎？
A: No, I like it. 不，我覺得很棒。

＊「使人不安」、「使人驚慌」、「令人厭煩」這些的英文說法是 bother。建議各位讀者把它記起來，保證不會後悔的。

### 還有這種說法唷！

Do you drive well? 你的駕駛技術好嗎？

Can you drive me downtown? 你可以載我到市區嗎？

You're driving too fast. 你開得太快了。

# ⑬ eat

02-13.mp3

　　eat 只有一種含義，不管是吃植物還是吃動物都是「吃」的意思。還有另一個大家熟知的動詞也有「吃」的意思，就是 "have"。不過，「吃」這個意思的元祖就是 eat。

## Time to eat.
用餐時間到了。

A: Time to eat. 開飯了。

B: I'm not hungry. 我不餓耶。

A: I cooked for you! 我為妳煮的耶！

B: I'm sorry. I'll eat it later. 對不起，我晚一點吃好了。

＊ "Time to eat." 是 "It's time to eat." 的簡單說法，適合用在和關係親近的人的對話。

## What would you like to eat?
你想吃什麼呢？

A: What would you like to eat? 您想吃什麼呢？

B: I'll have an 8-ounce steak. 我要一份 8 盎斯的牛排。

A: Very well. Would you like anything to drink? 沒問題。要喝什麼飲料嗎？

＊點牛排的時候，可能需要指定想要的大小。雖然可能並不常用到這句話，不過，若是能夠先有點概念，到需要用上時或許能減少點錯的機率。

### 還有這種說法唷！

You eat a lot. 你吃得很多。

＊奉勸男士們，這句話千萬別對女伴說唷。

I want to eat something. 我想要吃點東西。

I think I ate too much. 我想我吃得太多了。

# get

02-14.mp3

　　沒有其他的單字像 get 一樣，能夠表達那麼多種含義。因此，坊間有很多專門探討 get 的英語學習書，更有人因為鑽研 get 取得博士學位，get 這個單字的變化無常由此可見。不過，這裡只為各位讀者簡單介紹必須知道的部分。請某人接電話時，get 可解釋為「接」；get 也可以用來表示「得到、拿到」某樣東西。你以為只有這樣而已嗎？它還可以用來表示「到達」某處的意思喔。

## Get some milk.
**買些牛奶回來。**

A: Are you going to the store? 妳要去商店嗎？
B: Yes. Do you need anything? 是啊，你需要什麼嗎？
A: Get some milk. 買些牛奶回來吧。

## I'm getting a new computer.
**我要買一台電腦。**

A: I'm getting a new computer. 我要買一台電腦。
B: What kind of computer? 哪一種電腦？
A: I don't know. 還不知道。

### 還有這種說法唷！

Get the phone, would you? 接一下電話，好嗎？

Get out of my face. 從我的眼前消失。

＊如果你有機會非常非常生氣地向對方說「從我的眼前消失」，記得要用動詞 "get"，整句的說法是 "Get out of here." 或是 "Get out of my face."。

Get the waiter over here. 把服務生叫過來。

# ⑮ give

02-15.mp3

　　記得以前流行著一首嘻哈歌曲，連續唱了五次 "give me"，究竟這 "give" 意味著什麼呢？沒錯，就是「給」的意思。某個人「給」我某樣東西的時候，我們可以說 "give me"。此外，把錢或物品交「給」某個人的時候，用 "give" 就對了。各位覺得如何？很簡單對不對？千萬要記得啊，學英文用不著那麼辛苦。

## Give me.
給我。

A: Give me your attention. 注意聽我說。

B: I'm listening. 我在聽啊。

A: You're watching TV! 妳明明在看電視！

B: Yes, but I'm listening. 沒錯，可是我在聽啊。

\* 看電視要說 "watching TV"，聽音樂就要說 "listening to music" 或是 "listening to the radio"，去看電影可以說 "going to the movies" 或是 "seeing a movie"。

## Give Joe back his bike.
把腳踏車還給喬。

A: Give Joe back his bike. 把腳踏車還給喬。

B: He let me borrow it for a week. 他讓我借一個禮拜。

A: Oh, I didn't know that. 是喔，我不知道。

\* 一般來說，腳踏車叫做 "bike"，那機車呢？可以說 "motorcycle"，但老外也把機車叫做 "bike"，有時候也會說 "motorbike"。

### 還有這種說法唷！

Give me the remote control. 把遙控器給我。

I'll give her this ring. 我要送給她這只戒指。

Give Robert back his toy. 把玩具還給羅伯特。

不久以前，我們在前面章節已經了解過 "come" 的用法了。接下來，我們要來看一下它的相反詞 "go"。"go" 也是一個非常簡單的單字。因為你只要對著某個人喊 "Go!"，他就真的會乖乖移動腳步了。好啦，這下子該換我們走了。

# I'm going to the store.
**我要去商店。**

A: Hey, Jimmy. Where are you going? 嘿，吉米，你要去哪裡啊？
B: Hi! I'm going to the store. 嗨！我要去商店。
A: Store? 商店？
B: Yeah. I want to get some milk. 嗯，我要去買些牛奶。

# Go fly a kite.
**去放風箏吧。**

A: I'm bored. What should I do? 好無聊喔。有什麼可做的？
B: Go fly a kite. 去放風箏啊。
A: I don't have a kite. 我沒有風箏。

\*風箏叫做 "kite"。台灣人學英文和日本韓國一樣有個共同點，那就是他們知道許多高難度的英語單字，可是卻有可能不知道像 "kite" 這麼簡單的單字。來，大家一起把它記下來，kite 指的是風箏喔！

### 還有這種說法唷！

That car is going really fast. 那部車跑得很快。

Go away. I'm busy. 走開，我正在忙。

# ⑰ hand

02-17.mp3

"hand" 當名詞時是「手」的意思，但是也經常用來表示「遞給」的動作。給人的時候說 "give"，接受的時候則說 "get" 或 "receive"，接著，我們要來看看 "hand" 的用法。如果你能使用這個動詞，老外一定會很驚訝：「初學入門的人怎麼可能懂得 hand 這種高級單字的用法？」大家一起來，「遞給」的英文是 "hand"。

## Hand over my money.
**把我的錢拿出來。**

A: Hand over my money. 把我的錢拿出來。

B: I don't have all your money yet. 我沒有你全部的錢。

A: Give me what you have. 妳有多少就給我多少。

## I'll hand it to you.
**我拿給你。**

A: Would you like a banana? 你要吃香蕉嗎？

B: Yes, throw it to me. 好啊，把它丟給我。

A: I'll hand it to you. I can't throw food. 我拿給你，我不能丟食物。

### 還有這種說法唷！

Hand me the wrench. 把扳手遞給我。

Hand over your keys. 把鑰匙給我。

＊在這裡，over 的角色可有可無。

Will you hand me that screwdriver? 把螺絲起子遞給我可以嗎？

# <sup>18</sup> have

02-18.mp3

讓我們先回到 "have" 的基本功能，原本 have 是指「擁有」的意思：「有」正在交往中的女朋友、「有」手錶、問朋友「有」沒有空，使用的動詞都是 "have"。啊…差點忘了，有些時候，have 也用在像是 "I'm having dinner." 這種意味「吃」的動作。

## I have a computer.
**我有一台電腦。**

A: Do you have a computer? 妳有電腦嗎？
B: Yes, I do. 有啊。
A: Can I use it? 我可以用一下嗎？
B: Sure. 可以啊。

## Do you have a pen I can use?
**我可以向你借一支筆嗎？**

這裡有一個我們必須了解的句型。即便在全然不同的句子裡，也很容易看出這樣的句型。舉例來說，Do you have a dollar I can borrow?（我可以向你借一塊美金嗎？）。怎麼樣？你找到以上兩個例句相同的地方了嗎？

A: Do you have a pen I can use? 我可以向你借一枝筆嗎？
B: No, I'm sorry, I don't. 不好意思，我沒有筆。
A: Are you sure? 你確定嗎？
B: …（這個人有疑心病不成？！）

### 還有這種說法唷！

I have three cats. 我養了 3 隻貓。

Do you have a computer? 你有電腦嗎？

I have good, strong teeth. 我的牙齒很好、很健康。

# ⑲ help

02-19.mp3

　　有很多教英語的老師，習慣在課堂上告訴學生所學的單字有各種不同的含義。即便把那麼多的含義硬是記在腦袋瓜裡，遇到真正需要用到時真能發揮出來嗎？在這裡，我們只要簡單地牢記一種意思就可以了。不管是在什麼樣的情境之下，help 永遠都是與「幫助」有關的單字。如果想對人說「幫幫我」，英文可以說 "Help me!"，「我會幫你」則是說 "I will help you."。

## Help me.
**幫幫我吧。**

A: Help me with my math, please. 請教我數學。
B: What's the problem? 有什麼問題？
A: I can't do this problem here. 我不會解這個問題。

## Help.
**來幫我。**

　　就算只是簡略地說 "Help!"，同樣能表示「來幫我」的意思。

A: Help, I'm stuck. 救救我，我被困住了。
B: I'll find someone to help you. 我去找人來幫妳。
A: Hurry! 快點！

＊在 "I'm stuck." 這句話中所提及的 "stuck" 是指被困在某個地方「動彈不得的狀態」，尤其是被堵在車陣當中，同樣可以用這個字來形容。

### 還有這種說法唷！

Help me! I'm drowning! 救救我！我快淹死了！
＊沉在水裡就快要淹死的英文就叫 "drowning"。

I help people in need. 我幫助需要幫助的人。

Help get this refrigerator off me! 幫忙把冰箱從我身上移開！

# ⁽²⁰⁾jump

02-20.mp3

"jump" 是指「朝天一躍、奮力跳起」的意思。各位讀者或許都看過 jump 後面加上 over 變成 "jump over" 的形式；如果後面加上的是 up，則變成 "jump up" 的形式。別緊張，沒有你想像中的難，只要記得它的意思是「跳起來」，就什麼都不用怕了。

## I can jump high.
**我可以跳得很高。**

A: Basketball players can jump high. 籃球選手能跳得很高。

B: Only some of them. 只有一些選手能。

A: That's true. Not all of them can. 妳說的對，並不是所有人都行。

＊唸英文的時候，牢記像是 some of them、all of them 或是 none of them、both of them 這些用詞，適時加以善用是很重要的。請各位讀者「用力」地將它記起來吧。

## Jump over this banana peel.
**跳過這塊香蕉皮。**

"banana peel" 是指香蕉皮，相信各位都知道香蕉皮很滑吧？「滑倒」的英文是 "slip"。而 "jump over" 是說「跳著越過」某處的意思。

A: Jump over this banana peel. 跳過這塊香蕉皮看看。

B: That's easy. I can do that. 很簡單，我做得到。

A: Don't slip on it! 可別滑倒了喲！

### 還有這種說法唷！

Jump as high as you can. 你能跳多高就跳多高。

Jump up and touch the ceiling. 跳起來去碰天花板。

Jump over the crack. 跳過那個裂縫。

# ㉑ keep

"keep" 有兩種含義，其一是「繼續做（某件事）」，另一個是「持續保有某件物品」。「繼續做某事」的句型是 "keep + V-ing"，持續保有（某件）物品則可以說 "I keep something."。

## Keep running.
繼續跑。

A: Keep running. 繼續跑。
B: But I'm so tired! 但是我很累了耶！
A: I said keep running! 我說繼續跑！

＊不管是說 "keep running" 或是 "keep working"，各位只要把它當做一句話學起來就行了，這樣就不需要再去思考 keep 後面的動詞要不要接 -ing 之類傷腦筋的問題。

## You keep this condom.
你要隨身攜帶這個保險套。

A: Hey! Jonny. You keep this condom.
　　嘿！強尼，你要把這個保險套帶在身上。
B: What? Condom? 啊？保險套？
A: Yeah! You'll need that some day. 沒錯！有一天你會需要它的。

### 還有這種說法唷！

I want you to keep it. 我希望你能帶著它。

You should keep that money for college. 你應該將那筆錢留來唸大學。

Keep out of here. 離這裡遠一點。（別想靠近這裡半步。）

＊ "Keep out of here." 也可以和相同含義的 "Stay out of here." 互換使用。

# <sup>22</sup> leave

02-22.mp3

我曾經看過這樣的電影畫面：一處幽暗的公寓，突然有個男人一邊高聲喊叫，一邊死命地跑，而這個男人的身後有一群女人快步追上他。最後，那一群女人圍著倒臥在地上的男人，用力扯開他身上的衣服，這時候男人大喊："Please leave me alone."。這句話是什麼意思呢？是「放開我、離我遠一點、別理我」的意思。除了這種特殊情況的用法，所有的"leave"都可以用來表示「離開」的意思。對了，還有一件事，"leave"的過去式是"left"。

## Leave here now.
### 現在就離開這裡。

A: Leave here now. 現在馬上離開這裡。
B: Fine, I'll go. 很好，我這就走。
A: Don't come back. 再也不要回來。

## Should I leave?
### 我該離開嗎？

在一場許多人聚集的重要會議中，有這麼一個不相干的人在場。當會議即將進行之際，這人可能會問 "Should I leave?"，意思是：「我應該離開嗎？」

A: Should I leave? 我該離開嗎？
B: No, please stay. 不，請留下來。
A: Okay. I'll stay. 好吧，我留下來。

### 還有這種說法唷！

I stood up and left. 我起身離開了。

He left only a minute ago. 他剛剛才離開。

Leave the book on the table. 把書留在桌上。

# ㉓ **let**

02-23.mp3

　　學校教我們 let 是使役動詞，不過，我們別去管它是使役還是奴役了，只用簡單的方式來了解 let 這個字。"I want to go." 是指「我想走了。」，是我主動要去的；那麼，"Let me go." 又是指什麼呢？雖然並不全然是說話者可以決定的，不過，這也有「想走」的意思喔。"let" 是「讓我去做」，有請求的意思。"Let me go." 則是「讓我走吧」。

## I'll let you go.
**我會讓你去。**

A: Please, can I go to the party? 拜託，我可以去派對嗎？
B: I guess I'll let you go. 我想我會讓妳去的。
A: Oh, thank you, daddy! Thank you! 噢，謝謝你，爸爸！謝謝你！

## Let me help you with that.
**讓我來幫你吧。**

　　"Let me help you." 是指「讓我幫你」的意思。

A: I can't open this jar. 我打不開這個罐子。
B: Let me help you with that. 讓我幫你打開。
A: Thanks. You're stronger than me (I). 謝謝。妳比我要強壯。

### 還有這種說法唷！

Let me carry your groceries. 讓我幫你搬這些（食品類）貨物。

I won't let her treat me like this. 我不會讓她這樣對待我。

Don't let your father down. 別讓你父親失望了。

# <sup>24</sup>look

02-24.mp3

有一件事情讓我感到很不可思議，就是中國人居然比美國人更懂得用理論區分 see、look 和 watch 的用法。可是，為什麼實際上就是不太會用呢？老實說，我自己並不懂如何在理論上明辨 see、look 還有 watch。不過，我可以很肯定地告訴各位讀者，see 就像 meet 一樣有「見到」的意思，或者也可以用來表示「看電影」的意思。而 look 可以用在像是 "Have a look." 這樣的說法，表示「看一下」的意思。"look at" 則是指「注視著…」的意思。

## Look at me.
**看看我。**

A: Look at me. 看看我嘛。
B: No. 不要
A: Why won't you look at me? 妳為什麼不看我呢？

## Don't look right at it.
**不要直視它。**

A: The sun is pretty. 太陽真美。
B: Don't look right at it. 不要直視它喔。
A: Why? 為什麼？
B: It will damage your eyes. 它會傷害你的眼睛。

### 還有這種說法唷！

Look at the boat in the water! 看海上的那艘遊艇！

Don't look directly at the sun. 不要直視太陽。

I can't look at the dead body. 我無法正眼看屍體。

Look to your left. 看你的左手邊。

# ㉕ make

02-25.mp3

用木材「製作」書桌的英文是 "make"，為心愛的另一半「製作」愛心便當也是 "make"，甚至是上床睡覺之前「鋪」棉被的動作也可以用 "make"。不管做什麼，只要是類似「製作」的動作，統統都可用 "make" 表達喔。另外，表示「使某人做…」時所用的動詞也是 "make"。

## I'll make you dinner.
我來為你準備晚餐。

A: I'm hungry. 我肚子餓扁了。
B: I'll make you dinner. 我來為妳準備晚餐。
A: What are you making? 你要做什麼吃的呢？

＊當你回家進了家門，發現嬌妻正在準備晚餐，你或許會靜悄悄地走到她身後，溫柔地抱住她，然後在她耳畔輕聲地這麼說吧？ "Honey! I love you. What are you making?"。

## Did you make your bed?
你整理好床鋪了嗎？

起床後整理床鋪，或是晚上就寢前鋪床等舉動，在英文裡都叫做 "make bed"。

A: Did you clean your room? 你清理房間了嗎？
B: Yes, mommy. 好了，媽咪。
A: Did you make your bed? 床鋪整理了嗎？
B: I forgot to do that. 那個我倒忘了耶。

### 還有這種說法唷！

I'll make dinner for you. 我來為你準備晚餐。

I'll make some food. 我來做些吃的。

Make him stop bothering me. 叫他別再騷擾我。

# ²⁶ move

02-26.mp3

　　所有「移動」的舉動都可以用 "move" 來表達；當然，正在移動中的英文是 moving。乘車時想請同車的人挪動位置時也可以用 "move" 表達。

## My dog isn't moving!
**我的小狗一動也不動耶！**

A: My dog isn't moving! 我的小狗一動也不動耶！
B: Maybe he's sleeping. 也許他睡著了吧。
A: No, I think he's dead. 不，我想他已經死了。

## We're moving to California.
**我們要搬到加州去了。**

　　搬家也可以用 move 這個字表達，因此，搬家用的卡車英文就叫 "moving truck"。

A: We're moving to California. 我們要搬到加州去了。
B: I'm sorry to see you go. 我有點捨不得妳走呢。
A: I'm sorry to leave. 我也捨不得離開。

### 還有這種說法唷！

Move to the left a little. 往左邊移一些。

He isn't moving. He's dead. 他一動也不動。他死了。

We're moving down south. 我們要往南方移動了。

# ²⁷ pass

02-27.mp3

　　這幾年足球運動相當風行，大家在踢足球或觀賞足球賽時，第一個聯想到的單字可能是 soccer，其次可能就是 pass 這個字了。pass 是很大眾化的用詞，好比說在球場上兩隊人馬把球傳來傳去，吃飯時為家人遞胡椒粉或接過一盤菠菜，都會用到 pass 這個字。pass 還有另外一個含義，就是指「通過考試」。

## Pass me the ball.
把球傳給我。

A: Pass me the ball. 把球傳給我。
B: No, you're not good at this game. 不要，你不太行。
A: You're not very nice. 妳人真壞。

## Did you pass the class?
那一門課你及格了嗎？

　　在美國，成績是以 "ABCDE" 來計算的，相當於國內的「優甲乙丙丁」。對美國人來說，得到 C 以上才算及格。

A: Did you pass the class? 那一門課你及格了嗎？
B: Yes, I got a C! 嗯，幸好得了個 C！
A: That's great. I knew you could do it. 太好了。我就知道你可以。

### 還有這種說法唷！

He never passes his classes. 他從沒及格過。

I hope I'm going to pass my math test. 我希望我的數學會及格。

My grandfather passed away. 我爺爺去世了。

＊ pass away 是指「去世」，是敬重對方的用詞。談及長輩去世時，不可以使用 "die" 這個字。

# pull

02-28.mp3

　　有些門上會寫著 pull 或是 push 這兩個單字，不過，看英文判斷要把門「推開」或「拉開」的人恐怕不多吧，即便是時常跑去國外生活的我，有時候還是會把這兩個字的含義給弄混了。以後各位讀者要是看見門口貼著 "pull"，請把門「拉開」吧。

## Pull the rope tight.
**把繩子拉緊。**

A: Pull the rope tight. 把繩子拉緊。

B: I am. It's tight already. 我在拉啊，它已經很緊了。

A: Pull harder. 再拉緊一點。

## Pull open the lid (on the can).
**把罐頭上的拉環打開。**

　　上面例句中的 "can" 是指罐裝食物，我們每天都會喝上一、兩罐的可樂或汽水也是，而 lid 指的是開口的部分。

A: Pull open the lid on the can. 把罐頭上的拉環打開。

B: It's stuck. 它卡住了。

A: How will we get it open? 我們要怎麼樣才打得開呢？

### 還有這種說法唷！

Pull on my arm. 拉我的手臂。

Pull my finger. 拉我的手指。

I got pulled over by a cop. 我被警察攔了下來。

＊許多人有過因為違規或超速而被警察「攔車」的經驗，那種情況的英文說法就是 "pull over"。

# 29 **push**

02-29.mp3

　　"push" 有兩個含義，第一個是把某人「推開」，或是從高處往下「推」；第二個是強行把他人「推向」所希望的方向。不過話說回來，我們絕對不應該強行 push 別人，因為這樣做是不禮貌的。

## Push the button.
**按下那個按鈕。**

A: Push the button. 按下那個按鈕。

B: What does the button do? 這個按鈕有什麼作用？

A: I don't know. 我不知道。

B: Then I'm not pushing it. 那麼，我就不按了。

＊在 push the button 這個例句中，可以將 push 換成 hit，特別是在電梯裡，可以説 push the button 或 hit the button，請別人幫忙按下樓層的按鈕。

## Don't push me.
**別推我。**

A: Hey, don't push me. 嘿，別推我。

B: Want to fight? 想打一架嗎？

A: No, I don't. 不要，我不想。

B: You're weak! 膽小鬼！

＊ push 這個字用在身體上是指「推擠」的意思，用在意識上的傳達則有「強迫」的意味。

### 還有這種說法唷！

He tried to push me into doing what he wanted. 他試圖強迫我照他的意思去做。

I got pushed into doing his work for him. 我被強迫去幫他做他的工作。

Push the table against the wall. 把這張茶几靠在牆邊。

# put

02-30.mp3

　　要求把物品「放在某個地方」時，我們會用到 "put" 這個字，各位讀者若是能夠適時使用 "put"，就可以說出很夠水準的英文。put 可以和 down 或是 away 一起搭配使用，不過，即便多加了這些單字，put 本身的含義並不會受影響，也不會改變，請各位讀者切記。

## Put the box down here.
**把箱子放在這裡。**

A: Put the box down here. 把箱子放在這裡。
B: Where? 哪裡？
A: Here, where I'm standing. 這裡，我站著的地方。

## Put down the gun.
**把槍放下。**

A: Put down the gun, John. 約翰，把槍放下。
B: I'll shoot you! 我要殺了妳！
A: Please, put it down. 求求你，把它放下來。
B: No! 不要！

### 還有這種說法唷！

Don't put that there! 別把那個放在那裡！

I put your mail on the table. 我把你的信放在桌上。

Put the money on the ground. 把錢放在地上。

Put away your toys. 把你的玩具收拾好。

# <sup>31</sup> run

02-31.mp3

應該不會有人不知道 run 是指「跑」的意思吧。對了，run 的過去式是 ran，各位一定要記住喔。

## I love to run.

### 我喜歡跑步。

A: I love to run. 我喜歡跑步。

B: Running is good for you. 跑步對你不錯。

A: It also relieves stress. 它還能解除壓力。

＊跑步真的很不錯唷…我也習慣每天晚上到戶外慢跑 30 分鐘。呃，該怎麼説呢，跑步的時候我發現腦袋瓜會變得什麼都不想，只是專心一意為跑步而跑步，心情就會不知不覺輕鬆起來，這在英語的説法叫 "relieve stress"（消除壓力）。

## He's running away!

### 他跑走了！

"run away" 是指「逃跑」的意思，不知道各位讀者是否看過 Runaway Bride（落跑新娘）這部電影？是理查吉爾和茱莉亞羅勃茲主演的喔。

A: He's running away! 他跑走了！

B: Get him! 抓住他！

A: I'll call the police! 我去叫警察來！

### 還有這種說法唷！

I ran all the way home. 我一路跑回家。

＊ run all the way home 是指「一路跑回家」，還沒有到家之前都不停下來。

Keep running. 繼續跑。

I'm a runner. 我是個跑者。

He ran for the Olympics. 他在奧運會上賽跑。

# send

02-32.mp3

各位應該都認得 "send" 吧？是「發送」的意思喔。"send" 的過去式是 "sent"。所以造句的時候，若是「我寄出去」就說 "I send"，若是「我寄出去了」，則要說 "I sent"，若是「我將要寄出去」就要說 "I'll send"。好了！我決定，今天下班要 "send a flower" 給親愛的太太！

## I sent you a birthday card.
**我寄了生日卡片給你。**

A: I sent you a birthday card. 我寄了生日卡片給妳。
B: I didn't receive it. 我沒收到耶。
A: Maybe it hasn't gotten there yet. 也許還沒有寄到吧。

## I sent you a present.
**我寄了禮物給你。**

A: I sent you a present. 我寄了禮物給你。
B: I got it. Thank you, dear! 我收到了，謝謝妳，親愛的！
A: Of course. 那是我應該做的。

### 還有這種說法唷！

He sent me his laundry. 他寄了他的換洗衣物給我。

I sent you a letter. 我寄了一封信給你。

I will send for you when I'm available. 我有空的時候再派人去請你過來。

Send him away. 把他送走。

# ③③ show

02-33.mp3



好萊塢影片裡所有事件的起因幾乎都和金錢有關，所以影片中常會出現 "Show me the money." 這句對白。這句話的意思是「沒什麼好談的，把錢拿出來就對了」。把某種東西「秀」出來時，用 show 這個動詞準沒錯。

## I'll show you something.

**我給你看一樣東西。**

A: I'll show you something. 我給妳看一樣東西。

B: What is it? 是什麼？

A: It's a surprise. Close your eyes. 是一個驚喜，把眼睛閉上。

## Let me show you my dog.

**讓我給你看看我的小狗。**

A: Let me show you my dog. 讓我給你看看我的小狗。

B: I heard she's beautiful. 我聽說她很漂亮喔。

A: Of course she is. 那當然囉。

**還有這種說法唷！**

He showed me his guest house. 他讓我參觀客房。

Show me your goods. 讓我看看你的商品。

I was shown into a large room. 我被帶到一間大房間參觀。

# ³⁴ shut

02-34.mp3

當你在跟別人說話或是看英文書時,只要看到 "shut" 出現,就可以確定一定是以下兩個意思中的一個,通常這樣的推測很準確。

"shut" 的第一個意思是指「關上」,也就是和 close 的意思一樣,但是比 close 還要強烈一點。所以, "Shut the door!" 的中文意思是「把門給我關上」,是有點生氣的語氣。

"shut" 的另一個意思是請人「閉嘴」。在美國, "Shut up!" 是經常會聽到的一句話,是以強烈的語氣要求對方閉嘴。

## Shut the door, please.
請把門關上。

A: Shut the door, please. 請把門關上。
B: It's hot in here. 屋裡很熱耶。
A: There are bugs outside. 外面有蟲子啊。

## Shut up!
閉嘴!

A: Hey, why don't you shut up? 嘿,妳能不能閉嘴啊?
B: You shut up, man. 你才該閉嘴,你這傢伙。
A: Let's go outside. 我們去外頭單挑。

### 還有這種說法唷!

The door is shut. 門被關上了。

Shut up. You're dumb. 閉嘴,你這愚蠢的傢伙。

Shut your mouth. 閉上你的鳥嘴。

Just shut out the noise. 把噪音隔開就對了。

# ㉟ sit

02-35.mp3

我相信包括正在讀這一頁的讀者在內，應該沒有人不知道 "sit down" 這個用詞。誠如我們早已熟知的含義，sit 是指「坐下」的意思。除此之外，sit 這個字搭配不同的詞語，就能表達「坐到我身邊來」和「坐在那裡」的意思。

## Sit on the floor.
坐在地板上。

A: Where do I sit? 我要坐在哪裡？

B: Sit on the floor. 就坐地板上吧。

A: Where are your chairs? 你家裡的椅子都到哪裡去了？

B: I sold them for beer money. 我拿去換啤酒喝了。

＊在此，beer money 是指「用來買啤酒的錢」。

## Are you sitting down?
你坐好了嗎？

sitting 是 sit 的現在進行式，有「坐著」的意思。所以，這句中文應該翻譯成「你坐好了嗎」。

A: Are you sitting down? 你坐好了嗎？

B: Yes, why? 好了，什麼事啊？

A: I have some bad news. 我有一些壞消息。

### 還有這種說法唷！

Sit down by me. 坐到我身邊來。

Sit down on the couch. 坐在沙發上吧。

I'd better sit down. 我最好坐下來。

Sit down if you're feeling sick. 你如果不舒服就坐下來吧。

# <sup>36</sup> start

02-36.mp3

翻開字典你可能會看到一長串文字，說明 begin 與 start 之間的差異，坦白說，那只會讓人更霧裡看花，愈看愈不明白。我認為並不需要去搞懂 begin 和 start 的差別，只需要知道它們都有「開始」的意思就行了。

## Start the car.
**發動汽車吧。**

A: Start the car. 發動車子吧。

B: Hurry. 動作快一點。

A: I'll be there in a minute. 我很快就會到。

## I don't want to start a fight.
**我不想吵架。**

在美國生活，有時候難免會遇到老外不懷好意的挑釁，我在這裡告訴各位一些妙招。第一，千萬別想用英文和老外吵架；第二，用英文爭吵時裝作聽不懂；第三，要拉大嗓門；第四，不論任何狀況，絕對動口不動手，要不然後果會很嚴重。一定要大聲嚷嚷，想辦法刺激對方動武。運氣好的話，或許就能賺到一筆留學的生活費呢。

A: I don't want to start a fight. 我並不想吵架。

B: Then maybe you shouldn't have insulted me. 那妳就不應該對我無禮啊。

A: I'm sorry. 對不起。

### 還有這種說法唷！

Start running. 起跑。

Start peeling the potatoes. 開始削馬鈴薯的皮。

Start the lawn mower. 發動割草機。

＊ "lawn mower" 是割草的機器，"lawnmower man" 是指割草的人。

# ③⑦stop

02-37.mp3

在酒店正喝得興致高昂時，若有個喝醉酒的傢伙靠過來發酒瘋，這個時候可以疾言厲色地向對方說 "Stop it!"。這麼一來，大部分的老外都會當下就溜之大吉，當然，可別忘了表情要狠一點才有效喔。就像這樣，「停止」或「中斷」某個舉動時，都可以用 stop 當動詞。走在路上時常可見寫著 "STOP" 的交通標誌，也是「停下來」的意思。

## Stop it!
**住手！**

A: Kiss me, baby. 陪我玩親親，小妞。
B: Stop it! 住手！
A: What's the matter? 有什麼關係？

## Would you stop the car?
**請你停車可以嗎？**

以 "Would you ..." 開頭的疑問句，中文意思是「請你…可以嗎」，是禮貌的請求及詢問。

A: Would you stop the car? 請妳停車好嗎？
B: Are you getting out? 你想下車嗎？
A: Yes, I need to get out. 是啊，我要下車。

＊在英文的說法裡，搭乘一般轎車時，上車叫 "get in"，下車叫 "get out"；搭乘公車或火車時，上車叫 "get on"，下車叫 "get off"。這些情形都使用 "get" 這個動詞唷。

### 還有這種說法唷！

Stop eating so much. 別再吃了。　　Stop bothering me. 別再煩我了。

Stop the washing machine. 關掉洗衣機。

Stop the match! 停止比賽！

＊ match 是名詞，意指「火柴」，但也可以像這個例句一樣用來指「運動競賽」。

# ㊳take

關於 take 我想就不必口沫橫飛地講一大堆了，我簡單扼要地把它的意思歸納為 4 種。牽手時表示 hold 的含義，進食時表示 eat 或是 have 的含義，某人帶走某樣物品時表示 take 的含義，還有一個是把人帶走的意思。各別的中文意思就是抓（hold），吃（eat or have），拎走，帶走。

## Take my hand.
**牽我的手。**

A: Take my hand. 牽我的手。

B: Are you afraid? 你害怕嗎？

A: No, I just want to know you're here. 不，我只是想知道妳確實在我身邊。

## Take only two cookies.
**只能吃兩塊餅乾。**

A: Take only two cookies. 只能吃兩塊餅乾喔。

B: But I want more cookies. 但我想多吃幾塊。

A: No, take only two. 不行，只能吃兩塊。

B: But I want more. 我想再多吃幾塊嘛。

### 還有這種說法唷！

Take this turkey to your mother. 把這隻火雞拿去給你媽媽。

Take this note to Theresa. 把這張留言拿給泰瑞莎。

I'll take him to the store. 我要把他帶到店裡去。

# ③⁹ talk

02-39.mp3

　　tell 是指某人「告訴」對方一件事，而 talk 則偏重互相交談或討論。另外，tell 後面可以直接接告訴的對象或內容，talk 後面則必須用到介系詞 to 或是 about。

## Talk to me.

**告訴我。**

A: I need to tell you something. 我有件事情要告訴你。
B: Sure. Talk to me. 好啊，跟我說。
A: I love you. 我愛你。
B: Well, I already knew that. 哦，我已經知道了。

## I like talking to you.

**我喜歡和你聊天。**

A: I like talking to you. 我喜歡和你聊天。
B: I like talking to you, too. 我也是。
A: What should we talk about? 我們該聊什麼呢？

### 還有這種說法喲！

I like talking on the phone. 我喜歡講電話。

We talked all night long. 我們聊了一整夜。

You talk funny. 你講話真風趣。

Were you talking to that girl? 你那時在和那個女孩說話嗎？

# ⁴⁰ think

02-40.mp3

　　有些人習慣用像 consider 這種高難度的單字來描述「想」這件事，其實，這麼做並不見得高明。一切從簡吧，「想」這個字的英文說法用 think 就夠了。懂得用這個字，就已經夠厲害了，況且這個字不受用法上的限制，適用於所有的句型。

## I'm thinking.
**我正在思考。**

A: What are you doing? 你在幹嘛？
B: I'm thinking. 我在想事情。
A: Don't think too much. 別想太多。

## I want a thinking man.
**我想要一個懂得思考的男人。**

A: I want a thinking man. 我想要一個會思考的男人。
B: I want a strong man. 我想要一個強壯的男人。
A: Thinking men can be strong, too. 懂得思考的男人也可以是強壯的男人。

### 還有這種說法唷！

Think about it. 想想看。

Think before you act. 三思而後行。

Think of what we should do. 想想看我們該做什麼。

I'll think over my decision. 我會考慮一下自己的決定。

# ⁴¹throw

02-41.mp3

　　丟球的英文有兩種，一個是已經在前面章節提過的 pass，另一個則是 throw 這個字。相較於 pass 不限手或腳部的動作，throw 則僅限於手部的動作。明白了嗎？另外，throw 後面若是接 away 的話，中文的意思就是指「丟掉、丟棄」。

## Throw the ball.
丟球。

A: Throw the ball to Jason. 把球丟給傑森。
B: He isn't looking. 他沒在看這裡耶。
A: Yell at him. 大聲叫他啊。

## Throw me the ball.
把球丟給我。

　　"Throw the ball." 中間加上 me 就成了 "Throw me the ball."。
　　來，試著做個變化吧，"Throw him the ball."、"Throw her the ball."。

A: Throw me the ball. 把球丟給我。
B: You're too far away. 妳離我太遠了。
A: You can throw this far. 你可以丟這麼遠的。

### 還有這種說法唷！

You throw like a girl. 你丟得像個女孩子一樣。

Throw away your garbage. 把你的垃圾倒掉。

Don't throw away your life. 別看輕你的人生。（別輕易放棄你的人生。）

Let's throw her a party. 我們為她舉辦一場派對吧。

# ⁴²walk

02-42.mp3

看到這裡，可能有讀者會認為「怎麼都是些簡單到不行的單字啊」？先別急，不管你認為自己的英文有多行，最好還是從「根本」強化基礎。walk 在中文是指「走」的意思。那「跑」又該怎麼說呢？在前面學過了，是 "run"。

## Walk.
走路。

A: My car is broken. 我的車壞了。
B: Then walk. 那就用走路的吧。
A: I don't like to walk. 我不喜歡走路。

## I'm walking to Joe's house.
我要走到喬的家。

A: I'm walking to Joe's house. 我要走到喬的家。
B: Be home in time for dinner. 要準時回來吃晚飯喔。
A: I will. 我會的。

### 還有這種說法唷！

Walk this way, please. 請往這邊走。

I walked to the store. 我走到商店。

I walk in the mornings for exercise. 我每天早上走路當作運動。

Running is better than walking. 跑步比走路來得好。

02-43.mp3

# ㊸ **wear**

衣服或是任何可以往身上套的東西，記得英文的說法用 "wear" 就對了。當然，有些時候會用 put on 來表示「穿上衣服」，不過，請記得大致上用 wear 已足夠 cover 所有的情形。

## What's your favorite thing to wear?
**你最喜歡穿什麼樣的衣服？**

A: What's your favorite thing to wear? 妳最喜歡穿什麼樣的衣服？
B: T-shirts. T 恤。
A: Me too! 我也是耶！

＊ thing to wear 是指「可以穿戴的東西」，可用來表示衣物。

## I'm wearing only my underwear.
**我只穿著內衣。**

A: What do you have on？妳穿了什麼衣服？
B: I'm wearing only my underwear. 我只穿著內衣。

### 還有這種說法唷！

You have lots of clothes to wear. 你有很多衣服可以穿。

What are you wearing? 你穿著什麼衣服？

Wear this to the party. 穿這件衣服去派對吧。

You're wearing that to work? 你要穿這樣去上班嗎？

# ⁴⁴ work

02-44.mp3

　　警察一天到晚都得和歹徒交戰，人們每天都得埋首在繁瑣的工作中抱怨連連。真是讓人想不通，這麼做真正的意義是什麼！

　　工作的英文說法是 "work"，切記避免唸成 "walk"。請各位讀者熟悉以下的例句，如此一來，如果再碰到有關 work 的任何問題，絕對 No problem！

## Where do you work?
### 你在哪裡工作？

A: Where do you work? 妳在哪裡高就？
B: I'm a teacher at the high school. 我在高中教書。
A: That must be fun. 一定很有趣喔。
B: No, it's a terrible job. 不，那是個糟糕的工作。

## I like my work.
### 我喜愛我的工作。

A: I like my work. 我喜愛我的工作。
B: Really? What do you do? 真的嗎？妳是做什麼工作的呢？
A: I teach disabled children. 我教導身心障礙的兒童。
B: That sounds exciting. 聽起來很刺激。

＊ disabled children 是指「身心障礙兒童」的意思。

### 還有這種說法喔！

I work at the power company. 我在電力公司上班。

I don't want to work tonight. 我今晚不想工作。

Do you have a lot of work to do? 你有很多工作要做嗎？

I have a lot of work to do. 我有很多工作要做。

# ⁴⁵write

02-45.mp3

　　讀寫文字的英文說法是 read and write。我想大家應該對 write 很熟悉了，因此，在此一章節我就簡單舉幾個例句，檢視一下適當的用法。

## I love to write.
**我喜歡寫作。**

A: I love to write. 我喜歡寫作。
B: Me too. 我也一樣。
A: How long have you been writing? 妳寫作有多久了？
B: Five years. 五年。

## I'm a writer.
**我是個作家。**

A: I'm a writer. 我是個作家。
B: What kinds of things do you write? 妳寫哪一類的書呢？
A: I write novels, mostly. 大部分是小説。
B: I'd like to read them. 我想拜讀妳的作品。

### 還有這種說法唷！

I need to write a paper. 我得寫一篇報告。

Do you know how to write? 你知道怎麼寫嗎？

Writing can be fun. 寫作可以是件有趣的事。

I wish I could write like you. 我希望能夠寫得像你一樣好。

# Chapter 3

# 用 56 個核心句型，勇敢面對老外

注意觀察老外或是英文高手，你會發現他們其實都擅長使用固定的句型。由此可見，英語句子一定有固定的句型用法。

接下來，我們試著利用前面章節學過的基礎文法以及基本動詞來熟悉英文句型。這裡歸納出來的 56 種英文句型，一定會讓各位讀者感到既神奇又好用。只要使用固定的句型套用你需要的單字，馬上就會變成完整的「英文會話」。

所以，只要對句型用法建立了正確的概念，以後就再也不用擔心要面對老外了。各位應該都懂得舉一反三，透過這些英文句型，絕對有能力好好地加以活用。來吧，咱們開始吧！快把這些句型融會貫通，一定要讓老外刮目相看。

# ❶ Coffee, please.

### 請來杯咖啡。

03-01.mp3

就算英文實力不怎麼樣，只要懂得活用 please，就足夠應付簡單的要求或請求了。像是 coffee、beer 或是 water 這樣的單字，只需要在後面加個 please，就變成一個會話語句了。要說出讓老外讚美的英語，就從最簡單、活用度最高的 please 開始吧。

A: Can I help you? 請問要點什麼？
B: Coke, *please*. 請給我可樂。
A: Sure. 好的。

# ❷ Please help me.

### 請幫幫我。

03-02.mp3

"Help me." 。有一點「命令」的語氣，但是多了 please 語氣就緩和許多。please 可以放在句子的開頭或結尾。那麼，接著就來看看有關 please 的簡單例句。

A: *Please* let me go. 請讓我走吧。
B: I can't. 我做不到。
A: Why not? 為什麼？
B: Because I love you. 因為我愛妳。

＊ "Let me go." 的相關說明，我們將在後面的章節再講解。

A: Can I ask you a big favor? 我可以請你幫個大忙嗎？
B: Sure. What is it? 好啊，什麼事？
A: *Please* give me some money. 請給我一些錢。

## ❸ Let's go.

**我們走吧。**

03-03.mp3

Let's 是 let us 的縮寫，而 let 是「讓別人去做某事」的意思，那麼，"Let us ..." 就是「讓我們做…」的意思了，帶有提議或勸誘的意味。

A: Do you want to try? 你想試一下嗎？

B: Yes, *let's* do it. 好啊，我們就做吧。

A: Okay. 來吧。

### 還有這種說法唷！

Let's forget about it. 我們忘了它吧。

Let's see a movie. 我們去看電影吧。

## ❹ Let's go for it.

**我們放手一搏吧。**

03-04.mp3

看了活用 Let's 的句子之後，順帶了解一下 "Let's go for it." 的用法。照字面直譯有「讓我們向著它走吧」的意思，其實是採納他人建議或意見時普遍的說法。

A: We could beat him. 我們能夠贏過他。

B: *Let's* go for it. 放手一搏吧。

A: Okay, let's do it. 沒問題，就這麼辦吧。

＊這裡的 "Let's do it." 是將他人說的 "Let's go for it." 縮簡後的說法，不過也有很多時候會直接採用原來的句子。

### 還有這種說法唷！

A: Do you want to go for a ten-mile walk? 你要不要參加 10 英哩的競走比賽？

B: Let's go for the championship. 我們一定要得冠軍。

# ⑤ Let me **help you.**

讓我**來幫你。**

03-05.mp3

前面提過 let's 原來的形態是 "let us"，還記得嗎？接下來是關於 "Let me ..." 這個片語，中文有「讓我…」的意思。請務必記得，在一般會話中這個片語可用來表示「讓我來…」或是「我來做…」等的意思。

A: I wanna go home. 我想要回家。

B: Just *let me* finish this one and we can go. 讓我喝完這杯再走。

A: OK. 好吧。

\*這裡的 wanna 是 want to 比較口語的說法。

# ⑥ Let me **explain it.**

讓我**來說明。**

03-06.mp3

事實上，這是一個自願的動作，不過卻以尋求他人同意的語氣來表達，老外在措辭上謹慎的作風從 "Let me ..." 這個用法可以窺知一二。

A: See what I mean? 懂我在說什麼嗎？

B: I hear you. 我懂。

A: I don't think you did. *Let me* explain it again.

我不覺得你懂，讓我再解釋一次好了。

**還有這種說法唷！**

Let me tell you something. 讓我告訴你一件事。

Let me ask you something. 讓我問你一件事。

# ⑦ Do you think he's smart?

03-07.mp3

你認為**他聰明**嗎？

詢問他人的意見或想法時用 "Do you think ...?" 為開頭的疑問句即可，意思是「你認為⋯嗎」。think 在發音的時候，請留意 th 的發音要輕咬舌頭。

A: *Do you think* people are evil? 妳認為人性本惡嗎？

B: Not at all. 一點也不。

A: I agree with you. 我也是這麼想的。

### 還有這種說法喑！

Do you think I'm strange? 你覺得我很怪嗎？

Do you think you would go out with me? 妳覺得妳會跟我約會嗎？

# ⑧ Do you know the time?

03-08.mp3

你知道**現在幾點**嗎？

一定有人會說「這麼簡單的句子誰不知道啊」，不過事實上，遇到老外的時候真正能夠用 "Do you know ..." 問話的人並不多。藉著這次機會，讓我們把很多最基本卻又常用在日常會話的句型完全融會貫通吧。

A: *Do you know* who I am? 妳知道我是誰嗎？

B: No, I'm sorry. I don't. 不好意思，我不知道。

A: I'm your Uncle Martin! 我是妳的叔叔，馬丁啊！

B: I have an uncle? 我有個叔叔嗎？

＊在英文裡，叔叔稱做 uncle，舅舅也叫 uncle，不認識的叔叔也是 uncle；但是，沒有親戚關係隔壁鄰居的叔叔就要直呼姓名囉。

### 還有這種說法喑！

Do you know how tall you are? 你知道你多高嗎？

Do you know how to play baseball? 你知道怎麼打棒球嗎？

# ⑨ Do you mean you hate me?

03-09.mp3

### 你是說，你討厭我嗎？

　　不論是說中文還是英文，若對方一時沒能對說話者的談話即時反應過來，往往就會像這樣反問回來。接下來，請大聲練習 50 遍 "Do you mean ...?" 這句用來弄清楚對方語意的疑問句。

A: Take care, now. 保重喔。

B: *Do you mean* you're going now? 妳是說妳現在要走了嗎？

A: Yes, I have to. 是啊，我得走了。

#### 還有這種說法唷！

Do you mean I'm stupid? 你是說我很笨嗎？

Do you mean you want a divorce? 妳是說妳要離婚？

# ⑩ What do you mean by that?

03-10.mp3

### 你說的話是什麼意思？

　　詢問對方「是什麼意思」時普遍使用的英文說法就是 "What do you mean?"，若不熟練很容易會忘掉，因此，請確實牢記。

A: I'm going to work. 我要去上班了。

B: *What do you mean?* You lost your job. 你在說什麼啊？你失業了啊。

A: I'm starting a new one. 我要開始新的工作了。

#### 還有這種說法唷！

What do you mean you don't know me? 你說你不認識我是什麼意思？

What do you mean you made a cake? 你說你做了一個蛋糕是什麼意思？

# ⓫ Do we have to work?

03-11.mp3

### 我們必須去工作嗎？

「必須」去完成某件工作時的英文說法是 "have to"；"Do we have to ...? " 是疑問句型，各位讀者應該不難看出中文意思了吧？在這裡比較重要的並不是立即看得懂中文意思，實際上能夠說得出口才是重點。因為，日常會話中 "Do we have to ...? " 出現的頻率相當高。

A: *Do we have to* have this for dinner? 我們晚餐一定要吃這個嗎？
B: You can find your own dinner. 你可以找你愛吃的。
A: I'll order a pizza. 那我要訂披薩喔。

#### 還有這種說法唷！

Do we have to eat dinner now? 我們一定要現在吃晚飯嗎？

Do we have to wear these clothes? 我們一定要穿這樣嗎？

# ⓬ We don't have to go.

03-12.mp3

### 我們可以不用去。

「必須去做…」這個片語中若帶入 not 就會變成「不需要去做」的意思。"We don't have to ..." 把 we 換成 you 則有「你不需要去做…」的意思。當然，想換成 I 也是可以的。

A: *We don't have to* work today. 我們今天可以不用去上班。
B: Great！太棒了！
A: Today is a holiday. 因為今天是假日。

#### 還有這種說法唷！

You don't have to do this. 你可以不必做這件事。

We don't have to stay. 我們不需要留在這裡。

# ⓭ Do you have anything to **do**?

### 你有什麼事要**做**嗎？

03-13.mp3

詢問對方有什麼需要做的「事」時，英文的說法是 "Do you have anything to ...?"。這個句型比較長，別因為覺得困難就放棄，各位可以反覆練習再練習，直到能夠朗朗上口為止。

A: *Do you have anything to* eat? 妳有什麼可以吃的嗎？

B: No, my refrigerator is empty. 沒有，我的冰箱空空如也。

A: Go shopping then. 那就去買啊。

B: I'm out of money. 我沒錢了呀。

＊ out of money 是指錢花完了，out of oil 是指「汽油用盡了」。另外，在用法上稍微不同的 "out of order" 是指「脫離了秩序」，也就是「故障了」的意思。

# ⓮ Do you have anything to **open this lock?**

### 你有什麼工具可以**開這把鎖**嗎？

03-14.mp3

A: *Do you have anything to* cook with? 你有什麼工具可以用來做飯嗎？

B: I have several knives. 我有幾把菜刀。

A: That isn't enough. 那些不夠呀。

B: Sure it is. 那些絕對夠了啦。

＊ anything to cook with 是指「用來做料理的東西」，即料理用具的意思。

A: *Do you have anything to* share with me? 你有什麼要和我分享的嗎？

B: No, should I? 沒有，應該要有嗎？

A: I was just hoping you did. 我只是希望你有罷了。

# ⑮ Do you want to go to the movies?

**你想去看電影嗎？**

03-15.mp3

"Do you want to ...?" 開頭的句型，中文意指「你想…嗎」，還可以當作「你要不要…」的意思，用來詢問對方意願。相同含義的句型另有 "Do you like to ... ？"。

A: *Do you want to* go snowboarding? 妳想去玩滑雪板嗎？

B: I've never been snowboarding before. 我從來沒玩過滑雪板耶。

A: It's fun. 很好玩喔。

＊可能讓初學者比較感到困難的是上面例句中的 "I've never been snowboarding before."。請各位讀者記住，回答「有／沒有做過某件事的經驗」時，英文說法是 "I've been / I've never been"。只要牢記這些用法，就能在適當時機發揮絕妙的功用。來，讓我們一起大聲地唸一遍吧！

### 還有這種說法喏！

Do you want to play a game? 你要玩遊戲嗎？

Do you want to do something? 你要做點事嗎？

# ⑯ Do you want me to help you?

**你要我幫你嗎？**

03-16.mp3

大家普遍不懂得使用的句型之一 "Do you want me to ...？"，直譯是「你希望我…嗎」，實際上是表達自己想幫忙做什麼。

A: *Do you want me to* open the window? 你要我把窗戶打開嗎？

B: Yes, it's hot in here. 好啊，這裡面很悶熱。

A: Where's the window? 窗戶在哪裡呢？

### 還有這種說法喏！

Do you want me to shut up? 你要我閉嘴嗎？

Do you want me to bake a cake? 你要我烤蛋糕嗎？

# ⑰ How come you don't like me?

03-17.mp3

### 你怎麼會不喜歡我？

　　在台灣可能比較少聽見，但是在美國使用率頗高的句型之一就是 "How come ..." 開頭的句型，中文的意思是「你怎麼會…」。

A: *How come* I'm short? 我怎麼會這麼矮呢？

B: Because you aren't tall. 因為你不高啊。

A: That's a good answer. 回答得真好。

A: *How come* you're so mean? 妳說的話怎麼會這麼刻薄啊？

B: I'm not mean. 才不會。

A: Yes, you are. 妳就是這麼刻薄。

\*我們所知的 "mean" 是指「意味著…」，但是在美國有些時候會把 "mean" 用來表示「惡意的、刻薄的」。

### 還有這種說法唷！

How come you don't like pork? 你怎麼會不喜歡豬肉呢？

How come I'm so fat? 我怎麼會這麼胖呢？

# ⑱ How come?

03-18.mp3

### 怎麼會這樣？

　　"How come?" 可單獨用來表示「怎麼會這樣」，是帶有驚嘆語氣的用法。在台灣比較少機會聽見這樣的英文說法，不過，對「老外」來說是很便利的句型。

A: I broke up with my girlfriend. 我和女朋友分手了。

B: *How come*? 怎麼會這樣？

A: Her father didn't like me at all. 她爸爸根本不喜歡我。

B: That's the reason? 是那個原因嗎？

# ⑲ How about her?

**她看起來怎麼樣？**

03-19.mp3

向對方詢問「某人看來如何」或是「做…如何」的英文說法是 "How about ..."。但是，若是要表達「做…如何」的意思時，在 How about 之後要使用 -ing 的形式。

A: I'm bored. 好無聊啊。

B: *How about* rubbing my back? 幫我抓抓背怎麼樣啊？

A: You've got to be kidding! 你是開玩笑的吧！

＊即便是老外，他們也喜歡沒事就抓抓背享受一下。抓背的英文說法就是 "rubbing back"。

### 還有這種說法喲！

How about a favor? 幫個忙怎麼樣啊？

How about giving me some free money? 給我一些錢怎麼樣？

# ⑳ Why don't you eat some food?

**你何不吃一點東西呢？**

03-20.mp3

與剛剛才學過的「How about ...?」含義最接近的句型就是「Why don't you ...?」，中文的意思是「你何不…呢」。雖然聽起來有點像是「要求」的語句，但這個句型比較常用在「建議」的說法上。

A: I'm so fat. 我好胖喔。

B: *Why don't you* go on a diet? 你何不減肥呢？

A: Diets don't work for me. 減肥對我沒有用。

### 還有這種說法喲！

Why don't you go for a walk? 你何不去散散步呢？

Why don't you go away? 你何不走開？

# **21 What kind of food do you like?**

03-21.mp3

### 你喜歡吃什麼樣的食物？

早在唸國中的時候，眾多拚命記在腦袋瓜子裡的英文片語之一就是 "What kind of"。除了背誦以外，也要多找機會和老外實際練習看看。 "What sort of" 的意思也和 "What kind of" 相近。

A: *What kind of* doctor are you? 妳是哪一科的醫生？
B: I'm a physical therapist. 我是物理治療師。
A: That's a popular job. 那是個受歡迎的工作。

**還有這種說法唷！**

What kind of dog is he? 這隻狗是什麼品種？

What kind of person are you? 你是什麼樣的人呢？

# **22 What makes you so afraid?**

03-22.mp3

### 什麼讓你這麼害怕？

這是在詢問對方「究竟怎麼了」時常使用的一句話，so 用來強調「如此」。

A: *What makes you so* interesting? 是什麼讓你這麼有趣啊？
B: Maybe it's my French accent. 大概是我的法國腔吧。
A: No, I think it's something else. 不，我想是其他的原因。

**還有這種說法唷！**

What makes you so angry all the time? 什麼讓你一直如此生氣呢？

What makes you scared? 什麼令你這麼害怕呢？

03-23.mp3

# ㉓ What do you think of that girl?

**你覺得那個女孩怎麼樣？**

詢問對方「你覺得…如何」時的英文說法是 "What do you think of ...?"，這是一句很實用的英文。

A: *What do you think of* our football team? 妳覺得我們的足球隊怎麼樣？
B: I watched them play on Saturday. 我週六看了他們的比賽。
A: And ...? 然後呢？
B: They're pretty good. 很不錯啊。

### 還有這種說法唷！

What do you think of my wife? 你覺得我太太怎麼樣？

What do you think of the food here? 你覺得這裡的食物如何？

03-24.mp3

# ㉔ How do you like my clothes?

**我的穿著怎麼樣？**

這句話也可以說成 "What do you think of my clothes?"，不過，若是詢問對方關於服裝打扮或是物品的狀態，最好還是說 "How do you like ..." 比較符合習慣。回答時的英文說法則是 "I like it a lot." 或是 "It's great." 等。

A: *How do you like* my car? 我的車看起來怎麼樣？
B: It's great. 很棒。
A: I got it for my birthday. 是我的生日禮物耶。

### 還有這種說法唷！

How do you like school? 學校怎麼樣？

How do you like my cooking? 我的廚藝怎麼樣？

## ㉕ I can't believe you said that.

03-25.mp3

### 我不敢相信你會這麼說。

遇到情況出乎意料或是感到訝異時，有些人會說「我不敢相信」。英文的說法就是 "I can't believe ..."。

A: *I can't believe* it's Saturday already. 我不敢相信已經到週六了耶。

B: Time goes fast. 歲月如梭啊。

A: I want it to go slow. 真希望時間過得慢一些。

#### 還有這種說法唷！

I can't believe it's over. 我不敢相信已經結束了。

I can't believe this is so hard. 我不敢相信這是如此辛苦。

## ㉖ What time do you have to go?

03-26.mp3

### 你什麼時候必須走呢？

這是一句很簡短的問話，請各位讀者一定要牢記。

A: *What time do you* want to go? 你什麼時候要走呢？

B: How does 5:30 sound? 五點半怎麼樣？

A: That sounds good. 聽起來不錯。

＊ "How does 5:30 sound?" 這種說法老外常用，所以，希望各位讀者一定要牢記。

#### 還有這種說法唷！

What time do you leave in the morning? 你早上幾點離開呢？

What time do you like to get up? 你想幾點起床呢？

## ㉗ Can you help me?

03-27.mp3

### 你能幫我一下嗎？

如同 "Do you ...?"，在英文中另一個最常使用的句型就是 "Can you ...?"，含義跟 "Could you ...?" 是一樣的。藉由這次的練習，讓我們牢記在腦海裡，有機會就勇敢地和老外對話吧。

A: *Can you* do my work for me? 你能替我完成工作嗎？
B: I can, but I won't. 可以啊，但是我不會這麼做。
A: You're not a good friend. 你算什麼朋友。

＊ I won't 是 I will not 的縮寫；I will 是「我將做…」的意思，反之，當然就是不肯去做的意思囉。I will 和 I won't 都是日常會話當中經常使用的語句，尤其，I won't 的發音必須格外小心。

#### 還有這種說法唷！

Can you fix my car? 你能修理我的車嗎？

Can you go to the store for me? 你能替我去一趟商店嗎？

## ㉘ Can you tell me what color this is?

03-28.mp3

### 你能告訴我這是什麼顏色嗎？

雖然也可以直接問 "What color is this?"，但 "Can you tell me ..." 是表示禮貌地向對方詢問「你可以告訴我這是什麼顏色嗎」，有尊重對方的感覺。

A: *Can you tell me* what your name is? 請問芳名？
B: My name is Mary. 我叫瑪莉。
A: Oh, yes! I remember you, Mary! 噢，對了！我記得妳，瑪莉！

#### 還有這種說法唷！

Can you tell me where to find Paul? 你能告訴我哪裡可以找到保羅嗎？

Can you tell me how to fix my car? 你能告訴我怎麼修理我的車子嗎？

# ⓵ **How long is the song?**

03-29.mp3

### 這首歌有多長？

"How long?" 是指「有多長」的意思，上面的例句「這首歌有多長」，回答時可以很簡短地說 "Five minutes."。國人在英文的表達能力上說 "How long" 沒問題，比較吃虧的部分在於不懂接下來該怎麼說，希望各位讀者能夠在下面的例句中，發現自己的問題所在。

A: *How long* is your arm? 妳的手臂有多長啊？
B: A couple feet, I guess. 大概有兩英呎吧。
A: That's long! 還真長呀！

\* feet 這個長度單位在一般的字典附錄部分都找得到，請換算成公分看看。

#### 還有這種說法唷！

How long do you have to work? 你還要工作多久啊？

How long should the pizza cook? 披薩應該烤多久呢？

# ㉚ **How far is the airport?**

03-30.mp3

### 機場有多遠？

若說 How long 用來表示「長度」，那麼，How far 則用來詢問「距離」。

A: *How far* to the next city? 到下一個城市有多遠？
B: Three miles. 要三英哩。
A: Three miles isn't long. 三英哩不算長。

#### 還有這種說法唷！

How far do we have to go? 我們還要再走多遠？

How far is it? 距離有多遠？

## ㉛ How soon will I see you again?

03-31.mp3

### 我何時才會再見到你？

How soon 照字面上的解釋是「多快」的意思，其實就是指「何時」。而且，應該將「何時」看做是包含了「多快」的意思。

A: *How soon* can you be done? 妳何時能做完？（妳能多快結束？）
B: I don't know. It's a lot of work. 還不能確定，工作太多了。
A: Please hurry. 請快一點。

#### 還有這種說法喔！

How soon will we get there? 我們何時會到達那個地方？

How soon can we leave? 我們何時能出發？

## ㉜ How often do you go shopping?

03-32.mp3

### 你多久去購物一次？

在這幾個單元，我們看了 How 後面接 long（長度）、far（距離）、soon / often（時間）等詞語的用法。How soon 是「多快」、How often 則是「多常（每隔多久一次）」的意思。

A: *How often* do you play baseball? 你多久打一次棒球？
B: As often as I can. 只要一有空我就去打。
A: How often is that? 那是多久一次啊？

#### 還有這種說法喔！

How often do you sleep? 你多常睡覺？

How often do you go out? 你多久約會一次？

# ③ How much is this candy?

03-33.mp3

**這個糖果多少錢？**

連三歲小孩都會說這句話吧？大家都知道詢問價錢的英文說法是 How much，不過，各位可以記住所有詢問「量」的多寡的問題都可以用 "How much ...?" 這個句型。此外，想要問對方「你有多愛我」時也可以用 "How much ...?" 的句型。

A: *How much* do you like me? 妳有多喜歡我呢？
B: A little. Why? 一點點，為什麼問？
A: I'm just wondering. 我只是好奇。

### 還有這種說法唷！

How much is this pen? 這支筆要多少錢？

How much milk did you put in? 你加了多少牛奶？

# ③ How many friends do you have?

03-34.mp3

**你有多少朋友？**

像「麵粉」、「砂糖」還有「愛」這種不可數的物質名詞必須用 "How much"；相反地，像「餅乾」、「雞蛋」、「罐裝啤酒」等可數的名詞則要用 "How many"，請各位繼續往下看。

A: *How many* pets do you have? 你養了幾隻寵物呢？
B: I have a dog and two cats. 我有一隻狗，兩隻貓。
A: How old are they? 牠們多大了呢？

### 還有這種說法唷！

How many cookies can I have? 我可以吃幾塊餅乾呢？

How many drinks have you had? 你喝了幾杯？

# 35

# How long have you been married?

03-35.mp3

## 你結婚多久了？

在眾多現在完成式疑問句中，我們學得最多、練習最久的就是 "How long have you ...?" 開頭的句型。不過，也請各位讀者先別管它是不是現在完成式，只要牢記像是「結婚多久了」、「住在這裡有多久了」這類的疑問都用 "How long have you ...?" 這個句型即可。

A: *How long have you* lived here? 妳住在這裡多久了？
B: I moved here two years ago. 我兩年前搬來這裡。
A: How do you like it? 妳喜歡這裡嗎？

### 還有這種說法唷！

How long have you been here? 你在這裡多久了？

How long have you liked skiing? 你喜歡滑雪多久了？

# 36

# How long does it take to drive to school?

03-36.mp3

## 開車到學校要多久？

要到某個地方或是針對某件事詢問「要多久」時，"How long does it take to ...?" 是最簡單好用的英文說法。

A: *How long does it take to* clean a window? 清洗窗戶要多久時間？
B: Only about a minute. 大約只要 1 分鐘。
A: Good. 很好。

### 還有這種說法唷！

How long does it take to cook the meal? 做一次料理要花多久時間？

How long does it take to go to school? 到學校要多久？

# 37 How do you say dog in your language?

03-37.mp3

### 用你的語言怎麼説「狗」？

和老外講英文，一定免不了遇到對方問你這一類的問題。例如，「dog 的中文怎麼說」，當然是叫狗囉。適合這種情況的疑問句型就是 "How do you say ...?"。

A: *How do you say* church in Spanish? 用西班牙文怎麼説「教堂」？
B: Iglesia. Iglesia。
A: Thank you. 謝謝。

### 還有這種說法唷！

How do you say goat in French? 「山羊」的法文怎麼説？

How do you say horse in Japanese? 「馬」的日文怎麼説？

# 38 How do you spell your name?

03-38.mp3

### 你的名字怎麼拼？

第一次聽到老外的名字常會覺得很難；相對地，老外第一次聽到台灣人的名字也同樣會覺得很難聽懂。所以，以後要問老外的名字時，我們可以用 "How do you spell ..." 的句型確認拼法。

A: Your name? 你叫什麼名字？
B: Mulder. 穆德。
A: *How do you spell* your name? 怎麼拼呢？
B: M-U-L-D-E-R. M-U-L-D-E-R。

### 還有這種說法唷！

How do you spell your last name? 你的姓氏怎麼拼？

## ③⁹ How do I do this?

### 我該怎麼做？

03-39.mp3

　　詢問事情「該怎麼做」時的英文說法是 "How do I ...?"。另外，詢問別人「我看起來怎麼樣」時同樣可以用 "How do I ...?" 這個句型，變成 "How do I look?"。

A: *How do I* play baseball? 棒球應該怎麼打？
B: Watch and learn. 好好看著學。
A: I'll watch you play. 我會用心看妳打。

**還有這種說法喔！**

How do I get money? 要怎麼樣才能賺到錢？

How do I sleep without you? 沒有妳我怎麼睡得著？


## ④⁰ How can I get a good job?

### 怎麼做才能找到好工作呢？

03-40.mp3

　　「怎麼樣才能…」的英文說法用 "How can I ...?" 開頭就行了。例如，「怎麼做才能得到 A 呢」、「怎麼做才能見得到她呢？」等。

A: *How can I* get in better shape? 怎麼做身材才能比較好呢？
B: Exercise. 運動啊。
A: I don't like exercising. 我不喜歡運動。

**還有這種說法喔！**

How can I get an A in this class? 怎麼做才能在這門課拿到 A 呢？

How can I open this can? 怎麼做才能打開這個罐頭？

# ⁴¹ Would you mind if I sit down?

03-41.mp3

## 你介意**我坐下來**嗎？

這是很常在電影情節中聽到的對白。千萬別把它想得很難，各位只要以平常心看待就行了。雖然因為 mind 表示「介意」的關係，所以同意時要回答不介意，但我們只要記得可以簡單回答 Go ahead.（請便）就行了。

A: *Would you mind if* I lay down? 妳介意我躺下來嗎？
B: Go ahead. Are you feeling okay? 請便，你還好嗎？
A: My stomach hurts a little. 我的肚子有點痛。

> **還有這種說法唷！**
>
> Would you mind if I watch TV? 你介意我看電視嗎？
>
> Would you mind if I leave now? 你介意我現在離開嗎？

# ⁴² Do you mind if I borrow your car?

03-42.mp3

## 你介意**我向你借車**嗎？

用法和上面的 Would you mind if 是一樣的。

A: *Do you mind if I* ask you a favor? 你介意我請你幫忙一件事嗎？
B: Of course not. What is it? 當然不會，是什麼事情？
A: Give me a hug. 給我一個擁抱。

> **還有這種說法唷！**
>
> Do you mind if I get a drink of water? 你介意我喝杯水嗎？
>
> Do you mind if I smoke? 你介意我抽根煙嗎？

## ㊸ Would you like some tea?

03-43.mp3

### 你想喝杯茶嗎？

如果要詢問對方「你想做…嗎」，百分之一百放心大膽地說 "Would you like to...?" 或是下一個句型 "Do you like to ...?" 就對了。

A: *Would you like* to stay with me? 妳想暫時在我這裡嗎？
B: Yes, I'd love to. 是的，我很樂意。
A: You can have the guest room. 妳可以住在客房。

**還有這種說法唷！**

Would you like more potatoes? 你想再來一點馬鈴薯嗎？

Would you like a new car? 你想要一台新車嗎？

## ㊹ Do you like to work for me?

03-44.mp3

### 你想跟著我做事嗎？

很多時候，Would 開頭的句子比 Do 開頭的表達方式更加禮貌。不過，在一般輕鬆的對話中，兩種表達方式都可以使用。

A: *Do you like to* make some money? 你想賺點外快嗎？
B: How can I do that? 怎麼做呢？
A: Wash my car for me. 幫我洗車就行了。

**還有這種說法唷！**

Do you like to start your own business? 你想創業嗎？

# ⁴⁵ We'd better see what's up.

03-45.mp3

## 我們最好小心點（看看發生什麼事情）。

A: *We'd better* eat something. 我們最好吃點東西。

B: Yes, we haven't had food for a while. 是啊，我們有好一陣子沒吃東西了。

A: What should we eat? 該吃點什麼呢？

### 還有這種說法唷！

We'd better help them. 我們最好幫助他們。

We'd better see what's wrong. 我們最好看看問題出在哪裡。

# ⁴⁶ You'd better hurry.

03-46.mp3

## 你最好快一點。

"You'd better ..." 字面上是「你最好…」的意思。表面上說得很婉轉，事實上，即便理解成「去做…」這種命令的口吻其實也不為過。

A: *You'd better* do your work. 你最好去做功課。

B: I will. 我會的。

A: Hurry! 快去！

### 還有這種說法唷！

You'd better save your money. 你最好省一點錢。

You'd better leave me alone. 你最好別管我。

# ⁴⁷ I'd like to see you.

03-47.mp3

### 我想見你。

　　「我想…」的英文說法是 "I'd like to ..."，不用說，I'd 是 I would 的縮寫。事實上，請各位讀者注意 "d" 的發音並不是像中文「的」那麼明顯。另外，在會話中 see 當作「見面」的意思遠比當作「看見」的意思要來得常用。

A: Do you want to come to my house? 你要來我家嗎？
B: *I'd like to*, but I can't. 我很想，可是不行。
A: Why not? 為什麼不行？
B: I'm busy today. 我今天很忙。

#### 還有這種說法唷！

I'd like to tell you something. 我有話想對你說。

I'd like to go shopping. 我想去逛街。


# ⁴⁸ I want to go home.

03-48.mp3

### 我要回家。

　　剛剛才學過的 "I'd like to ..." 和 "I want to ..." 其實大同小異，意思很類似。不管採用哪一個句型，只要選擇自己說得順口的就行了。此外，"I need to ..." 也是相似的句型。如果說 "I want to ..." 是指「我想要…」的意思，那麼，"I don't want to ..." 當然是「我不想要…」的意思囉。

A: *I want to* listen to music. 我想聽音樂。
B: Then do it. 那就聽啊。
A: I don't have any music! 我沒有任何音樂耶！

#### 還有這種說法唷！

I want to go out and play. 我想要出去玩。

I need to get my hair cut. 我需要剪頭髮。

## ⑲ I'm not going to trust you.

03-49.mp3

### 我不打算相信你。

"I'm going to ..." 是指「我打算要…」的意思；那麼「我不打算要…」又該怎麼說呢？嗯，很簡單，只要把 not 放進去變成 "I'm not going to ..." 即可。be 動詞後面接 not 就會變成否定句，各位應該都還記得吧？

A: Do as I say. 照我說的去做。

B: *I'm not going to*. 我不要。

A: You have to! 你一定要！

**還有這種說法唷！**

I'm not going to help you. 我不會幫你的忙。

I'm not going to lie to you. 我不會騙你。

## ⑳ I was just going to go for a walk.

03-50.mp3

### 我正要去散步。

「我剛要去…」的英文說法是 "I was just going to ..."，若是能夠說出這樣的一句英文已經算是很厲害了。

A: What are you doing? 妳在做什麼啊？

B: *I was just going to* do my homework. 我正要做功課呢。

B: Okay. Carry on. 很好，繼續吧。

**還有這種說法唷！**

I was just going to the store. 我正要去那家商店。

I was just going to pet your dog. 我正要摸摸你的狗。

# ⑤ I've heard about you.

03-51.mp3

## 我聽說過關於你的事。

「我聽說某件事」，英文的說法是 "I've heard ..."，後面直接接句子，或者也可以接名詞，表示「聽說過某個對象」。若是有人天花亂墜地講一堆過去式、現在完成式之類的術語，各位可以一概不用理會。大家只需要將這個句型牢記在腦海裡就可以了。

A: *I've heard* you play music. 我聽說妳會演奏音樂。
B: Yes, I have a guitar. 是啊，我有一把吉他。
A: Play for me. 彈一段讓我聽聽吧。

### 還有這種說法唷！

I've heard this song. 我聽過這首歌。

I've heard that before. 我以前聽過。

# ㊜ Have you ever been to Hawaii?

03-52.mp3

## 你曾經去過夏威夷嗎？

想問對方「你曾經…嗎」，只要運用 "Have you ever ..." 的句型，那麼說出來的絕對是一句完美的英文喔。別把文法想得太複雜，只要記著這個句型一律都是接動詞的過去分詞就可以了。

A: *Have you ever* seen the movie "The Fugitive?"
  你看過「絕命追殺令」這部電影嗎？
B: Yes, that was a good movie. 有啊，那是部好電影。
A: I think so, too. 我也這麼覺得。

### 還有這種說法唷！

Have you ever been to a party? 你參加過派對嗎？

Have you ever eaten tuna fish? 你吃過鮪魚嗎？

# 53 I've got to do something.

03-53.mp3

**我應該做些事情。**

美國人有一句口頭禪 "I've got to ..."。既然是口頭禪，各位就別太在意 get 究竟是什麼意思，為什麼要用完成式之類的問題。因為這追根究柢起來可能三天三夜都說不完呢。美國人就是這麼做，所以我們也如法炮製就對了。

A: *I've got to* go to the post office. 我得跑一趟郵局。

B: Would you mail a letter for me? 可以請你幫我寄封信嗎？

A: Sure. Give it to me. 可以啊，給我吧。

## 還有這種說法唷！

I've got to write a letter. 我要寫一封信。

I've got to eat something. 我應該去吃些東西了。

# 54 We've got to warn people!

03-54.mp3

**我們得提醒大家！**

"I've got to ..." 本來源自英國，到了美國就變成了 "I gotta ..."，是「我該…」的意思。

A: A killer is on the loose. 殺人犯被放出來了。

B: *We've got to* warn people! 我們得提醒大家啊！

A: No, let's find the killer first. 不，我們先把殺人犯找出來吧。

A: *I've got to* save James. 我得去救詹姆士。

B: Why, where's James？ 為什麼，詹姆士在哪裡？

A: He's a prisoner. 他在牢房裡（他是囚犯）。

## 55 I don't know where to **go.**

03-55.mp3

我不知道該往哪裡**走**。

I don't know 後面接 "where to ..." 的意思是「在哪裡做…」；I don't know 後面接 "how to ..." 的意思是「不知道怎樣做…」。請牢記像 I don't know 後面接 where / how / what / when to 的各式句型，如此才能輕鬆應付各種狀況。

A: *I don't know where to* eat. 我不知道去哪裡吃飯。
B: I don't, either. 我也是。
A: Let's just find a place. 我們隨便找個地方吧。

### 還有這種說法唷！

I don't know where to sit down. 我不知道該坐在哪裡。

## 56 I don't know what to **do.**

03-56.mp3

我不知道該**做些什麼**。

"I don't know what to ..." 是間接疑問句型，如同 "I don't know where to ..." 一樣是常用的說法，中文意思當然是指「我不知道該…什麼」。

A: My dog died. 我的狗死了。
B: *I don't know what to* say. 我不知道該說些什麼。
A: It's okay. 沒有關係。

### 還有這種說法唷！

I don't know what to wear. 我不知道該穿什麼。

I don't know what to eat. 我不知道應該吃什麼。

# 用 365 個單字
# 說盡英語會話！

第 2 部分的內容為打招呼、對話、搭乘交通工具、飲食、購物、打電話、旅行還有居家用語等 8 種情境課程。只要認真閱讀此章，應付一般場合絕對沒問題。而且，你只需要說最簡單、最簡短的英語就行了。這些句型都是嚴選實際生活上能夠輕鬆應付老外的英語會話。

CH 4 → 不管遇見誰，招呼用語讓你自信滿滿

CH 5 → 言之有禮！贊同、反對用語說得大方

CH 6 → 無論去哪裡，交通用語無敵方便

CH 7 → 大快朵頤！飲食用語盡情享用

CH 8 → 就是要血拼，購物用語殺到底

CH 9 → 講電話支支吾吾？電話用語說得流利

CH 10 → 旅行靠自己，旅遊用語讓你信心倍增

CH 11 → 禮尚往來！居家、拜訪用語最感心

# Chapter 4
# 不管遇見誰，招呼用語讓你自信滿滿

據說學習者最有自信的英語是「招呼語」，但是，我認為沒有比招呼語更難的英語了。筆者在美國留學的期間，有好幾年都深深體悟到招呼語實在是十分奧妙的用語。

各位讀者，你們知道老外最常說的招呼語是什麼嗎？當然是 "Hi!" 這個簡短的用語。但是，當我們說 "Hi!" 向對方打招呼時，重點在於能否看著對方的眼睛，真心地打從心裡高興遇見對方而說 "Hi!"。心情好的時候，不好的時候，不好也不壞的時候，招呼用語其實都不一樣。事實上，同一種招呼語怎麼可能用來應付各種不同的情況呢？

好了，那麼請各位讀者現在就進入本文部分，親自體驗不同狀況的不同招呼語，順便檢視一下是否用得合宜。希望各位都能跟著例句大聲朗讀，並且認真學習。

# ① How are you doing?

04-01.mp3

### 近來好嗎？

一直以來，我們所知的招呼語都是 "How are you?"，不過，老外常說的則是多了 doing 的 "How are you doing?"。為什麼是 doing 呢？別管為什麼了，各位只管牢記就是了。所謂「說話」，著重的並不是規則，而是「實際生活上使用的言詞」，這才是學習會話的起點。

A: How are you doing? 近來怎麼樣？

B: I'm fine. How are you? 還不錯，你呢？

A: Great, thanks. 很好，謝謝妳的關心。

＊各位，可別看這句話很簡短就小看它。就像用中文跟人家打招呼通常也不會太冗長，老外在實際對話中大部分也都是像這樣簡短對答。

# How's it going?

### 過得好嗎？

與 "How are you doing?" 一樣，"How's it going?" 也是常用的問候語之一，請各位讀者務必銘記在心，有機會就對人說說看。（How's 是 How is 的縮寫，大家應該都沒問題吧？）

A: How's it going? 過得好嗎？

B: Not bad. How about you? 還好啦，妳呢？

A: It's going fine with me. 我過得還不錯。

B: I'm glad to hear that. 聽到妳這麼說我很高興。

＊我們常會聽到像 "It's going fine with me." 一樣加上 "with me" 的說法，關於這一點，我們只要當作是美國人的慣用說法就可以了。類似的用法還有 "It's okay with me."。

### 活用 365 個單字也能這麼說！

No money, no show. 沒有錢，不給看（不願意無酬演出）。

No pain, no gain. 一分耕耘，一分收穫。

# ❷ What's up?

### 過得怎麼樣？

課本不太會教，但美國年輕人最常說的招呼語就是 "What's up?"。我們即便知道怎麼說，也常害怕說出口，因為心裡有著「要是說錯發音，不就要被老外笑掉大牙」的不安心理。既然在這裡學到了，請各位讀者下次一定要說說看。

A: What's up? 過得怎麼樣？

B: Not much. 馬馬虎虎。

A: Not much here, either. 我也差不多。

＊回答句 Not much. 是說「過得馬馬虎虎」的意思。

# What's new?
**有什麼新鮮事嗎？**

這句話跟 "What's up?" 一樣是大家常用的招呼語，中文意思是「有沒有什麼新鮮事」，不過，只要簡單當成「最近怎麼樣」的意思就可以了。

A: Hey, there! 嘿，瞧誰來了！

B: Hey Jack! 嘿，傑克！

A: What's new? 有什麼新鮮事嗎？

B: Oh, not much, man. 噢，沒什麼特別的事耶。

＊如果想很自然地向對方打招呼，"Hey there!" 是很不錯的說法。在這句話裡，千萬別死腦筋地認為 there 一定是指「那裡」（地方副詞）。就像平時我們和朋友打招呼時常說「你那裡怎麼樣」，也是這樣的意思。

# How have you been?
**這段時間你過得如何？**

A: How have you been? 這段時間你過得如何？

B: I've been okay. 還可以。

A: How is your family? 家人都好吧？

B: They are good, too. 他們也都很好。

＊ "How have you been?" 和 "What's up" 或 "How are you?" 一樣，都有相同的中文含義。也可以簡化成 "How you been?"。

絕對派上用場！
最常用的情境單字！

## Emotions 情感

04-w1.mp3

| | | |
|---|---|---|
| tired [taɪrd] | adj. | 疲倦的 |
| sleepy [ˋslipɪ] | adj. | 想睡覺的 |
| exhausted [ɪgˋzɔstɪd] | adj. | 精疲力盡的 |
| hot [hɑt] | adj. | 熱的 |
| cold [kold] | adj. | 冷的 |
| hungry [ˋhʌŋgrɪ] | adj. | 飢餓的 |
| thirsty [ˋθɝstɪ] | adj. | 口渴的 |
| full [fʊl] | adj. | 飽的 |
| sick [sɪk] | adj. | 生病的 |
| happy [ˋhæpɪ] | adj. | 快樂的 |
| sad [sæd] | adj. | 傷心的 |
| disappointed [͵dɪsəˋpɔɪntɪd] | adj. | 失望的 |
| upset [ʌpˋsɛt] | adj. | 苦惱的 |
| angry [ˋæŋgrɪ] | adj. | 生氣的 |
| furious [ˋfjʊrɪəs] | adj. | 憤怒的 |
| disgusted [dɪsˋgʌstɪd] | adj. | 厭惡的 |
| surprised [səˋpraɪzd] | adj. | 驚訝的 |
| shocked [ʃɑkt] | adj. | 受到打擊的 |
| nervous [ˋnɝvəs] | adj. | 緊張的 |
| worried [ˋwɝɪd] | adj. | 擔心的 |
| scared [skɛrd] | adj. | 害怕的 |
| bored [bord] | adj. | 感到無聊的 |
| proud [praʊd] | adj. | 得意的 |
| embarrassed [ɪmˋbærəst] | adj. | 難堪的 |
| ashamed [əˋʃemd] | adj. | 慚愧的 |
| jealous [ˋdʒɛləs] | adj. | 妒忌的 |

# 3 Long time no see.

**好久不見。**

04-03.mp3

我們在學英文時，最大的滿足感來自於能夠學會以前以為很艱深，但其實很簡單的內容，然後運用在適當的時機。這裡介紹的 "Long time no see" 就是屬於這類的說法，了解之後是既簡單又實用。類似的句型還有 "Long time no talk."，中文意思是「好久沒聊了」，也就是說「很久沒見」。

A: Hi Tony! 嗨，湯尼！
B: Long time no see! 好久不見了！
A: It's been a while. 是滿久了。
B: How have you been? 最近在忙什麼呢？

## I haven't seen you for a long time.
**好久不見。**

和 "Long time no see." 一樣，都是指「好久不見」的意思。分開來解釋是這樣的：好久（for a long time）我沒見到你（I haven't seen you）。

A: I haven't seen you for a long time. 好久不見了。
B: Not for a few years. 應該有好多年了吧。
A: How have you been? 你過得好嗎？
B: Good. And yourself? 好啊，妳自己呢？

## I haven't seen you in years.
**好多年沒見到你了。**

A: I haven't seen you in years. 好多年沒見到妳了耶。
B: I've been very busy. 我過得很忙。
A: Doing what? 在忙什麼呢？
B: I'm working for a large corporation. 我在一家大公司上班。

# ④ It's been a long time.

04-04.mp3

好久不見。

如果說 "Long time no see." 是最普遍又實用的問候對方「好久不見」的說法，那麼，"It's been a long time." 這個句型則顯得比較高雅，也顯示出英文表達方式的多樣性。在這裡，It's 是 It has 的縮寫。

A: It's been a long time. 好久不見了。

B: Yes, it has. 是啊，是滿久了。

A: What have you been doing? 妳都在做什麼？

B: I've been going to school. 我在學校唸書。

## What have you been up to?

你過得好嗎？

繼 "It's been a long time." 之後，接著就可以說 "What have you been up to?"。這句話的簡短說法是 "What's up?"。

A: What have you been up to? 你過得好嗎？

B: Oh, not much. 噢，還可以啦。

## What a surprise to meet you here!

竟然在這裡遇到你！

A: What a surprise to meet you here! 竟然在這兒遇到妳！

B: Same here. 我也這麼想。

A: What are you doing here? 妳在這裡做什麼？

B: I was about to ask you the same thing. 我也正想問你呢。

＊在偶然的場合遇到某人時，我們可以很驚訝地表示 "What a surprise to meet you here!"。

絕對派上用場！
最常用的情境單字！

04-w2.mp3

## Family 家族稱謂

| | | |
|---|---|---|
| father [ˋfɑðɚ] | n. | 父親 |
| mother [ˋmʌðɚ] | n. | 母親 |
| wife [waɪf] | n. | 妻子 |
| husband [ˋhʌzbənd] | n. | 丈夫 |
| daughter [ˋdɔtɚ] | n. | 女兒 |
| son [sʌn] | n. | 兒子 |
| sister [ˋsɪstɚ] | n. | 姊姊、妹妹 |
| brother [ˋbrʌðɚ] | n. | 哥哥、弟弟 |
| baby [ˋbebɪ] | n. | 嬰兒 |
| grandfather [ˋgrænd͵fɑðɚ] | n. | （外）祖父 |
| grandmother [ˋgrænd͵mʌðɚ] | n. | （外）祖母 |
| granddaughter [ˋgrænd͵dɔtɚ] | n. | （外）孫女 |
| grandson [ˋgrænd͵sʌn] | n. | （外）孫子 |
| aunt [ænt] | n. | 阿姨、伯母、嬸嬸、姑媽、舅媽 |
| uncle [ˋʌŋkl̩] | n. | 舅舅、伯父、叔父 |
| niece [nis] | n. | 姪女、甥女 |
| nephew [ˋnɛfju] | n. | 姪子、外甥 |
| cousin [ˋkʌzn̩] | n. | 堂兄弟姊妹、表兄弟姊妹 |
| mother-in-law [ˋmʌðərɪn͵lɔ] | n. | 婆婆、岳母 |
| father-in-law [ˋfɑðərɪn͵lɔ] | n. | 公公、岳父 |
| son-in-law [ˋsʌnɪn͵lɔ] | n. | 女婿 |
| daughter-in-law [ˋdɔtərɪn͵lɔ] | n. | 媳婦 |
| brother-in-law [ˋbrʌðərɪn͵lɔ] | n. | 姊夫、妹婿 |
| sister-in-law [ˋsɪstərɪn͵lɔ] | n. | 嫂嫂、小姑、小姨子 |

# ⑤ Great!

很好！

04-05.mp3

說英文容易表達得不好的就是招呼語，尤其是回答句。照理說，心情壞就應該要說心情壞，心情好就應該要說心情好，不過，事情似乎總不是這麼容易呢。我們就別再只懂得說 "Fine, thank you. And you?" 這一句了。"Great!" 這個回答句是「心情很好」時可以說的話。

A: I'll see you tonight. 今晚見囉。
B: Great! 好啊！
A: See you later. 待會見。

## Very good.

非常好。

"Very good." 和 "Great!" 一樣，都是心情快樂得像飛起來一樣時所說的語句。

A: Look at this picture I drew. 看一下我畫的圖。
B: Very good. 畫得很好啊。
A: I'm proud of it. 我感到很自豪。

## ⑥ Just fine.

### 還可以。

向別人打招呼時，若是心情不好也不壞，可以說 "Just fine."。但是，即便早就想好要回答什麼，一旦面對老外，還是會說不出口，這真是令人傷腦筋。平時如果不勤加練習，實際上場最難應付的部分就是招呼語的回答。各位加油啊，一定要努力朗讀三、四次，再學習下個單元。

A: How are you? 你好嗎？
B: Just fine. 還可以啦。
A: I'm glad to hear that. 很高興聽你這麼說。

## Good.
### 很好。

good 這個字，在發音的時候要記得它的重音在 "goo"，後面的 "d" 很快帶過就行了。

A: I did what you told me to. 我把妳叫我做的事情做好了。
B: Good. 很好。
A: Can I do anything else for you? 還有其他我能幫你的嗎？

## Keeping busy.
### 過得很忙。

A: What have you been up to? 你過得還好吧？
B: Keeping busy. 過得挺忙的呢。
A: Doing what? 在忙些什麼？
B: I've been doing odd jobs. 我打了些零工。

＊ odd jobs 是指「零工」，而 Keeping busy. 則是「過得很忙」的意思。若不用點心思，這是絕對不會想到的回答句。要是能熟稔這些說法，你很快就會聽見別人說你是個「英文高手」了。

# ⑦ OK.

**還好。**

04-07.mp3

向別人打招呼時，若是心情不好也不壞，最適合說的就是像 "OK." 或 "Not bad."、"So-so." 之類的回答。

A: Hey, Frank! 嘿，法蘭克！
B: Joey! How're things going? 喬伊！妳好嗎？
A: Same as usual. How about you? 還是老樣子。你呢？
B: OK. 還可以。

# Not bad!

**還不錯！**

"Not bad!" 照字面上的解釋是「不壞」，所以，我們可以直接當它是「好」的意思。

A: Hello! 哈囉！
B: Hello! How's it going? 哈囉！最近怎麼樣？
A: Not bad. 還不錯啦。

# So-so.

**馬馬虎虎。**

A: How is your mother? 你媽媽好嗎？
B: So-so. 馬馬虎虎啦。
A: Is she sick? 她是不是病了？
B: A little. 一點點。

＊這是一句十分容易聽得到的招呼語，是指「還過得去」的意思。

# ⑧ Not so good!

## 不太妙！

04-08.mp3

當你和某人打招呼後，對方若是回答 "Not so good!"，可能表示情況不是很好，應對的時候可能要稍微留心了。事實上，老外並不常用 "Not so good!" 回答，因為即便自身的狀況真的不好，他們也不想讓人看見自己的窘迫。總之，記得下次回應別人問候時，不要輕易說 "Not so good!"。

A: How is your wife? 你太太還好嗎？
B: Not so good! 不太好！
A: I'm sorry. 我很遺憾聽你這麼說。

## Shitty.

**很差。**

這是比較粗俗的說法，雖然適合在心情不好的時候說，不過，這個字用在交情很好的朋友之間，聽起來才不會那麼刺耳。

A: How is the weather there? 那裡的天氣如何？
B: Shitty. 很差。
A: It's sunny here! 這裡可是陽光普照呢！
B: Good for you. 你可好了。

## Not so great!

**過得不太好！**

A: How are you? 你好嗎？
B: Not so great. 不太好。
A: Why? What's wrong? 怎麼回事？有什麼問題？

＊ Not so great! 和 Not so good! 一樣，都是形容不太好的狀況。

04-w3.mp3

## Weather & Seasons 天氣與季節

| | | |
|---|---|---|
| sunny [ˈsʌnɪ] | adj. | 晴天的 |
| cloudy [ˈklaʊdɪ] | adj. | 陰天的 |
| clear [klɪr] | adj. | 晴朗的 |
| foggy [ˈfɔgɪ] | adj. | 有霧的 |
| windy [ˈwɪndɪ] | adj. | 颱風的 |
| rainy [ˈrenɪ] | adj. | 下雨的 |
| snowy [ˈsnoɪ] | adj. | 下雪的 |
| snowstorm [ˈsnoˌstɔrm] | n. | 暴風雪 |
| typhoon [taɪˈfun] | n. | 颱風 |
| temperature [ˈtɛmprətʃɚ] | n. | 溫度 |
| thermometer [θəˈmɑmətɚ] | n. | 溫度計 |
| Fahrenheit [ˈfærənˌhaɪt] | adj. | 華氏的 |
| centigrade [ˈsɛntəˌgred] | adj. | 攝氏的 |
| hot [hɑt] | adj. | 熱的 |
| warm [wɔrm] | adj. | 暖和的 |
| cool [kul] | adj. | 涼爽的 |
| cold [kold] | adj. | 冷的 |
| freezing [ˈfriɪŋ] | adj. | 寒冷的 |
| summer [ˈsʌmɚ] | n. | 夏天 |
| fall [fɔl] / autumn [ˈɔtəm] | n. | 秋天 |
| winter [ˈwɪntɚ] | n. | 冬天 |
| spring [sprɪŋ] | n. | 春天 |

# **9 This is my friend Tom.**

04-09.mp3

### 這是我的朋友湯姆。

以前我們為了向別人介紹自己的朋友或同事，用 I'd like to 和 introduce 來造句而吃盡了苦頭。從今天起，就讓我們以 "This is my friend Tom." 這種簡單的方式來替朋友介紹吧。各位一定能感受到說英文是那麼簡單又輕鬆。

A: This is my friend Tom. 這是我的朋友湯姆。
B: How do you do, Tom? 你好嗎，湯姆？
C: I'm good, thanks. 我很好，謝謝。

## Susan, do you know Tom?
**蘇姍，妳認識湯姆嗎？**

A: Susan, do you know Tom? 蘇姍，妳認識湯姆嗎？
B: No, we haven't met. 不認識，我們沒見過。
A: Well, now you have! 這樣啊，現在認識囉！
B: Hi, Tom! 嗨，湯姆！

## I'd like you to meet my friend Tom.
**我想讓你認識一下我的朋友湯姆。**

A: I'd like you to meet my friend Tom. 我想讓你認識一下我的朋友湯姆。
B: Hi Tom. 嗨，湯姆。
C: Hi, how are you? 嗨，你好嗎？
B: Fine, thank you. 我很好，謝謝。

＊這句的字面意思是「我想讓你見我的朋友湯姆」，請注意，不要把這個句型誤解成「我喜歡你⋯」。

# ⑩ I've heard so much about you.

04-10.mp3

久仰您的大名。

彼此互相介紹時，有時會說「久仰您的大名」。英文也有類似的說法，是 "I've heard so much about you."。說這個句型的時候，必須強調 so much。若是透過 "Jason" 得知了相關的訊息，則英文可說 "I've heard so much about you from Jason."。

A: I've heard so much about you. 久仰您的大名。
B: All good, I hope! 但願都是好事！
A: Oh, of course. 噢，那當然囉。

## Jane has told me all about you.

珍告訴了我所有關於你的事情。

這個句子當然是表示透過某人得知的意思。

A: Jane has told me all about you. 珍告訴了我所有關於你的事。
B: I'm sure she has. 我想也是。
A: Please sit down. 請坐。

### 活用 365 個單字也能這麼說！

You saved my life. Thanks. 你救了我一命，謝謝。
＊感激涕零的情況下才適用這一句。

# ⑪ I didn't catch your name.

04-11.mp3

### 我沒聽清楚你的名字。

　　我們在和別人打招呼時，有時不會直視對方的眼睛說話，也不一定會好好問清楚對方的姓名。我個人認為那實在會很失禮，所以，我想為各位讀者推薦的用語就是 "I didn't catch your name."。當我們和老外互相認識時，實在很難馬上聽懂對方的英文發音，所以請務必牢記這一句話，以便日後派上用場。對了，還有另一種說法是 "I'm terrible at names."，意思是說「我最不擅長記名字了」。

A: I didn't catch your name. 我沒聽清楚你的名字。
B: Rudy. 魯迪。
A: Yes, Rudy. I won't forget again! 沒錯，魯迪。我不會再忘記了。
B: That's okay. 沒關係。（別介意。）

## I'm sorry, what was your name again?
**抱歉，能再說一次你的名字嗎？**

A: I'm sorry, what was your name again? 抱歉，能再說一次你的名字嗎？
B: Randolf. 藍道夫。
A: Hi, Randolf. 嗨，藍道夫。

### 活用 365 個單字也能這麼說！

I'm just killing time. 我只是在消磨時間。

You're dressed to kill. 妳真會穿衣服。

絕對派上用場！
最常用的情境單字！

## WORD BOX

04-w4.mp3

## Jobs 職業

| | | |
|---|---|---|
| accountant [ə`kaʊntənt] | n. | 會計 |
| actor [`æktə·] | n. | 演員 |
| actress [`æktrɪs] | n. | 女演員 |
| architect [`ɑrkə‚tɛkt] | n. | 建築師 |
| artist [`ɑrtɪst] | n. | 藝術家 |
| baker [`bekə·] | n. | 麵包師傅 |
| bus driver [`bʌs ‚draɪvə·] | n. | 司機 |
| bookkeeper [`bʊk‚kipə·] | n. | 簿記員 |
| butcher [`bʊtʃə·] | n. | 屠夫 |
| carpenter [`kɑrpəntə·] | n. | 木匠 |
| cashier [kæ`ʃɪr] | n. | 櫃台收帳員 |
| chef [ʃɛf] / cook [kʊk] | n. | 廚師 |
| construction worker [kən`strʌkʃən ‚wɝkə·] | n. | 建築工人 |
| custodian [kʌs`todɪən] / janitor [`dʒænətə·] | n. | 警衛 |
| delivery person [dɪ`lɪvərɪ ‚pɝsn̩] | n. | 送貨人員 |
| farmer [`fɑrmə·] | n. | 農夫 |
| fisherman [`fɪʃə·mən] | n. | 漁夫 |
| hairdresser [`hɛr‚drɛsə·] | n. | 美髮師 |
| housekeeper [`haʊs‚kipə·] | n. | 管家 |
| journalist [`dʒɝnlɪst] / reporter [rɪ`portə·] | n. | 記者 |

# ⑫ Bye.

再見。

不管是對熟人或初次見面的人，都可以說 "Bye."。對於不太熟的人或是長輩也可以這樣說，一定有很多人是現在才知道的吧？

A: I'll see you later! 待會見囉！
B: Bye. 再見。
A: Bye. 再見。

## See you again.

**下次見了。**

顧名思義，see you（見面）、again（再次）湊在一塊兒就是指「下次再見」的意思。

A: See you again. 下次再見囉。
B: When? 下次是什麼時候？
A: I'll call you. 我再打電話給你。

## See you later.

**下次見囉。**

A: See you later. 下次見囉。
B: Okay, see you! 好啊，再見！
A: Bye. 再見。

# ⑬ Take care.

保重。

04-13.mp3

在美國，同學或是年輕人在分開時，最常說的就是這句 "Take care."。"Take care." 其實是 "Take care of yourself." 的簡短說法，中文的意思是「保重」。

A: Take care. 要多保重喔。
B: You too, okay? 你也一樣，好嗎？
A: Of course. 好。

# Good to see you.
見到你真好。

A: Good to see you. 很高興見到你。
B: It's good to see you, too! 我也是！
A: I've missed you. 我很想念你呢。

# Catch you later.
下次見囉。

A: I have to go. 我得走了。
B: Catch you later. 下次見囉。
A: Later. 下次吧。

＊與 "Take care." 的意思相近，是指「下次見」的意思。"Catch you later." 較正式的說法應該是 "I'll catch you later."，而有時會聽到別人簡單地說 "Later."，其實這是從 "Catch you later." 中將 Catch you 省略的用法。

## 活用 365 個單字也能這麼說！

He's really popular. 他很出名。
＊ popular 是「有名的、受歡迎的」，流行歌曲是 popular song。

127

# ⑭ Let's keep in touch.

04-14.mp3

保持聯絡。

比較不一樣的道再見說法是 "Let's keep in touch."。"keep in touch" 照字面上的意思來看是指「繼續保持接觸的狀態」，換言之，就是「保持聯絡」的意思。

A: Let's keep in touch. 保持聯絡喔。
B: Do you have my phone number? 你有我的電話號碼嗎？
A: No, may I have it? 沒有，可以告訴我嗎？
B: Yes, here it is. 好，號碼在這裡。

## I'll be in touch.
保持聯絡囉。

從 keep in touch 裡去掉 keep 再換成 be，也是「保持聯絡」的意思。

A: I'll be in touch. 保持聯絡囉。
B: That sounds good. 好啊。
A: Take care! 保重！

## Call when you get there.
你到了之後打個電話給我。

A: Call when you get there. 妳到了之後打個電話給我。
B: I always do. 我都會這麼做呀。
A: I know, but I worry about you. 我知道，但是我會擔心嘛。

＊這是一句稍作變化的道再見說法，請各位讀者記住這種用法。只要平時多思考各種不同的說法，英文絕對會有所進步的。

# COOL ENGLISH

## 時下美國年輕人常用的招呼語

04-x1.mp3

## Same old crap. 老樣子。

「大號」的英文怎麼說？答案是 crap。"Same old crap." 是說如同一直以來的「大號」一樣沒有太大的變化，換言之就是「一成不變」的意思。同樣的說法還有 "The usual."。

A: How was your day? 你今天怎麼樣？
B: Same old crap. 還不是老樣子。

## Howdy! 嗨！

大家較常用的打招呼用語是 "Hi!" 或是 "Hello!"，不過，老外卻常用 "Howdy!" 這個口語說法。"Howdy!" 和 "Hello!" 是相同的意思。

A: Howdy, friend. 你好嗎，朋友。
B: Hey, long time no see. 嘿，好久不見了。

## What's going on? 你好嗎？

這句話的意思是指「過得好嗎？沒什麼問題吧？」，大概有這樣的瞭解就夠了。

A: Hey, there! 嘿，你好啊！
B: Hey yourself! What's going on? 妳也是呀！過得怎麼樣？
A: Not much. 還可以。

## Bummer. 真糟糕。

意思與 "That's too bad."（那真是糟糕。）相近，是美國年輕人使用頻率非常高的說法。

A: Late night last night? 昨晚弄到很晚吧？
B: Yeah. I was up until 2 studying for my midterm.
　　嗯，為了準備期中考讀到凌晨 2 點。
A: Bummer. 真糟糕。

★請在以下空格中填入適當的單字★

Let's __1__ in touch. 我們保持聯絡。

What a __2__ to meet you here! 竟然在這裡見到你！

I've __3__ so much about you from Jason.
我從傑森那裡聽說很多你的事。

I didn't __4__ your name. 我沒有聽清楚你的名字。

__5__ me when you get there. 你到了之後打電話給我。

How's your __6__ ? 你家人好嗎？

Long time __7__ . 好久不見了。

How I've __8__ you! 我多想你啊！

How's the __9__ there? 那裡的天氣怎麼樣？

Jane has __10__ me all about you. 珍已告訴我所有關於你的事。

| 1. keep | 2. surprise | 3. heard | 4. catch |
| 5. Call | 6. family | 7. no see | 8. missed |
| 9. weather | 10. told | | |

★請在以下空格中填入適當的單字★

A: How's it going? 過得好嗎？

B: Not bad. __1__ 還不錯。你呢？

A: It's going fine with me. 我也還可以。

B: I'm glad to hear that. 很高興聽到你這麼說。

A: I haven't seen you for a long time. 好久不見。

B: Not for a few years. 大概好幾年沒見了。

A: __2__ 這段時間你過得如何？

B: Good. And yourself? 很好，你呢？

A: How is your mother? 你的母親好嗎？

B: __3__ 馬馬虎虎。

A: Is she sick? 她是不是生病了？

B: A little. 有一點。

A: Hey Frank! 嘿，法蘭克！

B: Joe! How're things going? 喬！你好嗎？

A: __4__ How about you? 還是老樣子，你呢？

B: OK. 還不錯。

| | |
|---|---|
| 1. How about you? | 2. How have you been? |
| 3. So-so. | 4. Same as usual. |

# Chapter 5

# 言之有禮！
# 贊同、反對
# 用語說得大方

各位讀者是否能夠很明確地分辨 "Excuse me." 和 "Excuse me?"，還有 "I'm sorry." 以及 "I'm sorry?" 的適用時機？給各位一點時間思考一下好了。大家剛開始一定覺得這沒什麼，不過仔細想想應該會發覺其實不太容易。

此外，與對方交談時要遵守什麼樣的禮節？想同意或反對對方說的話時，英文到底要怎麼說？這個部分，可就不簡單了。

就像「打招呼」一樣，在我們的印象裡最難的部分可能就是在還不熟悉英文的情況下要回應老外所說的話。在這一章，我們要針對基本對話所需的英文用語，以及必須遵守的英文禮節詳加探討。

另外，關於 "I'm sorry" 與 "I'm sorry?" 之間的相異處和相似處，也會為各位讀者詳盡介紹。

# ① Can I talk to you?

05-01.mp3

## 我可以和你說句話嗎？

有些人到現在仍然堅持 "May I talk to you?" 才是正確的，"Can I talk to you?" 是沒禮貌的說法。不需要考慮這麼多，想向某個人說「我可以跟你說句話嗎」時，只要靠過去輕鬆地說 "Can I talk to you?" 就行了，這是很正常的說法。

A: Can I talk to you? 我可以和妳說句話嗎？

B: Yes, what is it? 可以啊，有什麼事嗎？

A: We need to speak about your father. 我們得聊一聊有關妳父親的事。

# Got a minute?
## 你有空嗎？

"Got a minute?" 和 "Can I talk to you?" 一樣都是用來表示希望能夠和對方說話的意願。

A: Got a minute? 你有空嗎？

B: I'm kind of busy right now. 我現在有點忙。

A: Okay. I'll catch you later. 好吧，下次再找你囉。

＊在上面的例句中，kind of 的中文是「有一點…的狀態」的意思。

# I need to talk.
## 我需要談談。

A: I need to talk. 我需要談談。

B: To me? 和我嗎？

A: Yes, I need to talk to you. 是啊，我需要和妳談一下。

＊如果有人突然用嚴肅的語氣說「我要和你談一下」，是不是會覺得心裡不安呢？沒錯，這一句就是想要檢討問題時說的。

05-02.mp3

# ② Let's talk.

我們來談一談。

　　"Let's talk." 可以表示略帶輕鬆語氣說「我們來聊天」的意思。彼此之間有事情要商談，聚在一起開始對話時同樣可以說 "Let's talk."。當然，也可以在商務會議即將進行時對所有與會者說 "Let's talk."。

A: Let's talk. 我們來聊一聊。
B: Okay. 好啊。
A: How have you been? 最近過得怎麼樣？

## Hey, let's chat.
嘿，我們來聊一聊。

　　通常，chat 普遍用來指「聊天」，但有些時候也當作與 talk 相同的含義來使用。

A: Hey, let's chat. 嘿，我們來聊天。
B: I can't right now. I'm busy. 現在不行，我在忙。
A: Oh, okay. 噢，好吧。
B: I'm sorry. 我很抱歉。

### 活用 365 個單字也能這麼說！

My ears are burning. 我的耳朵好癢。（＊有人在說我壞話？耳朵在發癢。）

He's kind of slow. 他有點慢半拍。

＊ kind of 指「有一點」。

絕對派上用場！
最常用的情境單字！

# Everyday Activities 日常作息

| | | |
|---|---|---|
| get up | phr. | 起床 |
| take a shower | phr. | 淋浴 |
| brush my teeth | phr. | 刷牙 |
| shave [ʃev] | v. | 刮鬍子 |
| get dressed | phr. | 穿衣服 |
| wash my face | phr. | 洗臉 |
| put on makeup | phr. | 化粧 |
| brush / comb my hair | phr. | 梳頭髮 |
| make the bed | phr. | 整理床鋪 |
| get undressed | phr. | 換衣服 |
| take a bath | phr. | 洗澡、泡澡 |
| go to bed | phr. | 上床睡覺 |
| sleep [slip] | v. | 睡覺 |
| make breakfast | phr. | 做早餐 |
| have lunch | phr. | 吃午餐 |
| clean your apartment | phr. | 打掃公寓 |
| sweep the floor | phr. | 掃地 |
| vacuum [ˋvækjʊəm] | v. | 用吸塵器清掃 |
| wash the dishes | phr. | 洗碗 |
| do the laundry | phr. | 洗衣服 |
| feed the baby | phr. | 餵食嬰兒 |
| watch TV | phr. | 看電視 |
| listen to the radio | phr. | 聽收音機 |
| read [rid] | v. | 閱讀 |
| play [ple] | v. | 玩 |
| play basketball | phr. | 打籃球 |
| study [ˋstʌdɪ] | v. | 讀書 |

05-03.mp3

# ③ **Guess what?**

你知道嗎？

　　"Guess what?" 是把某件驚人或意想不到的事件告訴別人時，常用的開頭語。中文可以解釋為 1) 你知道嗎？ 2) 我跟你說。3) 事情是這樣子的。

A: Guess what? 妳知道嗎？
B: what? 什麼事？
A: I got fired from my job! 我被解雇了！
B: That's terrible! 那真糟糕！

\* get fired 是指在職場被解雇的意思。在上面的例句中，因為被「解雇」是已經發生的事實，所以用的是 get 的過去式 got，即 got fired。

## Did you hear what happened?
你聽說發生什麼事了嗎？

A: Did you hear what happened? 你聽到消息了嗎？
B: No, what happened? 沒有，什麼事情啊？
A: Ted got killed! 泰德被殺死了！

## You won't believe this, ...
你可能不會相信這件事，⋯

A: You won't believe this, but I won the lottery.
　　妳可能不會相信，但是我中了樂透耶。
B: You're kidding me. I don't believe you. 別開玩笑了，我才不相信呢。

# ❹ As you know, ...

你知道的，…

05-04.mp3

有時候，會想用英文說「你知道的」這句話。還好，它的英文和中文滿相近的，即便只唸過一次也能記得。「你知道的」英文的說法就是 "As you know"。

A: As you know, I'm your new boss. 妳知道的，我是妳的新老闆。
B: Yes sir, I know that. 是的，老闆，我知道。
A: I expect you to work hard for me. 我希望妳認真為我做事。

## As you may already know, ...
可能你早已知道，…

這個句型和上面的 "As you know" 是一樣的意思。

A: As you may already know, I'm getting married.
可能你已經知道，我快要結婚了。
B: I didn't know that. 我不知道那件事。
A: Well, anyway, we're moving to Boston together.
嗯，總之，我們要一起搬到波士頓去了。

## As you are aware, ...
你應該知道的，…

A: As you are aware, the country is at war.
妳應該知道的，國家正在戰爭狀態。
B: What about it? 你的意思是什麼？
A: You need to fight for your country. 妳必須為國家作戰。
B: I can't! 我辦不到！

＊ be aware 和 know 的意思相同。

05-05.mp3

# ⑤ Hey, are you listening?

嘿，你有在聽嗎？

常會見到這種情形，有人正在興高采烈地敘述某件事，而對方總是心不在焉的。這個時候要怎麼辦呢？抓起一支筆朝對方的臉丟過去嗎？這樣太極端了。我們可以說「嘿，你有在聽嗎」。同樣地，在英文的說法裡也有這麼一句 "Hey, are you listening?"。希望各位讀者能夠牢記。

A: Hey, are you listening? 嘿，妳有在聽嗎？
B: I'm sorry. What did you say? 對不起，你剛才說什麼？
A: Listen this time! 這次要注意聽喔！

## What are you thinking?
你在聽嗎？

"What are you thinking?" 可以是對坐在公園想事情的人說「你在想什麼」，也可以是和剛才的例句 "Are you listening?" 一樣，指「你有在聽我說話嗎」的意思。

A: What are you thinking? 你在聽嗎？
B: Hey, I'm listening. 有啊。
A: Okay. 那好。

## Hello? Are you there?
哈囉？你在聽嗎？

A: Hello? Are you there? 哈囉？妳在聽嗎？
B: Oh, I'm sorry. 噢，抱歉。
A: That's okay. 不要緊。

＊當你興高采烈地說話時，如果對方一副心不在焉的樣子，你可以說 "Hello? Are you there?"。

# **6 Can you keep a secret?**

05-06.mp3

你能保守祕密嗎？

　　人說天底下沒有祕密，但是大家都無法抗拒「祕密」所驅使的好奇心，因而對此議論紛紛。舉凡政治、經濟、娛樂八卦…都讓人愛不釋「口」。無論如何，如果想要問對方「你能保守祕密嗎」，你可以說 "Can you keep a secret?"，這裡的 keep 是指「守住」的意思。

A: Can you keep a secret? 妳能保守祕密嗎？
B: Yes. 當然。
A: I'm not a man. I'm a woman. 其實我不是男人，我是女人。
B: No! 天哪！

## **Just between you and me.**
只有你知我知。

A: Please don't tell anyone. 請不要告訴任何人。
B: It's our secret. 這是我們之間的祕密。
A: Just between you and me. 只有你知我知。
B: Yes. 當然。

## **Don't tell anybody.**
別告訴任何人。

A: Don't tell anybody. 別告訴任何人喔。
B: I won't tell a soul. 我誰都不會說。
A: Thank you. 謝謝。

05-07.mp3

# **7 Let me repeat myself.**

**我再說一遍。**

正在發表演說或高談闊論一番時，若是另一頭有人在呼呼大睡或注意力在其他地方，導致你必須重複說過的話，這種情況的英文說法就是 "Let me repeat myself."。repeat 指「重複」的意思，而 myself 是指「我自己」，換言之就是「重複自己的話」，清楚了嗎？

A: Let me repeat myself. 我再說一次。
B: You don't need to do that. 你不需要重複。
A: I think I do. 我認為有必要（重複）。

＊老外很常說 "You don't have to ..." 或是 "You don't need to ..." 這兩種句型。雖然這兩種說法字面上是「你沒必要…」的意思，但實際上這些句型表達的是某種略帶期望和肯定的含義。所以，在這段對話中，A 想說就說是沒問題的。

## Let's go over this again.
**我們再檢視一次。**

go over 的意思和 repeat 相同，也可以換成 "Let's repeat this again." 的說法，中文的意思是「我們再重複一次」或「我們再檢視一次」。

A: Let's go over this again. 我們再檢視一次。
B: No, let's not. 不需要。
A: We need to. 我們必須這麼做。

## How many times do I have to tell you?
**到底要我說幾次你才會懂呢？**

A: How many times do I have to tell you? 到底要我說幾次妳才會懂？
B: Sorry. 對不起。

＊大家一定覺得這句話很耳熟吧？沒錯，就是當我們還是小朋友的時候，媽媽一邊用藤條抽打，一邊責備我們的話。

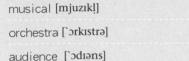

絕對派上用場！
最常用的情境單字！

# Entertainment & Hobbies
# 娛樂與嗜好

05-w2.mp3

| musical [`mjuzɪkl] | n. | 歌舞劇 |
| orchestra [`ɔrkɪstrə] | n. | 管弦樂 |
| audience [`ɔdɪəns] | n. | 觀眾、聽眾 |
| stage [stedʒ] | n. | 舞台 |
| balcony [`bælkənɪ] | n. | 包廂 |
| ballet dancer | phr. | 芭蕾舞者 |
| opera singer | phr. | 歌劇演員 |
| classical music | phr. | 古典樂 |
| popular music | phr. | 流行樂 |
| rock music | phr. | 搖滾樂 |
| jazz [dʒæz] | n. | 爵士 |
| heavy metal | phr. | 重金屬樂 |
| reggae [`rɛge] | n. | 雷鬼樂 |
| drama [`drɑmə] | n. | 戲劇 |
| western [`wɛstɚn] | n. | 西部片 |
| animation [ˌænə`meʃən] | n. | 動畫片 |
| adventure movie | phr. | 冒險片 |
| war movie | phr. | 戰爭片 |
| science fiction movie | phr. | 科幻片 |
| painting [`pentɪŋ] | n. | 繪畫 |
| coin collecting | phr. | 蒐集錢幣 |
| stamp collecting | phr. | 集郵 |
| photography [fə`tɑgrəfɪ] | n. | 攝影 |
| game [gem] | n. | 遊戲 |

# ⑧ Excuse me?

## 你剛才説什麼？

05-08.mp3

如果沒有聽見對方談話的內容，或是擔心聽錯了會造成誤會，我們是不是應該弄個清楚呢？這時英文可以簡單地説 "Excuse me?" 或是 "I'm sorry?"，也可以更簡潔地説 "Sorry?" 等。不過，很重要的一點是語尾必須「上揚」，這才是正確的表達方式。若是以平順的語氣説 "Excuse me." 或是 "I'm sorry."，就沒有詢問的意味了。

A: I need your wife. 我需要你的太太。

B: Excuse me? 你再説一次？

A: I want her to help me find a dress for my wife.
　 我希望她能幫我挑件洋裝送給我太太。

B: Oh, I see. 噢，我知道了。

＊上面的例句中，有人沒頭沒腦地説 "I need your wife." 造成了不必要的誤會。這種情況必須當下就問個明白，所以才説 "Excuse me?"。

## I'm sorry?

### 抱歉，你説什麼？

這個句型和 "Excuse me?" 的意思是相同的。

A: Did you call the police? 妳叫警察了嗎？

B: I'm sorry? 抱歉，你説什麼？

A: About your husband missing. 關於妳先生失蹤的事啊。

B: Oh, I'm sure he will be home soon. 噢，我相信他很快就會回家了。

## Say again?

### 能不能再説一次？

A: Say again? 能不能再説一次？

B: I said I want you to help me. 我是説我希望你能幫我一個忙。

A: What do you need help with? 幫妳什麼忙呢？

# ⑨ What do you mean?

05-09.mp3

### 你指的是什麼？

不是因為沒聽清楚，而是沒聽懂對方的意思時，可以說 "What do you mean?"。

A: He is a strange man. 他是個奇怪的人。

B: What do you mean? 什麼意思？

A: Well, you should meet him yourself. 嗯，你應該親自見見他。

## What's your point?

### 你想說的重點是什麼？

對一個說話拐彎抹角的人說 "What's your point?"，意思是「你的重點是什麼」、「你講話的用意是什麼」等。

A: What's your point? 你想說的重點是什麼？

B: I'm saying that we should leave now. 我是說我們現在應該離開了。

A: I don't think we should. 我不認為該那麼做。

## What are you talking about?

### 你到底在說什麼？

A: What are you talking about? 妳到底在說什麼？

B: Don't you understand English? 你聽不懂英文嗎？

A: Yes, but you are not making sense! 聽得懂啊，可是妳的話讓人無法理解！

＊ make sense 的中文意思是「說的話可以讓人理解」。所以，講的話讓人聽不懂或沒道理，就可以說 "It doesn't make sense."。

# ⑩ Do you know what I mean?

05-10.mp3

### 你懂我的意思嗎？

老外最常說的句型裡頭，這一句 "Do you know what I mean?" 是其中之一，意思是「你懂我的意思嗎」，還可以直接簡短地說 "You know what I mean?"。當你和別人說話時，可以用 "Do you know what I mean?" 來確定一下對方有沒有在注意聽你說話。

A: Do you know what I mean? 妳懂我的意思嗎？
B: Yes, I understand. 是的，我懂。
A: I'm glad you do. 很高興妳懂。

## Do you understand?
你了解嗎？

這是我們再熟悉不過的句子，回答句當然是 "Yes, I do." 或是 "No, I don't."。不過，也可以如同以下的例句那樣，在 "I do." 前面加上 "I think"，是比較時髦的說法，讓語氣顯得不那麼斬釘截鐵。

A: Do you understand? 你了解嗎？
B: I think I do. 我想我懂。
A: What do you mean by that? 你那樣說是什麼意思？
B: I don't know ... 不知道耶…

## Get it?
懂了嗎？

A: Get it? 懂了嗎？
B: Yes, I understand. 嗯，懂了。
A: Good. We are clear, then. 那好，沒事了。

＊ "Get it?" 在英文短句裡也是很普遍的說法，和 "Do you understand?" 是相同的意思。

絕對派上用場！
最常用的情境單字！

WORD BOX

05-w3.mp3

## Sports & Exercises 體育和運動

| jogging [ˋdʒɑgɪŋ] | n. | 慢跑 |
|---|---|---|
| running [ˋrʌnɪŋ] | n. | 跑步 |
| roller skating | phr. | 溜直排輪 |
| cycling [ˋsaɪklɪŋ] | n. | 騎自行車 |
| skateboarding [ˋsketˌbɔrdɪŋ] | n. | 滑板 |
| bowling [ˋbolɪŋ] | n. | 保齡球 |
| horseback riding | phr. | 騎馬 |
| skydiving [ˋskaɪˌdaɪvɪŋ] | n. | 跳傘 |
| golf [gɑlf] | n. | 高爾夫球 |
| tennis [ˋtɛnɪs] | n. | 網球 |
| squash [skwɑʃ] | n. | 迴力球 |
| ping-pong [ˋpɪŋˌpɑŋ] | n. | 桌球 |
| darts [dɑrts] | n. | 飛鏢 |
| pool [pul] | n. | 撞球 |
| weight lifting | phr. | 舉重 |
| work out | phr. | 健身 |
| hit [hɪt] | v. | 打擊 |
| pitch [pɪtʃ] | v. | 投球 |
| throw [θro] | v. | 擲出 |
| kick [kɪk] | v. | 踢 |
| stretch [strɛtʃ] | v. | 伸展 |
| hop [hɑp] | v. | 單腳跳 |
| jump [dʒʌmp] | v. | 跳躍 |
| lie down | phr. | 後仰 |
| push-up | phr. | 伏地挺身 |
| sit-up | phr. | 仰臥起坐 |

# ⑪ I don't think so.

### 我不這麼認為。

05-11.mp3

　　不能認同或同意對方的言論，或是拒絕對方的要求時，我們可以簡單地說 "I don't think so."。我剛到美國學校上課時，覺得當地學生的言論文化簡直令人咋舌。他們會直接當著對方的面反駁對方所說的話，彼此吐槽。要是換成在台灣，這樣的行為可能會讓人大感吃不消呢。

A: Will you help me? 幫我一個忙可以嗎？
B: I don't think so. 我不覺得應該幫妳。
A: Please! 拜託你！

## I don't get it.
**我不懂。**

　　在前面章節我們提到過有關 "Get it?" 的用法，各位還記得它的意思嗎？沒錯，就是在問對方「懂了嗎」。如果還沒有弄懂對方的意思，可以回答說 "I don't get it."。

A: I don't get it. 我不懂。
B: What don't you understand? 妳對哪個部分不了解呢？
A: The part about the horse. 關於馬的那個部分。
B: I will explain again. 我再說明一次好了。

## I don't understand.
**我無法理解。**

A: I don't understand. 我無法理解。
B: It's so simple! 這很簡單耶！
A: It isn't simple for me. 對我來說並不簡單。

＊這個句子與 "I don't get it." 的意思相同。

146

## ⑫ **Uh-huh.**

嗯。

05-12.mp3

有句話說和他人說話的時候，與其當個 good speaker，還不如做個 good listener 更容易建立彼此之間的融洽關係。沒有比用心聆聽對方說話更美好的心意了。若是能在適當時機做個回應，那更是錦上添花。代表性的回應用詞就是 "Uh-huh."，也可以說 "Yes"。

A: You're Jacob, right? 你就是雅各，對嗎？
B: Uh-huh. 是的。
A: I need to speak to you, Jacob. 我需要和你說句話。
B: About what? 說什麼呢？

## That's right.
**沒錯。**

"That's right!" 同樣也可以當作回應對方的用語，是「沒錯」的意思。

A: You're the new mayor? 您就是新上任的市長嗎？
B: That's right! 沒錯。

## Yeah.
**嗯。**

A: Do you love me? 你愛不愛我？
B: Yeah. 愛呀。
A: Then say it! 那你說（愛我）！
B: No. My mom is listening. 不要啦，我媽媽會聽到的。

＊ Yeah. 是 Yes. 更簡短而年輕、親密的說法。

147

絕對派上用場！
最常用的情境單字！

05-w4.mp3

# Describing People & Things
# 描述人與事物的用詞

| | | |
|---|---|---|
| tall [tɔl] / short [ʃɔrt] | adj. | 高 / 矮 |
| long [lɔŋ] / short [ʃɔrt] | adj. | 長 / 短 |
| large [lɑrdʒ] / small [smɔl] | adj. | 多 / 少 |
| heavy [ˋhɛvɪ] / light [laɪt] | adj. | 重 / 輕 |
| high [haɪ] / low [lo] | adj. | 高 / 低 |
| loose [lus] / tight [taɪt] | adj. | 鬆弛 / 緊縮 |
| fast [fæst] / slow [slo] | adj. | 快 / 慢 |
| wide [waɪd] / narrow [ˋnæro] | adj. | 寬大 / 狹窄 |
| thick [θɪk] / thin [θɪn] | adj. | 厚實 / 輕薄 |
| dark [dɑrk] / light [laɪt] | adj. | 幽暗 / 明亮 |
| new [nju] / old [old] | adj. | 新 / 舊 |
| young [jʌŋ] / old [old] | adj. | 年輕 / 年老 |
| good [gʊd] / bad [bæd] | adj. | 好 / 壞 |
| smooth [smuð] / rough [rʌf] | adj. | 柔和 / 粗獷 |
| neat [nit] / messy [ˋmɛsɪ] | adj. | 井然有序 / 雜亂無章 |
| noisy [ˋnɔɪzɪ] / quiet [ˋkwaɪət] | adj. | 吵雜 / 寧靜 |
| rich [rɪtʃ] / poor [pʊr] | adj. | 富有 / 貧窮 |
| sharp [ʃɑrp] / dull [dʌl] | adj. | 尖銳 / 遲鈍 |

# ⑬ Oh, look at the time!

05-13.mp3

噢，時間已經差不多了呀！

聊天聊到一半，突然要起身離開其實並不容易辦到，也沒辦法請求人家閉嘴或自己默默走開。此時，我們可以誇張地看看時鐘，然後口中唸唸有詞地說「噢，時間已經這麼晚了呀」，接著很自然地向在座的人告辭。這句話的英文說法是 "Oh, look at the time!"。

A: Oh, look at the time! 哎唷，時間已經差不多了呀！
B: Do you need to leave? 你要走了嗎？
A: Yes, I must go. 是啊，我必須走了。
B: Go, then. 那就先走吧。

## I really have to go.

我真的必須離開了。

強烈表達必須先行離開的處境時，英文的說法是 "I really have to go."。

A: I really have to go. 我真的必須先走了。
B: If you must. 如果妳真的需要的話。
A: We'll see each other again. 我們下次再見囉。

## Oh, I gotta go.

噢，我得走了。

A: Oh, I gotta go. 噢，我得走了。
B: Why? 為什麼呢？
A: I need to see my doctor. 我必須要看醫生。

\* gotta 是 got to 的口語說法，是「必須」的意思。

# COOL ENGLISH

時下美國年輕人常用的說法

05-x1.mp3

## Got a match? 借個火吧？

這句話的意思與 "You got a lighter?" 相同，是指「借個火吧」的意思。

A: Excuse me, got a match? 借個火吧？

B: Sure, here you go. 當然，這裡。

## Are you taking off? 你要走了啊？

這裡的 take off 並不是指我們常聽到的飛機起飛，而是指某人「離開或起身」的意思。

A: Are you taking off? 你現在就要走了啊？

B: Yeah, I've got class at 4. 嗯，四點有課要上。

## I agree with you 100%. 我完全同意。

美國人認同或贊成對方所說的話時，他們會說 100%，這句話的意思是「對於你說的話我表示百分之百的同意」。

A: This nightclub is the best I've been in a long time.
　　這間夜店是長久以來我到過最好的一家。

B: I agree with you 100%. 我完全贊同。

## Number one or number two? 小號還是大號？

小號叫做 number one，大號叫做 number two。這是一種朋友之間很俏皮的說法。

A: Number one or number two? 你要去上小號還是大號？

B: I have to do both. 兩個我都想。

# COOL ENGLISH

時下美國年輕人常用的說法

05-x2.mp3

## She is a knockout. 她真是美呆了。

一個女孩子能夠美到 knock out（將人擊倒），可見是絕世美女了。

A: She is a knockout. 她真是美呆了耶。
B: Yeah, that is true. 對啊，說得是。

## Let's cut to the chase. 我們有話直說。

chase 是「追逐」之意，而這一句是「停止追逐」的意思，換言之，是指「該說重點了」。

A: Let's cut to the chase. What do you want?
　　我們有話直說，你想怎麼樣？
B: I need a raise. At least $1 per hour.
　　我要求加薪，至少每小時加一美元。

## Hold your horses. 冷靜下來。

這一句「拉住你的馬」是指「冷靜下來」。

A: Are you ready yet? 你準備好了嗎？
B: Nope. 還沒。
A: Well, hurry up, or we're gonna be late.
　　那就快一點，要不然我們就要遲到了。
B: Hold your horses. We got plenty of time.
　　冷靜一點，我們還有足夠的時間。

## I heard you the first 10 times.
## 我聽過不下十次了。

「我聽過不下十次了」，意即「夠了」的意思。

A: You have to study hard. 妳必須好好的用功讀書。
B: I heard you the first 10 times. 這句話我聽過不下十次了。
A: Don't you talk back to me. 不要跟我頂嘴。

★請在以下空格中填入適當的單字★

Did you hear what __1__? 你聽到發生什麼事了嗎？

Let me __2__ myself. 我再說一遍。

What's your __3__? 你的重點是什麼？

What are you __4__ about? 你究竟在說什麼？

Do you know what I __5__? 你懂我的意思嗎？

Just __6__ you and me. 只有你知我知。

I'm kind of __7__ right now. 我現在有點忙。

How many __8__ do I have to tell you?
到底要我講幾次你才懂呢？

Let's __9__ over this again. 我們再檢視一次。

I have to __10__ my doctor. 我必須去看我的醫生。

---

1. happened　　2. repeat　　3. point　　4. talking
5. mean　　　　6. between　　7. busy　　8. times
9. go　　　　　10. see

# T E S T 2

★請在以下空格中填入適當的單字★

A: __1__ , I'm your new boss. 你知道的，我是你的新老闆。

B: Yes sir, I know that. 是的，老闆，我知道。

A: I expect you to work hard for me. 我希望你認真為我做事。

A: Hey, are you listening? 嘿，你有在聽嗎？

B: I'm sorry. __2__ 對不起。你剛才說什麼？

A: Listen this time. 這次要注意聽喔。

A: Did you call the police? 妳通知警察了嗎？

B: __3__ 抱歉，你說什麼？

A: About your husband missing. 關於妳先生失蹤的事啊。

B: Oh, I'm sure he will be home soon.

　　噢，我相信他很快就會回家了。

A: __4__ 我需要談談。

B: To me? 和我嗎？

A: Yes, I need to talk to you. 是啊，我需要和你談一下。

A: __5__ 你能保守祕密嗎？

B: Yes. 當然。

A: I'm not a man. I'm a woman. 我不是男人，我是個女的。

B: No! 天哪！

---

1. As you know
2. What did you say?
3. I'm sorry?
4. I need to talk.
5. Can you keep a secret?

# Chapter 6

# 無論去哪裡，
# 交通用語無敵方便

　　在國外旅行，和搭乘飛機或租車比起來，巴士或計程車還是比較方便。但是，很多人只要一想到上下車時該説什麼，就會覺得擔心。

　　有鑑於此，筆者想告訴各位，比起在前面幾章中學過的招呼語或一般對話，這些和交通有關的用語反倒容易學習。在這一章，我們從搭計程車時最簡單的 "Airport, please." 開始，一直學到比較長而複雜的 "Does this bus go downtown?"。另外，搭公車時詢問「這裡有人坐嗎」等用語，筆者也會為各位讀者一一分析説明。

　　了解之前覺得很難，懂了之後就會很簡單了。你會發現長久以來，我們都把英文想得太難了。

# **① Excuse me, where's the bus stop?**

06-01.mp3

## 不好意思，請問公車站牌怎麼走？

　　bus stop 是公車站牌，而 bus terminal 則是指客運總站。在路上如果想找車站，就找個經過的路人靠過去，先做 eye-contact（眼神交會），然後以禮貌的語氣說 "Excuse me."，緊接著問 "Where's the bus stop?" 就可以了。

A: Excuse me, where's the bus stop? 不好意思，請問公車站牌怎麼走？
B: Right over there. 就在那裡。
A: Thank you. 謝謝。

# **Is this bus to Linden Street?**
## 這班車有到林登街嗎？

A: Is this bus to Linden Street? 這班車有到林登街嗎？
B: No, the other bus goes there. 沒有，另一班車會到。
A: Thank you. 謝謝。

# **Does this bus go downtown?**
## 這班車會到市區嗎？

A: Does this bus go downtown? 這班車會到市區嗎？
B: No. 不會。
A: I need to go downtown. 我必須到市區去呢。
B: You're on the wrong bus! 你搭錯車了！

＊坊間有些英語學習書會特別說明 downtown 和 uptown 之間的差別，反而讓初學者感到一頭霧水。我建議，關於這個部分，讀者只要記住 downtown（市區）就夠了。有別於我國，美國人的市區和人們居住的住宅區（residential area）劃分得非常清楚。市區裡的高樓大廈可是櫛比鱗次的呢。

## ❷ Which bus goes to Grand Park?

06-02.mp3

**請問哪一路公車會到格蘭公園？**

公車都會沿著固定路線（route）每個小時或是幾分鐘發一次車。此外，詢問「班次」的英文說法不能用 "what bus"，而要說 "which bus" 才正確。

A: Which bus goes to Grand Park? 請問哪一路公車會到格蘭公園？
B: Bus number 13. 13 路公車。
A: That bus isn't here. 這裡好像沒有那一路車耶。

## Which line goes downtown?
**搭幾路公車可以到市區？**

剛剛在前面提過 "route"，表達相同含義的還有 "line" 這個字。簡單的說法是 "Which line goes downtown?"。

A: Which line goes downtown? 搭幾路公車可以到市區？
B: Get in that line over there. 搭那邊的那一路公車。
A: Okay, thank you. 好的，謝謝你。

### 活用 365 個單字也能這麼說！

I wanna go get a pop. 我想去買一瓶汽水。
* pop 是指「蘇打飲料」。
Are you making fun of me? 你是在拿我尋開心嗎？

156

# **❸ What stop is next?**

## 請問下一站是哪裡？

06-03.mp3

　學英文時，自信心和勇氣是首要條件。你是寧願下錯站而不敢開口問別人，還是就算英文說得不好也要鼓起勇氣詢問別人呢？ "What stop is next?" 是指「請問下一站是哪裡」的意思。

A: What stop is next? 請問下一站是哪裡？
B: The airport, I believe. 我想是機場。
A: And after the airport? 那機場之後的下一站呢？
B: I'm afraid I don't know. 我不清楚耶。

# **Where is Grand Avenue?**

## 格蘭大道在哪裡？

　　想向路人問「格蘭大道」在哪裡時，只要大膽地將 Where is 置於句首發問就行了。

A: Where is Grand Avenue? 格蘭大道在哪裡？
B: Grand Avenue is off 13th Street. 格蘭大道在 13 街的盡頭。
A: Where is 13th Street? 13 街又在哪裡呢？

＊還會在哪裡，當然是在格蘭大道的前面啊！（ ^^; ）

# **Where do I get off for New York Station?**

## 要在哪一站下車才能到紐約車站呢？

A: Where do I get off for New York Station?
　　要在哪一站下車才能到紐約車站呢？
B: Get off on Parker Avenue. 可以在帕克大道下車。
A: Are you sure? 妳確定？
B: Yes, I'm sure. 我確定。

＊從公車上下來的英文說法是 get off.

> 絕對派上用場！
> 最常用的情境單字！

## WORD BOX

06-w1.mp3

# Public Transportation 大眾運輸工具

### TRAIN 火車

| | | |
|---|---|---|
| train station | phr. | 火車站 |
| ticket window | phr. | 售票口 |
| information booth | phr. | 服務台 |
| schedule [`skɛdʒʊl] / timetable [`taɪm͵tebl̩] | n. | 時刻表 |
| track [træk] | n. | 軌道 |
| passenger [`pæsn̩dʒɚ] | n. | 乘客 |
| luggage [`lʌgɪdʒ] / baggage [`bægɪdʒ] | n. | 行李、旅行袋 |
| dining car | phr. | 餐車 |

### BUS 公車

| | | |
|---|---|---|
| luggage compartment | phr. | 行李廂 |
| bus driver | phr. | 公車司機 |
| bus station | phr. | 公車站 |
| ticket counter | phr. | 售票口 |
| bus stop | phr. | 公車站牌 |

### TAXI 計程車

| | | |
|---|---|---|
| taxi stand | phr. | 計程車招呼站 |
| meter [`mitɚ] | n. | 計程表 |
| fare [fɛr] | n. | 車資 |
| cab driver / taxi driver | phr. | 計程車司機 |

# ❹ How much?

多少錢？

06-04.mp3

包括美國在內，大部分國家的公車司機並不在車上準備零錢備用，所以，出國旅行搭乘公車最好自己先帶些零錢。國外車站附近都會有售票亭或是販售代幣，你可以先買好帶著，以免因為溝通不良而發生問題。公車車費的英文說法是 "bus fare"，請各位留意。

A: Pay your fare. 請投入車費。
B: How much? 多少錢？
A: Fifty cents. 五十分。
B: Here you go. 在這裡。

# What's the fare?

車費是多少？

A: What's the fare? 車費是多少？
B: One dollar. 一塊美金。
A: I only have a five dollar bill. 我只有一張五塊美金的鈔票耶。

# How much is the fare?

車費要多少錢？

A: How much is the fare? 車費要多少錢？
B: Two dollars. 兩塊美金。
A: I don't have that much. 我沒有那麼多錢。
B: Then get off the bus! 那麼請你下車！

＊請各位讀者自行感受一下用 what 與 how much 詢問有何差異。其實，幾乎是沒有差別的。如果說 how much 是比較正式的表達用語，那麼 what 因為較簡短，所以有比較年輕的感覺。

# ⑤ Is this seat taken?

### 這個座位有人坐嗎？

　　有時候我們會在公車上問別人身旁的座位「有沒有人坐」，但是美國人的說法就不大一樣。仔細解析這句 "Is this seat taken?"，中文是指「這個座位是否已經有人佔用」的意思，回答時當然不是 Yes 就是 No。各位讀者一定要確定聽到 No 才可以坐下去。不只是在巴士上，即便到了電影院、麥當勞或是公園也都一樣，記得一定要先問過，確定不會有問題才可以坐。因為，要是不小心惹火了美國人，他們可是會變成「綠巨人浩克」呢！

A: Is this seat taken? 這個座位有人坐嗎？
B: No. 沒有。
A: May I sit down? 我可以坐嗎？
B: Of course you may. 當然可以。

## Is anyone sitting here?
### 這裡有人坐嗎？

A: Is anyone sitting here? 這裡有人坐嗎？
B: Yes, a friend of mine is. 有，我的一個朋友坐在這裡。
A: I see. 我知道了。

## Is this seat occupied?
### 這個座位有人佔用嗎？

A: Is this seat occupied? 這個座位有人佔用嗎？
B: No, it isn't. 沒有。
A: I'll take it, then. 那我要坐了。

＊這個句型也同樣是表達「這個座位有人坐嗎」的疑問說法。另外，「我要坐了」的英文說法是 "I will take it."。

# **⑥ After you.**

你先。

06-06.mp3

　　上、下公車時禮讓老弱婦孺是基本的禮儀，需要說「你先上／下車吧」時，英文可以說 "After you."。不過，有一點必須注意，最好別顯露出不耐煩的樣子，而是真正發自內心向對方說 "After you." 才行喔。這樣，對方才會以真心的笑容回應你 "Thank you."。

A: Are you getting off? 你要下車了嗎？
B: After you. 妳先。
A: Oh, thank you. 噢，真謝謝你。

# **Do you want to sit here?**

你要不要坐這裡？

　　聽說美國人非常懂得禮讓座位，但是有人覺得國人卻不太樂於這麼做。哪天叫老外也來過過像我們每天都在為生活忙碌奔波、充滿壓力與競爭的生活，看他們還會不會有「與世無爭」的禮讓心情，呵呵…。

A: Do you want to sit here? 你要不要坐這裡？
B: Yes, may I? 好啊，可以嗎？
A: Sure. 當然。
B: Thank you. 謝謝妳。

# **Excuse me, driver (sir), I missed my stop.**

不好意思，司機（先生），我坐過站了。

A: Excuse me, driver, I missed my stop. 不好意思，司機，我坐過站了。
B: You'll have to wait to the next stop. 那你必須等下一站再下車喔。
A: Can't you go back? 不能回頭嗎？
B: No, I can't. 不行。

＊錯過下車站的英文説法是 "missed my stop"。此時，一定不能慌張，請司機停車好讓你下車就可以了。

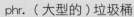

絕對派上用場！
最常用的情境單字！

# The City & Streets 都市與街道

06-w2.mp3

| | | |
|---|---|---|
| trash container | phr. | （大型的）垃圾桶 |
| bench [bɛntʃ] | n. | 長椅 |
| street light | phr. | 路燈 |
| sidewalk | phr. | 人行道 |
| manhole [`mæn‚hol] | n. | 下水道孔 |
| parking meter | phr. | 停車計費表 |
| phone booth | phr. | 電話亭 |
| street sign | phr. | 路標 |
| intersection [‚ɪntə`sɛkʃən] | n. | 十字路口 |
| crosswalk [`krɔs‚wɔk] | n. | 行人穿越道 |
| pedestrian [pə`dɛstrɪən] | n. | 行人 |
| traffic light | phr. | 紅綠燈 |
| newsstand [`njuz‚stænd] | n. | 書報攤 |
| street vendor | phr. | 路邊攤 |

# **⑦ Airport, please.**

### 到機場，謝謝。

06-07.mp3

我們搭計程車時可能會擔心「等一下要付多少車錢」、「這個司機能把我安全帶到目的地嗎」等等，但這些擔憂是沒必要的。如果本身的英文能力不夠，只要在想要到達的地名之後多附帶一句 "please" 就可以了。如果這樣還行不通的話，也可以寫在紙上遞給司機看。

A: Airport, please. 麻煩到機場，謝謝。

B: Yes, sir. 好的，先生。

A: How much will it cost? 車費大概要多少？

B: About ten dollars. 大概十塊美金。

## I need to go to Main Street.
### 我要到大街。

對於只說 please 覺得太小兒科的讀者們，不妨用 "I need to ..." 這個說法。

A: I need to go to Main Street. 我要到大街。

B: What part of Main Street? 您要到大街的哪個地方？

A: Main Street and Orchard Lane. 我要到大街和果園巷的路口。

＊美國的路有 Road, Street, Boulevard, Circle, Lane 等名稱。

## Take me to the airport, please.
### 請帶我到機場。

A: Take me to the airport, please. 請帶我到機場。

B: Which airport? 哪一個機場呢？

A: The nearest one. 離這裡最近的機場。

＊想用英文說「請到機場」這句話時，可以簡單地說 "Airport, please."，也可以加 take 變成 "Take me to the airport, please."。"Airport, please." 就是省略了 "Take me to the ..." 的部分。

# How much will it cost to the airport?

06-08.mp3

### 到機場要多少錢？

要是不確定在車上能否流利地說出這句話，其實也可以先問問住在附近的鄰居，然後下次搭車的時候只要照著跳表顯示的金額給付就沒問題了（不過前提是司機沒有坑你）。當然，若是能給司機 2、3 塊美金的小費那更好。但要是遇到沒有人情味的司機，小費就可免了。

A: How much will it cost to the airport? 到機場要多少錢？
B: Ten dollars. 十塊美金。
A: Exactly? 十塊美金整嗎？
B: Yes. 是的。

## This fare's much higher than usual.
車資比平時貴很多。

搭乘計程車到達目的地之後，如果發現比平時多付了車資，這時應向司機反應說 "This fare's much higher than usual."。不然，多付的就當是做善事囉。

A: This fare's much higher than usual. 車資比平時貴很多。
B: I raised my rates. 我調高了收費。
A: Why? 為什麼呢？
B: So I would make more money! 這樣子我才能多賺一些錢嘛！

### 活用 365 個單字也能這麼說！

This is killer steak. 這個牛排入口即化。
＊指食物美味無比。

There's no free rides. 天下沒有白吃的午餐。
＊ ride 是指搭乘交通工具。

# **9** **Could you please send a cab over right away?**

06-09.mp3

## 你能馬上派輛車來嗎？

以前美國擁有最多計程車的公司叫做 Yellow Cab，顧名思義，他們旗下所有的計程車全都是黃色的。當你需要叫輛計程車，可以打電話給計程車行，然後利用剛才的例句來叫車。

A: Could you please send a cab over right away?

妳能馬上派輛計程車來嗎？

B: Certainly. 沒問題。

A: Thank you. 謝謝。

＊上面的會話例句省略了詢問「目的地、姓名」的部分。關於它們的詢問，在此提供給各位讀者參考：Where is your destination?（您想到什麼地方？），What's your name, sir?（先生，您貴姓大名？）。

## Could you send a cab to the Taipei Hotel?

### 能否請你派輛車到台北飯店來？

這句話是要求「派輛計程車到台北飯店來」的意思。請注意這也是以 could you（please）開頭的詢問句。

A: Could you send a cab to the Taipei Hotel?

能否請你派一輛計程車到台北飯店來？

B: A cab can be there in ten minutes. 車子 10 分鐘後會到。

A: That's good enough. 很好。

### 活用 365 個單字也能這麼說！

I can't get hold of him. 我無法見到他（跟他說話）。

06-w3.mp3

## Places Around Town 市中心的商店

| | | |
|---|---|---|
| car dealer | phr. | 汽車展示場 |
| bakery [`bekərɪ] | n. | 烘焙坊 |
| bank [bæŋk] | n. | 銀行 |
| barber shop | phr. | （男士）理髮店 |
| bookstore [`bʊk͵stor] | phr. | 書店 |
| cafeteria [͵kæfə`tɪrɪə] | n. | 自助餐廳 |
| child-care center | phr. | 幼稚園 |
| cleaners [`klinəz] / | n. | 洗衣店 |
| laundromat [`lɔndrəmæt] | | |
| donut shop | phr. | 甜甜圈專賣店 |
| coffee shop | phr. | 咖啡館 |
| deli [`dɛli] | n. | 熟食店 |
| drugstore | phr. | 藥局 |
| flower shop / florist [`florɪst] | n. | 花店 |
| grocery store | phr. | 雜貨店 |
| hair salon | phr. | 美容院 |
| health club | phr. | 健身俱樂部 |
| movie theater | phr. | 電影院 |
| parking lot | phr. | 停車場 |
| photo shop | phr. | 照相館 |
| shopping mall | phr. | 購物中心 |
| travel agency | phr. | 旅行社 |
| vision center | phr. | 眼鏡行 |

# ⑩ I'm late, please hurry.

06-10.mp3

我遲到了，請快一點。

「快一點」的英文 "Hurry up." 是大家較熟悉也滿常用的說法。同樣地，將 hurry 用在搭乘計程車時，也表示「請快一點」的意思。

A: I'm late, please hurry. 我遲到了，請開快一點。

B: I'm going as fast as I can. 我已經盡量快了。

A: Go faster. 再快一點嘛。

B: I won't exceed the speed limit. 我不能超速。

\* speed limit 是指限速規定，而 exceed 則是指「超速」的意思。

## Please, make it quick.
### 拜託，開快一點。

要求「開快一點」的英文說法中，"make it quick" 也是其中一個。

A: Please, make it quick. 請開快一點。

B: Yes, sir. 好的，先生。

A: Don't drive so fast! 別開那麼快啦！

B: You said to make it quick. 你說要快一點的啊。

## Step on it, please.
### 請開快一點。

A: Step on it, please. 請開快一點。

B: I have the pedal to the metal already! 我已經把油門踩到底囉！

A: This car won't go any faster? 不能再快一點嗎？

# ⑪ Slow down, please.

06-11.mp3

**請開慢一點。**

在國外搭計程車，有時候難免會遇到一臉兇相的老外司機，把一般計程車當賽車開的情況。有生以來第一次踏上美國土地，若是不幸碰到這種計程車司機，你可以對司機明確地說 "Slow down, please."，以保障自身的權益。老實說，一個人的開車習慣大都是本身個性使然。

A: Slow down, please. 請開慢一點。
B: Don't tell me how to drive. 別指使我怎麼開車。
A: I'm the one paying you! 我可是付錢的人耶！

## Please drive safely.
**請小心開車。**

想要求司機開車小心一點時，可以很勇敢地對他說 "Please drive safely."。

A: Please drive safely. 請你小心開車。
B: I will. 我會的。
A: I don't want you to go too fast. 我不希望你開太快。

## There is no need to hurry.
**不必趕時間。**

A: There is no need to hurry. 不必趕時間。
B: Yes, there is. I'm in a hurry. 有必要，我在趕時間。
A: That isn't my fault. 那不是我的錯。

＊這是告知對方「不用趕時間」，可以「慢慢來」的意思。

168

# 12 Could you turn on the air conditioner?

06-12.mp3

## 請你把冷氣打開好嗎？

街上來來往往的計程車何其多，有冷氣開放的計程車，也有把四個車窗都開到底，讓你那抹上慕絲的時髦髮型被風吹得東倒西歪的計程車。身為乘客，當然應該向司機提出「開冷氣」、「打開窗戶」或是「關上窗戶」之類的要求。

A: Could you turn on the air conditioner? 請妳開一下冷氣好嗎？
B: Are you hot? 你會熱是嗎？
A: Yes, it's very hot back here. 是啊，後座滿熱的呢。
B: It's cold up front. 可是前座滿冷的耶。

# It's too cold in here.
## 車子裡太冷了。

因為車內冷氣全開而溫度過冷時，「車裡太冷了」的英文說法也請確實牢記。

A: It's too cold in here. 車子裡太冷了。
B: Put on a jacket. 穿上外套啊。
A: Take off your jacket. 把你的外套脫下來吧。

# Could you turn that heat up?
## 請你把溫度調高一點可以嗎？

A: Could you turn that heat up? 請妳把溫度調高一點可以嗎？
B: Certainly. 當然可以啊。
A: Thanks. 謝謝。
B: Is that hot enough? 現在的溫度夠暖嗎？

# ⑬ Can you pull over there?

06-13.mp3

可以請你在那裡停車嗎？

通常準備下車時說 "Could you stop over there?" 是十分正確的說法。不過，大部分的老外比較習慣用 "Can you pull over there?" 這個說法。

A: Can you pull over there? 可以請妳在那裡停車嗎？
B: No, I can't stop on this road. 不行，我不能在這條路停車。
A: Why not? 為什麼不行呢？
B: It's illegal. 那會違反交通規定。

## Can you drop me at the intersection ahead?
可以請你在前面的十字路口讓我下車嗎？

「下車」在英文的說法裡常用 drop，舉例來說，「讓我下車」是 "drop me off"，這句話裡提到的 "off" 其實可以說，也可以省略，全看個人的用字習慣。

A: Can you drop me at the intersection ahead?
　　可以請你在前面的十字路口讓我下車嗎？
B: Sure. 當然可以。

## Please wait here.
請在這裡等一下。

A: Please wait here. 請在這裡等一下。
B: How long will I have to wait? 我要等多久呢？
A: Just a few minutes. 幾分鐘就好。
B: Okay. 好的。

＊坐在計程車裡突然想去小號或是需要去找某個人，可以向司機說 "Please wait here."。不過，必須注意的一點是現在的計程車即便是等待時間也照樣計費。

170

絕對派上用場！
最常用的情境單字！

## Car 　與汽車相關的名詞 I

06-w4.mp3

| | | |
|---|---|---|
| headlight [`hɛd͵laɪt] | n. | 車頭燈 |
| bumper [`bʌmpɚ] | n. | 汽車保險桿 |
| turn signal | phr. | 方向燈 |
| tire [taɪr] | n. | 輪胎 |
| hood [hʊd] | n. | 引擎蓋 |
| windshield wipers | phr. | 雨刷 |
| side mirror | phr. | （兩側的）後照鏡 |
| sunroof [`sʌn͵ruf] | n. | 天窗 |
| trunk [trʌŋk] | n. | 後車廂 |
| license plate | phr. | 車牌 |
| spare tire | phr. | 備胎 |
| speedometer [spi`dɑmətɚ] | n. | 里程表 |
| steering wheel | phr. | 方向盤 |
| horn [hɔrn] | n. | 喇叭 |
| brake [brek] | n. | 煞車 |
| accelerator [æk`sɛlə͵retɚ] | n. | 油門 |
| seat belt | phr. | 安全帶 |
| sedan [sɪ`dæn] | n. | 轎車 |
| sports car | phr. | 跑車 |
| convertible [kən`vɝtəbl] | n. | 敞篷車 |
| jeep [dʒip] | n. | 吉普車 |
| pick-up truck | phr. | 貨車 |

171

## ⑭ Fill her up, please.

**請把油加滿。**

06-14.mp3

　　美國的加油站（gas station）經營形態分為 full service 和 self service
兩種。full service 是由加油站員服務，self service 則是自助式加油。「汽油」
的英文是 gas，而「把油加滿」的英文是 "Fill her up."。

A: Fill her up, please. 請把油加滿。
B: With regular or supreme? 要加普通汽油還是高級汽油？
A: Regular. 普通汽油。

## Please, fill it up.
**請加滿。**

A: Please, fill it up. 請加滿。
B: Would you open the gas cap? 麻煩把油箱蓋打開好嗎？
A: Ah, yes. 噢，不好意思。

＊用 it 替代 her 當然可以囉。Gas cap 是指油箱蓋。

## Regular, please.
**請幫我加普通汽油。**

A: What would you like? 你要加哪一種汽油？
B: Regular, please. 普通汽油。
A: Fill it up? 要加滿嗎？
B: No, ten dollars' worth. 不，加十塊美金就好。

＊汽油的種類有無鉛汽油（Unleaded）、普通汽油（Regular）和高級汽油（Super 或
　Premium）。
＊要求加油站員只要加到十塊美金的英文說法是 "Ten dollars' worth."。

**15** # Would you check my tires?

06-15.mp3

你能幫我檢查一下輪胎嗎？

　　美國的加油站設有幫顧客檢查輪胎和引擎油的服務，不過，必須多付費用。其實，一家服務周到的加油站收費本來就會比較高一些。

A: Would you check my tires? 你能幫我檢查一下輪胎嗎？
B: They look okay to me. 它們看起來沒有問題啊。
A: Please check them. 還是請你檢查一下。
B: Do you want me to kick them? 妳要我用力踢一下輪胎嗎？

## Would you check the oil?

你能幫我檢查一下引擎油嗎？

　　這裡所說的 "oil" 是指引擎油。

A: Would you check the oil? 妳能幫我檢查一下引擎油嗎？
B: Sure. 好的。
A: I've popped the hood. 我已經把引擎蓋打開了。

＊ "pop the hood" 中的 hood 是指蓋住引擎的車蓋，pop 則是指打開 hood 時發出的「啪」的聲音。

## Would you check the battery?

你能幫我檢查一下電池嗎？

A: Would you check the battery? 你能幫我檢查一下電池嗎？
B: I don't know how. 我不知道該怎麼檢查耶。
A: Oh, I see. 噢，這樣啊。

06-16.mp3

# ⑯ Can I park here?

## 我可以把車子停在這裡嗎？

停放車子的英文叫做 "park"。在大城市裡想要停車一定要很小心，因為違規停車不但會被罰很多錢，甚至連愛車都可能會被拖吊（tow）。所以囉，既然捨不得花錢，還是把愛車停在收費停車場或是汽車專用停車格比較保險。此外，若是把愛車停在路邊的計時停車格時，一定要仔細看過使用說明，以免被開罰單。

A: Can I park here? 我可以把車子停在這裡嗎？

B: You can park here for 15 minutes. 你可以停十五分鐘。

A: Okay. I'll be gone soon. 好的，我很快就會開走。

# Would you mind backing up, please?

### 能不能請你把車子往後退一點？

請後面的車主將車子向後退一些騰出空間的時候，可以說 "back up"。

A: Would you mind backing up, please? 能不能請你把車子往後退一點？

B: Why? 為什麼？

A: I need to pull out. 我要把車開出來。

# How much is it per hour?

### 停車費一個小時多少錢？

A: How much is it per hour? 停車費每小時多少錢？

B: $20 per hour. 每小時二十塊美金。

A: That's a lot! 好貴啊！

＊打算在收費停車場停放愛車的時候，必須先知道收費方式，這時候需要的英文說法就是 "How much is it per hour?"。

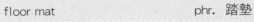

絕對派上用場！
最常用的情境單字！

# Car 與汽車相關的名詞 II

06-w5.mp3

| | | |
|---|---|---|
| floor mat | phr. | 踏墊 |
| ice scraper | phr. | 刮雪器 |
| antifreeze [ˌæntɪˋfriz] | n. | 防凍劑 |
| steering wheel cover | phr. | 方向盤護套 |
| tinting [ˋtɪntɪŋ] | n. | 汽車烤漆 |
| engine oil filter | phr. | 引擎油過濾器 |
| fuse [fjuz] | n. | 保險絲 |
| car wash | phr. | 洗車 |
| parking [ˋpɑrkɪŋ] | n. | 停車場 |
| car brochure | phr. | 汽車使用手冊 |
| stick [stɪk] | n. | 手動變速 |
| jack [dʒæk] | n. | 千斤頂 |
| car title | phr. | 汽車行照 |
| car registration | phr. | 汽車牌照 |
| car dealership | phr. | 汽車代理商 |
| import car | phr. | 進口車 |
| domestic car | phr. | 國產車 |
| finance [faɪˋnæns] | n. | 融資 |
| cosigner [koˋsaɪnɚ] | n. | 保證人 |
| muffler [ˋmʌflɚ] | n. | 消音器 |
| coolant [ˋkulənt] | n. | 冷卻劑 |

# ⑰ I need a jump.
### 我的車子需要充電。

06-17.mp3

汽車的電池沒電而需要充電時，英文的說法是 "jump"。充電用的纜繩叫做 "jump cable"。此外，電池耗盡的情形叫做 "die" 或是 "dead"。

A: I need a jump. 我的車子需要充電。

B: Your battery died? 你的電池沒電了嗎？

A: Yes. 是啊。

## I need a tow.
**我的車子需要拖吊。**

拖吊的英文說法是 "tow"，在美國若是愛車被拖吊，又不懂英文時，就會在精神、時間以及物質上遭受很大的損失。如果可能，應該避免將愛車停在會被拖吊的區域。

A: I need a tow. 我的車子需要拖吊。

B: To the nearest service station? 拖吊到最近的加油站嗎？

A: Yes, that would be fine. 是啊，可以。

＊加油站的英文說法是 "gas station"，附設維修保養等服務的加油站則是 "service station"。

## It won't start.
**車子發不動。**

A: It won't start. 車子發不動了。

B: Is the battery dead? 是不是電池沒電了？

A: I don't know. 我不知道。

＊汽車無法發動的英文的說法是 "It won't start."。

# ⑱ I'm locked out of my car.

**我把車鑰匙鎖在車子裡了。**

06-18.mp3

把汽車鑰匙反鎖在車子裡了，這種事有可能發生在任何人的身上。這種情況的英文說法是 "lock out of the car"。如果「苦主」是自己，則英文應該說 "I'm locked out of my car."。這時不是自己拿 jimmy（鐵撬）把車門撬開取出鑰匙，就是要把 locksmith（鎖匠）找來，雖然收費不便宜⋯。

A: I'm locked out of my car. 我把車鑰匙鎖在車子裡了。

B: Break a window. 打破車窗吧。

A: Can you pick the lock? 你能把鎖撬開嗎？

B: No, but I can break the window. 沒辦法，但是我能打破車窗。

＊ "Can you pick the lock?" 是指「你能夠撬開鎖嗎」的意思。

## I have a flat tire.
**我的車子爆胎了。**

輪胎爆胎的英文說法是 "I have a flat tire."。flat 是「平坦的」，所以直譯這個句子意思是「我有平坦的輪胎」，也就是說「我的車子爆胎了」。

A: I have a flat tire. 我的車子爆胎了。

B: Do you have a spare? 有備胎嗎？

A: Yes, in my trunk. 有，在後車廂。

B: Put that on. 那就換上備胎吧。

## I need an oil change.
**我要換引擎油。**

A: I need an oil change. 我要換引擎油。

B: What kind of oil do you need? 要換哪一種？

A: I don't know. 我不知道耶。

B: I'll check the oil cap. 我看一下油箱蓋。

# COOL ENGLISH

時下美國年輕人常用的交通用語

06-x1.mp3

## Would you like to take it for a spin?
### 你想開看看嗎？

take it for a spin 的意思和 take it for a drive 一樣，都是指「嘗試開看看」的意思。

A: I really love your car. 我真的超愛你的車子。

B: Would you like to take it for a spin? 妳想開看看嗎？

## My battery is dead. 電池沒電了。

battery 已經 "dead" 了，意思是「電力沒了」。

A: Why doesn't the car start? 為什麼車子不能發動了呢？

B: My battery is dead. 電池沒電了。

## He's a Sunday driver. 他專門開慢車。

開車速度過慢，使得其他駕駛人感到不耐煩的司機，我們說他是 "Sunday driver"。

A: I can't believe your dad driving so slowly.
   真不敢相信你爸爸開車這麼慢。

B: He's a Sunday driver. 他專門開慢車。

## Traffic is really backed-up.
### 交通真的動彈不得了。

backed-up 是指車子被堵得動彈不得的情況。

A: Those cars look really backed-up. 看來那些車真的被堵住了。

B: Yeah. 對啊。

# COOL ENGLISH

時下美國年輕人常用的交通用語

06-x2.mp3

## I had a little fender-bender.
我發生了一點小擦撞。

輕微的車身擦撞事故稱為 fender-bender。

A: I had a little fender-bender this morning.
今天早上我發生了小小的擦撞事故。
B: Are you okay? 你有沒有怎麼樣？


## Can I have a ride? 可以載我一程嗎？

讓人搭順風車的英文是 "ride"。英式英文會以 lift 替代 ride。

A: Can I have a ride? 可以載我一程嗎？
B: Yeah, where're you going? 好啊，妳要去哪裡？


## I want a seat up close. 請給我前排的座位。

飛機前排座位的英文是 "seat up close."。

A: I want a seat up close. 請給我前排的座位。
B: Okay, no problem. 好的，沒問題。


## My ears are popping. 我耳鳴了。

因飛機起飛時艙壓升高而引起的耳鳴現象，英文叫做 "popping"。

A: How do you feel now? 妳現在覺得怎麼樣？
B: My ears are popping. 我耳鳴了。

━┤ T │ E │ S │ T │ 1 ├━

★請在以下空格中填入適當的單字★

Does this bus __1__ downtown? 這班車會到市區嗎？

Where do I __2__ for New York Station?
我要在哪裡下車才能到紐約車站呢？

Is this seat __3__ ? 這個座位有人坐嗎？

Excuse me, driver, I __4__ my stop.
不好意思，司機，我坐過站了。

__5__ me to the airport, please. 請帶我到機場。

What's the __6__ ? 車費是多少？

Please drive __7__ . 請小心開車。

Can you __8__ me at the intersection?
可以請你在十字路口讓我下車嗎？

Please __9__ her up. 請幫我的車加滿油。

Would you __10__ the battery? 你能幫我檢查一下電池嗎？

| | | | |
|---|---|---|---|
| 1. go | 2. get off | 3. taken | 4. missed |
| 5. Take | 6. fare | 7. safely | 8. drop |
| 9. fill | 10. check | | |

## ┤ T | E | S | T | 2 ├

★請在以下空格中填入適當的單字★

A: __1__ 車費要多少錢？

B: Two dollars. 兩塊美金。

A: I don't have that much. 我沒帶那麼多錢耶。

B: Then get off the bus. 那就只好請你下車了。

A: __2__ 你要不要坐這裡？

B: Yes, may I? 好啊，可以嗎？

A: Sure. 當然可以。

B: Thank you. 謝謝。

A: Please, __3__ . 拜託，開快一點。

B: Yes, sir. 好的，先生。

A: Don't drive so fast! 別開那麼快！

B: You said to make it quick. 你說要開快一點的啊。

A: __4__ 這班車會到市區嗎？

B: No. 不會。

A: I need to go downtown. 我必須到市區耶。

B: You're on the wrong bus. 你搭錯車了。

1. How much is the fare?
2. Do you want to sit here?
3. make it quick
4. Does this bus go downtown?

# Chapter 7

# 大快朵頤！
# 飲食用語盡情享用

只要是有人居住的地方，就會有食物。我還不曾聽說過有人在旅行英語系國家時餓死。

不過，我們學英文又不是為了怕餓死，而是為了讓生活更便利，在面對老外的時候不用縮頭縮尾，可以抬頭挺胸。為了讓自己有一天真能如此，我們至少該懂得運用以下的基本英文用語。

走進燈光美、氣氛佳的餐廳，想找個靠窗的座位時要會說 "Can I have a table by the window?"，若不想喝含咖啡因的咖啡，應該對服務生說 "I'd like some decaf."。能夠應付以上這些狀況才算是具備了基本的英文功夫。好了，接下來，我們就直搗飲食方面的幾個重要說法，讓自己有機會去美國時能盡享美食。

# ① Would you like to go out for lunch with me?

07-01.mp3

## 你想和我一起出去吃午餐嗎？

"go out" 有幾個不同的含義，首先是「出去約會」，再來是指為了「喝咖啡或是吃東西」而外出，換言之就是「外食」。如果需要以正經認真的態度詢問別人意願時，可以用 "Would you like to ...?" 開頭的句型。

A: Would you like to go out for lunch with me? 妳想和我一起出去吃午餐嗎？
B: I'd love to. 好啊。
A: Where do you want to eat? 那妳想到哪裡吃呢？

## May I take you to dinner tomorrow?

### 我明天可以約你一起晚餐嗎？

這個句型同樣是表示「邀請用餐」的意思。

A: May I take you to dinner tomorrow? 我明天可以約你一起晚餐嗎？
B: I have other plans. 我有其他的安排了。
A: How about the day after that? 那後天呢？
B: I have plans. 後天也有事耶。

＊在上面的對話中，"I have other plans." 與其說是有要事在身，不如說是「藉口」比較貼切。

## Let's go out for lunch.

### 我們去吃午餐吧。

A: Let's go out for lunch. 我們去吃午餐吧。
B: I don't have any money. 我沒有錢吃飯。
A: I'll pay for you. 我請客。
B: I couldn't let you do that. 我不能讓你破費。

＊這是很普遍使用的簡單句型。

## ➋ Do you want to eat something?

07-02.mp3

### 要不要去吃東西？

這是朋友或熟人之間的用語，中文是指「要不要去吃東西」的意思。這裡所說的 something，表示「不特定的事物」。此外，沒有胃口或是不想吃的時候，只要說 "I don't feel like eating." 就行了。

A: Do you want to eat something? 要不要去吃東西？
B: I don't feel like eating. 我沒有胃口。
A: Me neither, actually. 其實我也是。

## Do you want to grab a bite?

### 你想去吃點東西嗎？

對初學者來說，"grab a bite" 是有點難度的句型，不過在美國是相當常用的說法。a bite 是指「一口」，grab 則是「抓住」的意思，所以 "grab a bite" 就是「吃一口」的意思了。

A: Do you want to grab a bite? 你想去吃點東西嗎？
B: I don't want to get fast food. 我可不想吃速食。
A: We could go inside and eat. 那就上館子吃好了。
B: That sounds better. 聽起來比較好。

＊ "We could go inside and eat." 照字面直譯是「我們可以進去吃」的意思，其實就是「我們可以到餐廳裡面吃」。

### 活用 365 個單字也能這麼說！

I've got to take a dump. 我要去上大號。
＊ 這裡的 "dump" 請與貨車聯想在一起。

I've got to take a piss. 我要去上小號。
＊ "take a piss" 是指小便。

184

# ③ Did you bring your lunch?

07-03.mp3

## 你帶午餐了嗎？

在澳洲，一到午餐時刻大家會一手拿著三明治，一手拿著名為 Foster 的澳洲啤酒在戶外大啖起來。而在美國，大家都習慣訂速食店的外賣。在台灣則是吃餐盒的飯食或是麵食…不過，任何一個國家也都有人每餐必備便當。「你帶午餐了嗎」的英文說法還有一句是 "Did you brown-bag it today?"。brown-bag 這個說法的由來是裝三明治的再生紙袋。

A: Did you bring your lunch? 妳帶午餐了嗎？
B: No, could I have some of yours? 沒有，我可以吃一點你的嗎？
A: No, I'm hungry! 不行，我很餓！

# I brought my lunch.

## 我帶了午餐。

在前面章節曾經跟各位說過 bring 是「帶來」的意思對吧？「我帶了午餐」簡單的英文說法就是 "I brought my lunch."。

A: I brought my lunch. 我帶了午餐。
B: Good for you. 太好了。
A: This is the first time I remembered to. 這是我第一次記得這麼做耶。

絕對派上用場！
最常用的情境單字！

07-w1.mp3

# Food 食物

## APPETIZERS 開胃菜

| | | |
|---|---|---|
| fruit cup | phr. | 水果盅 |
| tomato juice | phr. | 蕃茄汁 |
| chicken wings | phr. | 烤雞翅 |
| nachos | n. | 起司玉米片 |
| potato skins | phr. | 烤薯皮 |

## MAIN COURSES 主菜

| | | |
|---|---|---|
| meat loaf | phr. | 碎肉捲 |
| roast beef | phr. | 烤牛肉 |
| baked chicken | phr. | 烤雞 |
| broiled fish | phr. | 烤魚 |
| spaghetti and meatballs | phr. | 肉丸義大利麵 |
| steak [stek] | n. | 牛排 |

## SIDE DISHES 配菜

| | | |
|---|---|---|
| a baked potato | phr. | 烤馬鈴薯 |
| mashed potatoes | phr. | 馬鈴薯泥 |
| french fries | phr. | 薯條 |
| rice [raɪs] | n. | 米飯 |
| noodle [nudl] | n. | 麵條 |

## DESSERTS 點心

| | | |
|---|---|---|
| chocolate cake | phr. | 巧克力蛋糕 |
| apple pie | phr. | 蘋果派 |
| ice cream | phr. | 冰淇淋 |

# ④ I'd like to make a dinner reservation.

07-04.mp3

我想訂晚餐的座位。

　　一般來說，在美國若是想到餐廳用餐，必須要先訂位。預訂晚餐席位簡單的說法是 dinner reservation。另外，"I'd like to ..." 比較難發音，所以可以用 "I wanna ..." 來代替。

A: I'd like to make a dinner reservation. 我想訂晚餐的座位。
B: How many? 請問幾位？
A: Three. 三位。
B: What time? 想訂幾點鐘呢？
A: Seven. 七點。

## I'd like to reserve a table for tonight.
**我想訂今晚的席位。**

A: I'd like to reserve a table for tonight. 我想預訂今晚的席位。
B: Very good, sir. How many people are in the party?
　　好的，先生。請問有幾位？
A: Three. 三位。

## I'd like to make a reservation.
**我想要訂位。**

A: I'd like to make a reservation. 我想訂晚餐座位。
B: I'm sorry. We are full. 抱歉，訂位已經滿了。
A: When will you have a table open? 何時會有空位呢？

＊這是最簡單的訂位說法。"When will you have a table open?" 是個相當有趣的說法，若能牢記一定派得上用場。

## 5 I have a reservation for this evening.

07-05.mp3

我訂了今晚的座位。

進到餐廳通常會有 receptionist 走過來核對訂位資料，此時只要從容地走過去說 "I have a reservation for this evening." 就可以了。

A: I have a reservation for this evening.
　我訂了今晚的座位。
B: What is your name? 請問大名？
A: Donner. 唐納。
B: Yes, Mr. Donner, we have a table for you.
　好的，唐納先生。我們已經為您保留了座位。

## I have a reservation for Shirley Wang.
我有用王雪莉這個名字訂位。

A: I have a reservation for Shirley Wang. 我有用王雪莉這個名字訂位。
B: Are you Ms. Wang? 您就是王小姐嗎？
A: Yes. 是啊。
B: We have a table for you. 我們已為您留了座位。

## We need a table for two.
我們需要兩人的座位。

A: We need a table for two. 我們需要兩人的座位。
B: Right this way. 這邊請。
A: Great. 謝謝。

＊萬一沒有先預訂就到了餐廳，可以說 "We need a table for two." 等候服務生帶位。但是，
　一到星期五，可能就得忍受排隊等候的不方便了。

188

07-06.mp3

# 6 Could we have a booth?

有包廂嗎？

一般來說，餐廳的座位分為 table 和 booth 兩種；table 是指在開放的座位用餐，booth 則是指在包廂裡用餐。如果有特別中意的座位，可以事先要求，這是顧客的權利。

A: Could we have a booth? 有包廂座位嗎？

B: I'm sorry, all the booths are taken. 抱歉，包廂已經客滿了。

A: That's okay. We'll have a table. 沒關係，我們坐一般座位就可以了。

# Can we have a table by the window?

可以給我們靠窗的位子嗎？

想和另一半在窗邊享受浪漫晚餐的人，可以向服務生說 "Can we have a table by the window?"，應該能很順利地坐到靠窗的位子。

A: Can we have a table by the window? 可以給我們靠窗的位子嗎？

B: I'm sure that can be arranged. 當然，可以安排。

A: Wonderful. 太好了。

B: Smoking or non-smoking? 要吸煙區還是非吸煙區呢？

# I'd like to sit in the non-smoking area.

我想坐在非吸煙區。

A: I'd like to sit in the non-smoking area. 我想坐在非吸煙區。

B: We only have smoking left. 我們只剩下吸煙區的座位了。

A: Forget it, then. I'm leaving. 那算了。我下次再來。

189

## ⑦ How long do we have to wait?

07-07.mp3

**我們得等多久？**

在美國，同樣也有食物美味而且生意超好的餐廳，不過不太容易馬上就有位子可坐。等待的時間短則 10 分鐘，長則 1 小時都有。遇到這種情況就不應該盲目地等下去，而是向服務人員詢問 "How long do we have to wait?" 才是明智之舉。

A: How long do we have to wait? 我們需要等多久？
B: About one hour. 大約一小時。
A: I'm not waiting that long! 我沒法等那麼久啊！
B: Shall I take you off the list? 要把您從等候名單取消嗎？

## When can we get a table?
**我們何時才會有座位？**

A: When can we get a table? 我們何時才會有座位？
B: About 20 minutes. 大約再等二十分鐘。
A: Okay, I will wait. 好，我等。
B: What's your name, sir? 請問您的大名？

## Can you put my name on the list?
**你可不可以把我的名字寫在名單上？**

A: Can you put my name on the list? 你可不可以把我的名字寫在名單上？
B: Yes, sir. What's your name? 好的，先生，您的名字是什麼？
A: Radcliffe. 雷德克里夫。

\* 一般來說，餐廳服務生會把候位的客人名字寫在名單上，有空位時就會呼叫名單上的人。
　名字部分可以簡單地以姓氏帶過。

絕對派上用場！
最常用的情境單字！

WORD BOX

07-w2.mp3

chapter 7

大快朵頤！飲食用語盡情享用

## Fruits & Vegetables 水果和蔬菜

| | | |
|---|---|---|
| apple [ˋæpl̩] | n. | 蘋果 |
| peach [pitʃ] | n. | 水蜜桃 |
| pear [pεr] | n. | 梨子 |
| kiwi [ˋkiwɪ] | n. | 奇異果 |
| pineapple [ˋpaɪnˏæpl̩] | n. | 鳳梨 |
| watermelon [ˋwɔtɚˏmεlən] | n. | 西瓜 |
| grapefruit [ˋgrepˏfrut] | n. | 葡萄柚 |
| orange [ˋɔrɪndʒ] | n. | 柳橙 |
| tangerine [ˏtændʒəˋrin] | n. | 橘子 |
| strawberry [ˋstrɔˏbεrɪ] | n. | 草莓 |
| lettuce [ˋlεtɪs] | n. | 萵苣 |
| cabbage [ˋkæbɪdʒ] | n. | 包心菜 |
| celery [ˋsεlərɪ] | n. | 芹菜 |
| corn [kɔrn] | n. | 玉蜀黍 |
| broccoli [ˋbrɑkəlɪ] | n. | 花椰菜 |
| spinach [ˋspɪnɪtʃ] | n. | 菠菜 |
| eggplant [ˋεgˏplænt] | n. | 茄子 |
| cucumber [ˋkjukʌmbɚ] | n. | 黃瓜 |
| tomato [təˋmeto] | n. | 蕃茄 |
| carrot [ˋkærət] | n. | 紅蘿蔔 |
| mushroom [ˋmʌʃrum] | n. | 蘑菇 |
| potato [pəˋteto] | n. | 馬鈴薯 |
| sweet potato | n. | 番薯 |
| green pepper | n. | 青椒 |
| onion [ˋʌnjən] | n. | 洋蔥 |
| green onion | n. | 蔥 |

# 8 I haven't decided yet.

**我還沒決定。**

坐定位之後，服務生會拿來菜單，然後問你要喝什麼飲料。此時可以告訴服務生自己想點的飲料，如果沒有特別中意的，不妨就對服務生說 "Just water, please." 或是 "Coffee, please."。過一會兒，服務生會再度過來問你要不要點餐，這時如果還沒有決定要吃什麼，就可以說 "I haven't decided yet."。

A: What will you have today? 請問您今天要點什麼？
B: I haven't decided yet. 我還沒有決定。
A: I'll come back in a few minutes. 那我待會再過來。

## I need a couple more minutes to decide.
**讓我再想想。**

當然，也可以用 "I need a couple more minutes to decide." 來取代 "I haven't decided yet."，中文有「我還需要一點時間作決定」的意思。

A: I need a couple more minutes to decide. 我再想想。
B: No problem. 好的。
A: Thanks. 謝謝。

## I'm not ready to order.
**我還沒有準備要點餐。**

A: I'm not ready to order. 我還沒有準備要點餐。
B: You still aren't ready? 您還在考慮是嗎？
A: No, sorry. 是啊，不好意思。
B: I'll be back in two minutes. 那我過兩分鐘再來。

192

# ⑨ I'd like the New York Steak.

07-09.mp3

**我要一客紐約牛排。**

美國的牛排分成 New York Steak 和 Rib-eye Steak 兩種，當然也會有各位愛吃的 T-bone Steak。對於不太了解牛肉種類差別的人來說，可能不會去講究 Steak 的種類，所以，點餐時選擇自己唸得順口的餐點就可以了。

A: I'd like the New York Steak. 我要一客紐約牛排。
B: Okay. 好的。
A: Does it really come from New York? 它真的是從紐約運來的嗎？
B: No, it doesn't. 當然不是。

## I'd like my steak medium-well, please.
**我的牛排要 7 分熟，謝謝。**

點牛排最重要的在於肉質的熟度。怕看到血水的人，都習慣吃 well-done（全熟）的牛排。不過，往後或許可以試著品嚐 medium-well 的牛排，也許會覺得非常合胃口喔。

A: How would you like your steak? 請問您的牛排要幾分熟？
B: I'd like my steak medium-well, please. 我要七分熟。
A: Would you like soup or salad? 您要濃湯還是沙拉？
B: Salad. 沙拉。

## I'll have this, please.
**我要點這個，謝謝。**

A: I'll have this, please. 我要點這個，謝謝。
B: The number three? 三號餐嗎？
A: Yes. 對。

# **⑩ Do you have any veggie plates?**

## 有沒有素食餐點？

世界在變，人對食物的要求也更多樣化。如今，素食主義者在我們的生活周遭經常可見。在老外進出的餐廳，普遍都會為素食者準備素食菜單，而這些餐點就叫做 veggie plate。veggie 是 vegetable 的縮寫，plate 在這裡是指「菜色、餐點」而不是盤子。

A: Do you have any veggie plates? 有沒有素食餐點？

B: Sorry, we don't. 抱歉，沒有。

A: I'm a vegetarian. Do you have any suggestions?
我是素食者，有沒有什麼推薦的餐點？

# **What do you recommend?**

## 你們推薦什麼？

點餐時如果實在不知道該點什麼，可以問服務生 "What do you recommend?"，對方應該會樂意為你說明的。

A: What do you recommend? 你們推薦什麼？

B: I don't know. I'm new here. 我不知道，我是新來的。

A: You aren't familiar with the dishes? 你對菜色不熟嗎？

B: No. 不熟。

# **I'd like some decaf.**

## 我要去咖啡因的咖啡。

A: Would you like some coffee? 您要來點咖啡嗎？

B: I'd like some decaf. 請給我去咖啡因的咖啡。

A: I'm sorry, we're out of decaf. 抱歉，去咖啡因的咖啡已經賣完了。

＊咖啡有分含咖啡因和去除咖啡因兩種，而去咖啡因的咖啡就叫做 decaf。

絕對派上用場！
最常用的情境單字！

07-w3.mp3

# Fast Foods 速食

| | | |
|---|---|---|
| Coke [kok] | n. | 可樂 |
| coffee [ˋkɔfɪ] | n. | 咖啡 |
| tea [ti] | n. | 茶 |
| milk [mɪlk] | n. | 牛奶 |
| tuna fish sandwich | phr. | 鮪魚三明治 |
| egg salad sandwich | phr. | 雞蛋沙拉三明治 |
| ham and cheese sandwich | phr. | 火腿起司三明治 |
| donut [ˋdo͵nʌt] | n. | 甜甜圈 |
| muffin [ˋmʌfɪn] | n. | 馬芬 |
| bagel [ˋbegəl] | n. | 焙果 |
| croissant [krwɑˋsɑn] | n. | 可頌 |
| hamburger [ˋhæmbɝgɚ] | n. | 漢堡 |
| hot dog | phr. | 熱狗 |
| taco [ˋtɑko] | n. | 炸玉米餅 |
| slice of pizza | phr. | 一塊披薩 |

# ⑪ **More coffee, please.**

### 我想再多些咖啡，謝謝。

07-11.mp3

在餐廳用餐，各位可能都曾遇過裡面的服務生三不五時靠過來不厭其煩地詢問：「您有需要點其他東西嗎？」各位可以考慮喝免費咖啡或是選擇有免費續杯的飲料。想再多來點咖啡時可以說 "More coffee, please."。

A: More coffee, please. 再多些咖啡，謝謝。

B: I'll have to charge you for another cup. 我必須向您收取另一杯的錢。

A: You don't give free refills? 你們不提供免費續杯嗎？

B: No. 沒有。

# Could I have some more coffee, please?

### 我能再來一些咖啡嗎？

A: Could I have some more coffee, please? 我能再來一些咖啡嗎？

B: I'll get your waitress. 我會吩咐您的服務生。

A: Thanks. 謝謝。

＊有些餐廳每一桌都有固定的服務生為客人服務。當服務生在桌邊為我們點餐時，可以快速地瞄一下名牌，這樣做不但便於事後找人服務，也可以表現出熟客的親密感。

# Could I have the A1 sauce?

### 可以給我 A1 醬嗎？

A: Could I have the A1 sauce? 可以給我 A1 醬嗎？

B: I thought I gave it to you. 我以為已經拿給您了。

A: No, you didn't. 沒有耶。

B: I'm sorry. I'll bring it right away. 不好意思，我馬上拿來。

＊ A1 醬是一種吃牛排時專用的佐醬，建議各位可以嚐嚐它的味道，會是一種不錯的體驗喔。

# ⑫ Doggie bag, please.

**請幫我打包，謝謝。**

07-12.mp3

在美國當地的餐廳用餐，或許是為了配合老外體型的緣故，食物的分量通常都會偏多。吃不完的食物可以打包外帶，此時，只要簡單地說 "Doggie bag, please." 就可以了。"Box, please." 也是相同的意思。

A: Doggie bag, please. 請替我打包，謝謝。
B: We don't have doggie bags here, sir. 先生，我們這裡沒有打包服務喔。
A: Are you sure? 妳確定嗎？
B: Yes, I'm very sure. 是的，我非常確定。

# Can you wrap this up, please?
**可以把剩菜打包嗎？**

超級市場用來包裝食物的 wrap 是指保鮮膜。"Can you wrap this up, please?" 中所提到的 wrap 就是指「包裝物品」。

A: Can you wrap this up, please? 可以把剩菜打包嗎？
B: Certainly. 當然。
A: I couldn't quite finish it. 我吃不完了。

# This isn't what I ordered.
**這不是我點的東西。**

A: This isn't what I ordered. 這不是我點的東西。
B: What did you order? 請問您點了什麼？
A: I ordered a steak. 我點了一客牛排。
B: I'll get your steak. 我幫您拿牛排來。

# ⑬ Look! This meat is still pink.

**你看！這肉根本沒熟。**

發現服務生端上來的肉根本沒有熟，反應這個情況的英文說法是 "This meat is still pink."。

A: Look! This meat is still pink. 妳看！這肉根本沒熟耶。

B: Do you like it well done? 您希望是全熟的嗎？

A: Yes. 是啊。

B: Sorry about that. 很抱歉。

## This meat isn't cooked right.

**這肉煮得半生不熟。**

與上一句 "This meat is still pink." 類似的說法就是這句 "This meat isn't cooked right."。

A: This meat isn't cooked right. 這肉煮得半生不熟耶。

B: What's wrong with it? 有什麼問題嗎？

A: It isn't cooked evenly. 它沒有熟透。

＊ evenly 是指「全面、均勻、平坦」的意思。

## Could I speak with the manager?

**我可以和經理說話嗎？**

A: Could I speak with the manager? 我可以和經理說話嗎？

B: Is there a problem? 有什麼問題嗎？

A: Yes, and I'd like to tell him about it. 有，而且我想跟他說。

B: I will fetch him immediately. 我馬上請他過來。

# The Kitchen 廚房

07-w4.mp3

| dishwasher [`dɪʃˌwɑʃɚ] | n. | 洗碗機 |
| faucet [`fɔsɪt] | n. | 水龍頭 |
| sink [sɪŋk] | n. | 水槽 |
| sponge [spʌndʒ] | n. | 海綿 |
| microwave [`maɪkrəˌwev] | n. | 微波爐 |
| cutting board | phr. | 砧板 |
| stove [stov] | n. | 瓦斯爐 |
| oven [`ʌvən] | n. | 烤箱 |
| toaster [`tostɚ] | n. | 烤麵包機 |
| can opener | phr. | 開罐器 |
| cookbook [`kʊkˌbʊk] | n. | 食譜 |
| refrigerator [rɪ`frɪdʒəˌretɚ] | n. | 冰箱 |
| refrigerator magnet | phr. | 冰箱磁鐵 |
| ice tray | phr. | 製冰盒 |
| kitchen table | phr. | 餐桌 |
| kitchen chair | phr. | 餐椅 |
| pot [pɑt] | n. | 鍋子 |

07-14.mp3

# ⑭ Could I buy you a drink?

### 我請你喝一杯如何？

請朋友或同僚「喝酒」的英文說法是 "Could I buy you a drink?"。以前聽別人說老外對於請別人喝酒這種事情很小氣，不過，後來發現原來也是因人而異的。出手闊綽、總愛替人買單的大有人在，當然也有只付自己帳單的人。但願大家都賺大錢，都有能力款待他人。

A: Could I buy you a drink? 我請妳喝一杯如何？
B: Yes, what are you having? 好啊，你想喝什麼？
A: I am having a tequila. 我要喝龍舌蘭酒。

## Let me buy you a drink.
**我請你喝一杯。**

這個句型和前一句 "Could I buy you a drink?" 是一樣的意思。"Let me ..." 句型的用法，對各位讀者來說是否已經很熟悉了呢？

A: Let me buy you a drink. 我請妳喝一杯。
B: I buy my own drinks, thanks. 我自己買單就行了。
A: Oh, okay. 噢，好吧。

### 活用365個單字也能這麼說！

Can you break a hundred? 你能把這一百塊美金找開嗎？

＊中文裡，把大鈔換成其他小單位的台幣時會用「找開」這個詞，英文則是使用 break 這個字來表示。

200

**⑮ Give me a beer.**

給我一杯啤酒。

07-15.mp3

到 pub 向酒保點酒時，不用拘泥什麼禮節，只要簡單地說 "Give me a beer." 就夠了。根據筆者自己的經驗，一般說來酒保的修養都還不錯，對於客人的抱怨、嘮叨都能一概照單全收。

A: Give me a beer. 給我一杯啤酒。

B: On the rocks? 要加冰塊嗎？

A: No rocks. 不要加冰塊。

\* on the rocks 是指在酒裡加入冰塊。不只是威士忌，其實啤酒也可以有 on the rocks 的喝法。

## I'll have a Bud.
給我一杯百威。

Bud 是指 Budweiser 或是 Bud Light，為一啤酒品牌。"I'll have a Bud." 是「想要喝 Budweiser 或是 Bud Light」的意思。

A: I'll have a Bud. 給我一杯百威。

B: We don't carry Budweiser. 我們沒有賣百威啤酒。

A: What do you have? 你們有賣什麼？

## Gimme a Scotch on the rocks.
給我一杯加冰塊的蘇格蘭威士忌。

A: Gimme a Scotch on the rocks. 給我一杯加冰塊的蘇格蘭威士忌。

B: One Scotch coming up. 一杯蘇格蘭威士忌來了。

A: Cool. 謝了。

\* Scotch 是指蘇格蘭威士忌，on the rocks 是指放入冰塊的意思。所以，例句的中文意思是要一杯加冰塊的 Scotch Whisky。 cool 除了清涼的意思之外也有 nice, thanks 等含義。一定要懂得視狀況使用 cool，才算是完成了一段還不錯的對話。

# ⑯ Here's to you!

### 為你乾杯！

　　喝酒時和在座的人互相乾杯是一定不能少的禮節，這一點似乎不論在哪個國家都一樣。只不過，因國度不同，所用的語言也不盡相同。在我國是說「乾杯」，在美國則是說 "Cheers!" 或 "Here's to you!"。

A: Here's to you! 為妳乾杯！
B: Thank you, friend! 謝了，朋友！

## Cheers!

**乾杯！**

　　有一部美國電視影集叫做 "Cheers!"，內容非常有趣，不曉得片名是不是取自高喊「乾杯」時的英文說法 "Cheers!"。

A: Cheers! 乾杯！
B: I'll drink to that! 為它乾杯！
A: Me too! 我也是！

## To life!

**為人生乾杯！**

A: To life! 為人生乾杯！
B: To life! 為人生乾杯！
A: Are you going to toast with us, Jake? 傑克，你要不要跟我們一起乾杯？

＊不管是男人還是女人，都要為自己的人生努力。"To life!"（為人生）乾杯！。toast 是邀請他人一起乾杯的英文說法。"I'd like to propose a toast." 是說「我們來乾杯」。

### 活用 365 個單字也能這麼說！

Show me the money. 把錢拿出來。

## ⑰ Is it strong?

這酒是不是很烈？

07-17.mp3

　　威士忌是一種相當濃烈的洋酒，但是，我發現有些習慣喝烈酒的人對這類酒卻是情有獨鍾。「這酒是不是很烈」的英文說法就是 "Is it strong?"。

A: Is it strong? 這酒是不是很烈？
B: Not bad. 口感還不錯。
A: I'll try some. 我也來試試。

## You've had enough already.

你已經喝得差不多了。

　　對於已經喝得爛醉如泥的朋友，你想告訴他「你已經喝得差不多了」，希望他別再喝酒時，英文的說法是 "You've had enough already."。

A: You've had enough already. 你已經喝得差不多囉。
B: I'll tell you when I've had enough! 喝夠的時候我會跟妳說的！
A: I'm not giving you any more. 我不會再讓你喝了。
B: Just one more glass? 再一杯就好？

### 活用 365 個單字也能這麼說！

Money talks! 有錢萬事足！（金錢勝過萬語千言！）

Money can't buy everything. 錢不是萬能的。（錢不能夠買到一切。）

# ⑱ Check, please.

**買單，謝謝。**

到了要買單的時候，老外不會像我們搶著付錢或是故意去綁鞋帶假裝很忙。通常，他們會事先講好結束時誰要買單或是自行結帳。請服務生「結帳」時的英文說法是 "Check, please."。

A: Check, please. 買單，謝謝。
B: I'll bring it right away. 我馬上把帳單拿過來。
A: Thank you. 謝了。

## Let me get this.
**讓我來付。**

一手接過帳單，另一手準備拿出皮夾時說 "Let me get this."，中文是「讓我來付」的意思。

A: Let me get this. 讓我來付。
B: Are you sure? 妳確定？
A: Yeah. 是啊。

## It's on me.
**我來買單吧。**

A: It's on me. 我來買單吧。
B: What's the occasion? 有什麼特別的理由嗎？
A: I got a new job. 我找到新工作了。
B: You did? 真的啊？

\* "What's the occasion?" 是用以詢問對方「是什麼特別日子」的英文說法。

# COOL ENGLISH

## 時下美國年輕人常用的飲食用語

07-x1.mp3

### Let's split the bill. 我們分開付吧。

split the bill 是指把帳單金額拆開來計算，也就是說「分開結算」的意思。

A: Oh my God. Today's lunch is really expensive.
我的天，今天的午餐好貴啊。
B: Okay. Let's split the bill. 那好，我們各付各的吧。

### My mother is a world-class cook.
### 我媽媽是世界級的廚師。

廚藝好到具有 world-class 的水準，可見是十分精湛。

A: My mother is a world-class cook. 我媽媽是世界級的廚師呢。
B: Oh, really? 噢，真的嗎？

### This tastes like shit. 好難吃。

表示食物味道奇差無比，簡直像在嚐糞（shit）。

A: This tastes like shit. 好難吃。
B: Then, don't eat it. 那就別吃了。

### You licked the plate clean. 你吃得好乾淨喔。

這句是形容肚子餓到連盤子都舔得乾乾淨淨。

A: You licked the plate clean. 你吃得好乾淨喔。
B: I hadn't eaten anything all day. 我一整天都沒吃東西啊。

★請在以下空格中填入適當的單字★

Let's __1__ for lunch. 我們去吃午餐吧。

I'd like to make a __2__ . 我想預訂晚餐座位。

Could we have a __3__ ? 可以給我們一間包廂嗎？

__4__ me a beer. 給我一杯啤酒。

It's __5__ me. 我來買單吧。

__6__ people are in the party? 請問有幾位？

I'm sorry, all the booths are __7__ .
抱歉，所有的包廂都客滿了。

__8__ , please. 請給我非吸煙區的座位。

Can you __9__ my name on the list?
可以請你把我的名字寫在等候名單上嗎？

I'll be __10__ in two minutes. 我 2 分鐘後再來。

| | | |
|---|---|---|
| 1. go | 2. dinner reservation | 3. booth |
| 4. Give | 5. on | 6. How many | 7. taken |
| 8. Non-smoking | 9. put | 10. back |

## T | E | S | T | 2

★請在以下空格中填入適當的單字★

A: Do you want to eat something? 你要不要去吃點什麼？
B: ___1___ 我沒有胃口。
A: Me neither, actually. 其實我也一樣。

A: ___2___ 我想坐在窗邊。
B: Do you have any window in mind?
　　您有特別喜歡哪一面窗戶嗎？
A: No, any of them is fine. 沒有，任何一面都可以。

A: ___3___ 買單。
B: I'll bring it right away. 我這就把帳單拿過來。
A: Thank you. 謝了。

A: ___4___ 你帶午餐了嗎？
B: No, could I have some of yours?
　　沒有，我可以吃一點你的嗎？
A: No, I'm hungry. 不行，我很餓耶。

A: What will you have today? 您今天想點什麼呢？
B: ___5___ 我還沒有決定耶。
A: I'll come back in a few minutes. 那我等會兒再來。

---

1. I don't feel like eating.　2. I'd like to sit by the window.
3. Check, please.　　　　　　4. Did you bring your lunch?
5. I haven't decided yet.

# Chapter 8

# 就是要血拼，
# 購物用語殺到底

　　我個人認為在英語會話中，和逛街有關的英文是最容易的。因為逛街的時候，只要實際去觸摸、試穿（試用），中意了就付錢買回家。只要錢帶足了，東西也挑對了，如果不需要特別去講價，即使一句英文都不會，也沒有什麼大問題。

　　有關逛街購物方面的英文會話，其實是可以如法炮製的。請各位讀者確實了解這一章出現的各種情境，相信購物之門不但會為各位敞開，而且不會再害怕老外店員，可以隨性地逛街、購物了。

　　這裡為各位讀者嚴選不可不知的購物用語表達，以及各種實用的情境。但願各位就當作是在吃東西一樣，一口接著一口細嚼慢嚥。

# ① Where is the chocolate milk?

08-01.mp3

### 巧克力牛奶在哪裡？

在購物中心或是便利商店想要找需要的物品時，英文也有固定的說法，其中一個就是以 "Where is ...?" 開頭的句型。

A: Where is the chocolate milk? 巧克力牛奶在哪裡？

B: Aisle 2. 在二號走道。

A: I already checked there. 那裡我已經找過了。

＊ aisle 是「走道、通道」的意思。在飛機上，「靠走道座位」也叫做 aisle seat。

## Where can I buy children's clothing?
**我可以在哪裡買童裝呢？**

當然，以 "Where can I buy ...?" 開頭的句型向別人詢問，一定也能買到自己想買的東西。

A: Where can I buy children's clothing? 我可以在哪裡買童裝呢？

B: Any clothes store should carry children's clothing.

只要是服飾店應該都有在賣童裝吧。

A: Any clothes store? 任何服飾店？

B: Well, yeah, pretty much. 是啊，大部分都有吧。

＊ pretty much 在此可不是指「價格昂貴」。照整句話的意思來看，應該是表示「大部分」的意思。

## What floor is the men's wear on?
**男裝在幾樓？**

A: What floor is the men's wear on? 男裝在幾樓？

B: It's on the second floor. 在二樓。

A: Thanks. 謝謝。

## ❷ I want to buy a gift for my son.

08-02.mp3

**我想買禮物送給我的兒子。**

"I want to buy ..." 是「我想買…」的意思，gift 是指「禮物」。買給誰的禮物呢？沒錯，是 my son，所以是要買給兒子的禮物。

A: I want to buy a gift for my son. 我想買禮物送給我的兒子。

B: Have you checked out Copland Sports?

您有逛過 Copland 運動用品店嗎？

A: Yes, I didn't see anything that looked good.

有啊，不過我沒有看到好看的耶。

## I need a swimsuit.
**我想買泳裝。**

A: I need a swimsuit. 我想買泳裝。

B: What size are you? 您穿幾號尺寸？

A: I guess I need to be measured. 我想可能需要先量一下喔。

＊ "I guess I need to be measured." 這種說法可能有人會覺得很難，不過那是自己嚇自己，這其實很容易的。

## Can I see some silk ties?
**我可以看一下絲質領帶嗎？**

A: Can I see some silk ties? 我可以看一下絲質領帶嗎？

B: Follow me. 請跟我來。

A: Do you have many? 你們種類多嗎？

B: Yes, we have a whole wall of silk ties.

是啊，我們有一整面牆的絲質領帶呢。

# ❸ **When do you open?**

你們幾點開門？

08-03.mp3

當筆者剛學英文時，最感困擾的一個問題是 open 究竟該當動詞還是形容詞。不過，比較瞭解英文後，我發現那其實並不重要。因此，建議大家在學英文的初期階段別太在意詞性。

A: When do you open? 你們幾點開門？
B: We open at 8 am. 我們早上八點開門。
A: I'll be back then. 我那時候再過來。

## What are your hours?
你們的營業時間是幾點？

這裡完全不用 open 這個字，也能完整地表達「營業時間是幾點」。

A: What are your hours? 你們的營業時間是幾點？
B: 9 am to 5 pm, Monday through Saturday.
　　早上九點到下午五點，周一到周六。
A: You aren't open on Sunday? 你們星期天不營業嗎？
B: No. 沒有。

## How late are you open?
你們營業到多晚？

A: How late are you open? 你們營業到多晚？
B: We are open until 11 o'clock tonight. 今晚十一點。
A: Good. 太好了。

＊問「開到幾點」也就是問「多晚打烊」，不是嗎？

211

絕對派上用場！
最常用的情境單字！

08-w1.mp3

## Supermarket 超級市場

| | | |
|---|---|---|
| cheese [tʃiz] | n. | 起司 |
| butter [`bʌtɚ] | n. | 奶油 |
| margarine [`mɑrdʒə͵rin] | n. | 乳瑪琳 |
| egg [ɛg] | n. | 雞蛋 |
| tuna fish | phr. | 鮪魚 |
| cookie [`kʊkɪ] | n. | 餅乾 |
| noodle [`nudl̩] | n. | 麵條 |
| sausage [`sɔsɪdʒ] | n. | 香腸 |
| bacon [`bekən] | n. | 培根 |
| shrimp [ʃrɪmp] | n. | 蝦 |
| lobster [`lɑbstɚ] | n. | 龍蝦 |
| bread [brɛd] | n. | 麵包 |
| ketchup [`kɛtʃəp] | n. | 番茄醬 |
| mustard [`mʌstɚd] | n. | 芥末 |
| mayonnaise [͵meə`nez] | n. | 美乃滋 |
| flour [flaʊr] | n. | 麵粉 |
| sugar [`ʃʊgɚ] | n. | 糖 |
| peanut butter | phr. | 花生醬 |
| napkin [`næpkɪn] | n. | 餐巾紙 |
| soap [sop] | n. | 香皂 |
| aluminum foil | phr. | 鋁箔紙 |
| shopping cart | phr. | 購物用手推車 |
| checkout counter | phr. | 收銀台 |
| plastic bag | phr. | 塑膠袋 |
| shopping basket | phr. | 菜籃 |

# 4 Do you have this in a larger size?

08-04.mp3

## 這件有沒有大一點的尺寸？

遇到中意的衣服，一定要先確定是否合身。如果感覺衣服有點緊就必須問店家「有沒有大一點的尺寸」，這句英文的說法是 "Do you have this in a larger size?"。

A: Do you have this in a larger size? 這件有沒有大一點的尺寸？

B: All we have is what you see. 我們有的就是你看到的了。

A: Will you be getting any more in? 你們會再進貨嗎？

B: We get shipments in twice a week. 我們一個星期進貨兩次。

＊ "All we have is what you see." 是很普遍的說法，指「這就是全部了」的意思。

## Do you have this in red?
### 這件有紅色的嗎？

如果想問店家「這件有沒有紅色的」時，英文的說法是 "Do you have this in red?"。

A: Do you have this in red? 這件有紅色的嗎？

B: I'll check the back. 我去後面找看看。

A: Would you check for green also? 順便幫我看看有沒有綠色的好嗎？

B: Sure. 沒問題。

## What colors do you have?
### 你們有些什麼顏色？

A: What colors do you have? 你們有些什麼顏色？

B: That comes in green and purple. 那個有綠色和紫色。

A: Not red? 沒有紅色的嗎？

B: No, not red. 沒有，沒有紅色的。

# ⑤ Can I try this on?

08-05.mp3

## 我可以試穿這件嗎？

即便現場有貨，尺寸看起來也差不多，在決定結帳之前還是應該試穿看看。尤其，老外店裡的衣服基本上都是老外身型的尺寸，所以穿在東方人身上多少都會有些差距。"Can I try this on?" 就是「我可以試穿嗎」的意思。

A: Can I try this on? 我可以試穿這件嗎？
B: Sure. I'll open a fitting room for you. 當然可以。我幫你開試衣間。
A: Thanks. 謝謝。

＊ fitting room 是「試衣間」。

# I want to try this on.
**我要試穿這件。**

這句話的意思和 "Can I try this on?" 很相近喔。

A: I want to try this on. 我要試穿這件。
B: The fitting rooms are straight that way. 試衣間在那邊直走。
A: Are they unlocked? 沒有上鎖吧？
B: Yes. 沒有。

＊ "Are they unlocked?" 的意思和 "Are they open?" 是一樣的。

# Let me try this on.
**讓我試穿看看。**

A: Let me try this on. 讓我試穿看看。
B: Let me know if you need any help. 如果需要幫忙請告訴我。
A: I will. 我會的。

＊ Let me 可以當作 I want 的意思，所以 Let me try this on. 和 I want to try this on. 是一樣的意思。

214

# ❻ It's too tight.

### 衣服太緊了。

08-06.mp3

　　試穿時可能會發現衣服太緊或是太鬆，然而如果英文不夠流利，就只能眼巴巴地束手無策。好好地把以下的例句牢記在腦海裡，總會有機會派上用場的。"It's too tight." 就是「衣服太緊」的意思。

A: It's too tight. 衣服太緊了。
B: I'll fetch you a larger size. 我拿給你大一點的尺寸。
A: I don't need a larger size! 不用了！

＊ fetch 和 bring 一樣都是指「拿過來」的意思，在前面的章節裡曾經出現過。

## It's too loose.
**衣服太鬆了。**

A: It's too loose. 衣服太鬆了。
B: Okay, I'll bring you a smaller one. 這樣啊，我拿小一點的給妳。
A: Thanks. 謝謝。

## It's too small.
**衣服太小了。**

A: It's too small. 這件太小了。
B: Try this larger one on. 試穿大一點的這件看看。
A: That looks about right. 看來應該會合身喔。

＊這句話的意思是指「衣服太小了」。那麼，相反的說法又是什麼呢？答案是 It's too big.。

### 活用 365 個單字也能這麼說！

What a small world! 世界真小呀！

絕對派上用場！
最常用的情境單字！

08-w2.mp3

## Department Store 百貨公司

| | | |
|---|---|---|
| escalator [ˋɛskəˌletɚ] | n. | 電扶梯 |
| elevator [ˋɛləˌvetɚ] | n. | 電梯 |
| men's room | phr. | 男士洗手間 |
| ladies' room | phr. | 女士洗手間 |
| Perfume Counter | phr. | 香水專櫃 |
| Women's Clothing Department | phr. | 女裝專櫃 |
| Children's Clothing Department | phr. | 童裝專櫃 |
| Electronics Department | phr. | 電器專櫃 |
| Customer Service Counter | phr. | 服務中心 |
| Gift-wrap Counter | phr. | 禮品包裝櫃台 |
| remote control | phr. | 遙控器 |
| camcorder [ˋkæmˌkordɚ] | n. | 手提攝影機 |
| speaker [ˋspikɚ] | n. | 喇叭 |

# ❼ It's a little pricey.

**有一點貴。**

美國的商品價格一般來說都是不二價。不過，有時會遇到可以殺價的店家。如果碰到這種商家，請各位盡量殺價。在店裡看到喜歡可是嫌價格貴的商品時，可以很有自信地說 "It's a little pricey." 或是 "It's too expensive."。

A: It's a little pricey. 有點貴耶。
B: We have one that's less expensive. 我們有比較不貴的。
A: Does it look like this one? 看起來跟這個（形狀或是顏色）一樣嗎？
B: Kind of. 類似。

## I think it's too expensive.
**我覺得它太貴了。**

A: I think it's too expensive. 我覺得它太貴了。
B: Are you sure? It's a good price. 是嗎？這個價格很實惠。
A: I can't pay $900 for it. 我不可能花九百塊美金買它。

### 活用 365 個單字也能這麼說！

I'm allergic to dust. 我對灰塵過敏。

I'm allergic to MSG. 我對味素過敏。

# 8 Do you have anything cheaper?

有沒有比較便宜的呢？

　　站在消費者的立場，永遠都希望東西愈便宜愈好，價錢昂貴就想盡辦法殺價。但是身在國外，因為英文不夠流利，所以既無法找到更便宜的商品，也無法隨心所欲地殺價，還有比這更慘的嗎？就讓筆者來告訴各位聰明應付這種狀況的幾種英文說法吧。首先是 "Do you have anything cheaper?"，表示「你有比較便宜的嗎」。

A: Do you have anything cheaper? 有沒有更便宜的呢？

B: No, try another store. 沒有耶，可以到其他的商店找找看。

A: Okay, fine. 好吧，謝謝。

## It's much cheaper here.
這裡便宜多了。

A: It's much cheaper here. 這裡便宜多了。

B: We pride ourselves on our low price. 我們就是以低價為傲的。

A: I can see that. 我發現到了。

## Can you come down a little?
能不能再便宜一點？

A: Can you come down a little? 能不能再便宜一點？

B: I'm afraid not. 恐怕不行喔。

A: I'll give you fifty for it. 我出五十塊美金好了。

B: Okay, how about fifty-five? 那好，五十五塊美金如何？

\* "come down a little" 是「價格再降一點」的意思。雖然 discount 也有折價的意思，不過，可以試著多用老外的習慣說法 "Can you come down a little?"。老外一聽，肯定會對你豎起大姆指，不過降不降價可就不敢保證囉。

絕對派上用場！
最常用的情境單字！

## Clothing 有關衣服的各種名詞

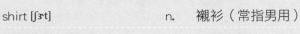

08-w3.mp3

| | | |
|---|---|---|
| shirt [ʃɝt] | n. | 襯衫（常指男用） |
| blouse [blaʊz] | n. | 女用襯衫 |
| pants [pænts] | n. | 褲子 |
| jeans [dʒinz] | n. | 牛仔褲 |
| skirt [skɝt] | n. | 裙子 |
| shorts [ʃɔrts] | n. | 短褲 |
| sweater [ˋswɛtɚ] | n. | 毛衣 |
| cardigan sweater | phr. | 羊毛衫 |
| suit [sut] | n. | 套裝 |
| vest [vɛst] | n. | 背心 |
| tie [taɪ] | n. | 領帶 |
| evening gown | phr. | 晚禮服 |
| pajamas [pəˋdʒæməz] | n. | 睡衣 |
| underpants [ˋʌndɚͺpænts] | n. | 內褲 |
| stockings [ˋstɑkɪŋz] | n. | 長襪 |
| socks [sɑks] | n. | 短襪 |
| shoes [ʃuz] | n. | 鞋子 |
| sneakers [ˋsnikɚz] | n. | 運動鞋 |
| sandals [ˋsændl̩z] | n. | 涼鞋 |
| boots [buts] | n. | 靴子 |
| coat [kot] | n. | 外套 |
| trench coat | phr. | 風衣 |
| glove [glʌv] | n. | 手套 |
| hat [hæt] | n. | 帽子 |
| baseball cap | phr. | 棒球帽 |

# ⑨ I'll take this.

08-09.mp3

### 我要買這個。

結束了殺價，到了結帳的時候，付款的方式分為現金支付和刷卡兩種。信用卡雖然比較方便，但若是跨國使用，手續費會比較貴。不過，預先考慮到這一點，就不會有什麼大問題。另外，發票或是收據請妥善保管。確定要把商品買下來的英文說法是 "I'll take this."。

A: I'll take this. 我要買這個。
B: Great. Will it be cash or charge? 好的，請問是付現還是刷卡？
A: Visa. 我用 Visa 卡。

## I like this one.
**我喜歡這個。**

「喜歡這個」這句話就足以用來表示「要購買」了。

A: I like this one. 我喜歡這個。
B: Me, too. 我也是。
A: Okay, I'll take this. 那就買這個吧。

## How much is it altogether?
**總共要多少錢？**

A: How much is it altogether? 總共要多少錢？
B: $159.76, including tax. 159 美元 76 美分，稅內含。
A: I only have $150 with me. 我身上只有 150 塊美金耶。

＊同時買了數件商品時，「全部」的英文說法是 altogether。

08-10.mp3

# ⑩ Can I write a check for this?

## 我可以開支票嗎？

有些老外會使用一種為個人發行的個人支票，類似我國的公司支票。

A: Can I write a check for this? 我可以開支票嗎？

B: Of course. 當然。

A: Who do I make it out to? 收款人該寫誰呢？

＊使用個人支票時，一定要在上面註明收款人的姓名，事後收支票的人才能到銀行兌現。給支票的人詢問收款人姓名時會說 "Who do I make it out to?"。

# Do you take Visa?

## 你們接受 Visa 卡嗎？

A: Do you take Visa? 你們接受 Visa 卡嗎？

B: We take all major credit cards. 我們接受所有主要的信用卡。

A: Here's my Visa. 這是我的 Visa 卡。

＊ major credit cards 有哪些呢？有 Visa、萬事達 (Master)、美國運通（American Express）、JCB 等。

### 活用 365 個單字也能這麼說！

Let's shop till we drop. 我們來逛一整天吧。

# Can I get this gift-wrapped?

08-11.mp3

## 可以幫我包裝嗎?

結帳之後希望把物品包裝起來的人可以到包裝櫃台去。有些包裝是免費的,有些包裝則必須支付費用。禮品包裝的英文是 "gift-wrap",請看下面的例句。

A: Can I get this gift-wrapped? 可以幫我包裝嗎?

B: Sure. Do you have a preference in wrapping?
沒問題。有特別想要的包裝樣式嗎?

A: Anything is fine. 都可以。

B: I'll use this one. 那我就用這個為您包裝了。

## Can you gift-wrap this?
### 你能替我包裝一下嗎?

A: Can you gift-wrap this? 你能替我包裝一下嗎?

B: Sure. I'll have Jenny do it. 當然可以,我請珍妮為您處理。

A: Where's Jenny? 珍妮在哪裡?

B: She's coming. 她來了。

## Would you please gift-wrap this?
### 可以請你幫我包裝嗎?

A: Would you please gift-wrap this? 可以請妳幫我包裝嗎?

B: I'm sorry, we don't gift-wrap. 抱歉,我們沒有這項服務。

A: Oh, I see. 噢,這樣啊。

B: We may start doing it in the future. 我們以後可能會有這項服務。

# COOL ENGLISH

## 時下美國年輕人常用的購物用語

08-x1.mp3

## I'm just browsing. 我只是隨便看看。

browsing 的意思和 looking 一樣，都是指進到店裡光看不買的意思。

A: May I help you with something? 我能為您效勞嗎？

B: I'm just browsing. 我只是隨便看看。

## This dress is so kinky. 這件禮服好性感喔。

kinky 是說衣服非常性感，很暴露的意思。

A: This dress is so kinky. 這件禮服好性感喔。

B: Yeah, it doesn't hide anything. 是啊，身體都露出來了。

## That's a rip-off. 簡直是在坑人嘛！

形容價格貴得離譜，英文可以說 rip-off。整句意思是指「那簡直是敲竹槓」。

A: A glass of juice in this hotel costs $10.

這家飯店一杯果汁要十塊美金耶。

B: That's a rip-off. 簡直是在坑人嘛。

## I've maxed out my plastic. 我的卡刷爆了。

這裡所說的 plastic 指的是信用卡，maxed out 則是把卡「刷到超過信用額度」的意思。

A: Do you have a credit card? 妳有信用卡嗎？

B: Yes, but I've maxed out my plastic. 有哇，不過已經被我刷爆了。

★請在以下空格中填入適當的單字★

Do you have this in a ___1___ ? 這件有沒有大一點的尺寸？

Can I ___2___ this ___2___ ? 我可以試穿這件嗎？

It's too ___3___ . 太鬆了。

Do you have anything ___4___ ? 你們有比較便宜的嗎？

Do you ___5___ Visa? 你們接受 Visa 卡嗎？

What ___6___ are you? 你穿幾號尺寸？

I think it's too ___7___ . 我覺得它太貴了。

Will it be ___8___ or charge? 是付現還是刷卡？

Who do I ___9___ it out to? 收款人該寫誰呢？

Can I get this ___10___ ? 可以幫我包裝嗎？

---

1. larger size    2. try on    3. loose    4. cheaper
5. take    6. size    7. expensive
8. cash    9. make    10. gift-wrapped

★請在以下空格中填入適當的單字★

A: __1__ some black jeans. 我想買一件黑色牛仔褲。

B: We don't carry black jeans. 我們沒有黑色牛仔褲耶。

A: Why not? 為什麼沒有啊？

A: __2__ 你們的營業時間是幾點？

B: 9 am to 5 pm, Monday through Saturday.
早上九點到下午五點，從週一到週六。

A: You aren't open on Sunday? 你們星期天不營業嗎？

B: No. 沒有。

A: __3__ 能不能再便宜一點？

B: I'm afraid not. 恐怕不行耶。

A: I'll give you fifty for it. 我付五十塊美金好了。

B: Okay, how about fifty-five? 既然這樣，五十五塊美金如何？

A: __4__ 我要買這個。

B: Great. Will it be cash or charge?
好的，您要付現還是刷卡？

A: Visa. 我用 Visa 卡。

---

1. I want to buy
2. What are your hours?
3. Can you come down a little?
4. I'll take this.

# Chapter 9

# 講電話支支吾吾？
# 電話用語說得流利

各位讀者，請先看以下與接聽電話有關的英文用語，看看這些用語自己懂得幾個：Speaking. / Who's calling, please? / Just a minute. / Can I take a message? ...。

如何？全都是你早已知道的嗎？那麼，接下來再看看另外一些用語：Yes, it is. / Who is this? / Hang on. / Any message? ...。

覺得怎麼樣？比一開始看到的幾個用語還要生澀、難懂嗎？讓我來為大家簡單說明一下。"Speaking." 和 "Yes, it is." 意思是一樣的，"Who's calling, please?" 和 "Who is this?"、"Just a minute." 和 "Hang on."、"Can I take a message?" 和 "Any message?" 的意思也都是各別相同的。

講電話的時候，無法看到對方的表情，只能將注意力放在話筒傳來的聲音上面，所以，更需要集中精神來聆聽。而且，每一個人都有獨特的表達方式以及說話聲調。好了，現在我們要一起去認識能教你趕跑電話恐懼症的英文電話用語。

# ❶ Who do you want to talk to?

09-01.mp3

### 請問找哪一位？

　　常聽很多人說電話英語很難，其實，我自己也是這麼覺得啦。面對面能夠看到對方臉上表情的變化，同時也聽到聲音，但是講電話只能聽見聲音而已。"Who do you want to talk to?" 是「你要找誰講話」的意思。

A: Who do you want to talk to? 請問要找誰？
B: George, please. 請接喬治，謝謝。
A: He isn't home. 他不在家喔。
B: When will he be home? 他什麼時候會在家？

## Who do you want to speak with?
**請問找哪一位？**

A: Who do you want to speak with? 請問找哪一位？
B: The head of the household. 我找戶主。
A: That would be me. 我就是。

\* the head of the household 是指「戶主」。

## I will get the phone.
**我來接電話。**

A: I will get the phone. 我來接電話。
B: No, I'll get it. It's for me. 不用了，我來接，那是找我的電話。
A: How do you know? 妳怎麼知道？

\*正當大家都在忙著手邊工作時，電話鈴突然響起。在廚房裡洗碗的阿花急忙走出來說 "I'll get the phone."，意思是「我來接」，因為她和男朋友講電話的時間到了！

# ❷ **Who is this?**

### 請問是誰？

接電話時簡單地說「請問哪裡找」，這是最常見的說法。不過，也可以用 "Who's calling?" 來詢問。

A: Who is this? 請問是誰？

B: This is your worst nightmare. 我是你最恐怖的惡夢。

A: Are you trying to scare me? 妳想嚇我啊？

＊這分明是打來惡作劇的，不然就是熟朋友間開的玩笑。

# Who's calling, please?

**請問哪裡找？**

A: Who's calling, please? 請問哪裡找？

B: Jacob. 我是雅各。

A: Just a minutes. 請等一下。

# Can I ask who is calling?

**可以請問是哪一位嗎？**

A: Can I ask who is calling? 可以請問是哪一位嗎？

B: This is his mother. 我是他的媽媽。

A: I'll let him know you called. 我會轉告他您來過電話。

### 活用 365 個單字也能這麼說！

M.Y.O.B

Mind your own business. 管好你自己吧。

# ❸ Can you hold?

### 請等一下好嗎（不要掛斷）？

09-03.mp3

「等一下」、「等一會兒」的英文是 "Can you hold?"。看起來很簡單，不過，真的接到老外打來的電話，大家可能還是會腦袋一片空白，所以平時一定要勤加練習。

A: Can you hold? 請等一下好嗎？
B: Okay. 好的。
A: Thank you. 謝謝。

# Hang on.

### 等一下喔。

與 "Can you hold?" 的意思相同，指「等一下」。

A: Is Bob there? 請問鮑伯在嗎？
B: Hang on. 等一下喔。
A: No need to disturb him if he's busy. 如果他在忙就不必叫他了。

＊ disturb 是「妨礙、打擾」的意思。

# Hold on, please.

### 請等一下。

A: Is Don there? 多恩在嗎？
B: Hold on, please. He's outside. 請等一下，他在外面。
A: No, I can leave a message. 沒關係，我留個話好了。

## 活用 365 個單字也能這麼說！

She has a big mouth. 她是個大嘴巴。

＊ "big mouth" 在這裡是指一個人很八卦、愛道人長短的意思。

09-04.mp3

# Can I take a message?

要不要留言？

詢問對方想不想留言，可以用 May 開頭說 "May I take a message?"。但是，就我個人來說，Can 比 May 更容易上口，所以在此向各位讀者推薦。

A: Can I take a message? 要留言嗎？

B: Would you let her know Jennifer called?

可以請你轉告她珍妮佛來過電話嗎？

A: Sure, I'll let her know. 當然，我會告訴她的。

## Any message?

**要留言嗎？**

A: Any message? 要留言嗎？

B: No, I'll call later. 不用了，我晚一點再打來好了。

A: Okay, bye. 好的，再見。

## You can reach him at 555-1213.

**你可以打 555-1213 這個電話號碼找他。**

A: You can reach him at 555-1213. 你可以打 555-1213 這個號碼找到他。

B: What's the area code? 區域號碼是多少呢？

A: The what? 什麼？

B: The three digits before 555. 撥 555 之前必須先撥的三位數。

＊請各位注意 reach 的用法，是指「找到、接通」的意思。而 the three digits 是指「三位數」。

# ⑤ He's not in.

他現在不在。

09-05.mp3

如果對方想找的人剛好不在，這裡有句實在很簡單的說法，那就是 "He's not in."。如果想要表現一下，拚了命也要藉機展現自己的英文才學，不妨就試試 "He's not here at the moment." 這個說法吧。

A: He's not in. 他現在不在。
B: Could you take a message? 可以請您轉告一聲嗎？
A: Certainly. Who's calling? 可以，請問您是哪位？

## He's not here at the moment.
**他現在不在。**

"at the moment" 是指「現在這個時候」。

A: He's not here at the moment. 他現在不在。
B: Do you know when he'll be back? 妳知道他什麼時候會回來嗎？
A: I have no idea. 我不清楚。

## I think he's out for lunch.
**我想他出去吃午餐了。**

A: I think he's out for lunch. 我想他出去吃午餐了。
B: How long is his lunch? 請問他會吃多久？
A: He'll be back by 1 o'clock. 一點之前會回來。

### 活用 365 個單字也能這麼說！

Would you cut it in half? 可以幫我對切嗎？

## Numbers 數字

| | | |
|---|---|---|
| 0 | zero | [ˋzɪro] |
| 1 | one | [wʌn] |
| 2 | two | [tu] |
| 3 | three | [θri] |
| 4 | four | [for] |
| 5 | five | [faɪv] |
| 6 | six | [sɪks] |
| 7 | seven | [ˋsɛvən] |
| 8 | eight | [et] |
| 9 | nine | [naɪn] |
| 10 | ten | [tɛn] |
| 11 | eleven | [ɪˋlɛvən] |
| 12 | twelve | [twɛlv] |
| 13 | thirteen | [θɝˋtin] |
| 14 | fourteen | [ˋforˋtin] |
| 15 | fifteen | [ˋfɪfˋtin] |
| 16 | sixteen | [ˋsɪksˋtin] |
| 17 | seventeen | [ˏsɛvn̩ˋtin] |
| 18 | eighteen | [ˋeˋtin] |
| 19 | nineteen | [ˋnaɪnˋtin] |
| 20 | twenty | [ˋtwɛntɪ] |
| 99 | ninety-nine | [ˋnaɪntɪˏnaɪn] |
| 100 | one hundred | [ˋhʌndrəd] |
| 1000 | one thousand | [ˋθaʊzn̩d] |

# ⑥ Wrong number.

你撥錯號碼了。

09-06.mp3

有一次我打電話到美國，結果不小心打錯了，話筒那頭傳來冷冷的聲音，很簡短地說 "Wrong number."，隨即就掛斷了。對於只熟悉 "You've got the wrong number." 的我來說，那樣的回答讓我有點錯愕。

A: Is Calvin there? 請問凱文在嗎？
B: Wrong number. 妳打錯了。
A: Oh, sorry. 噢，抱歉。

# You've got the wrong number.
你打錯電話了。

A: You've got the wrong number. 你打錯電話了。
B: Is this 555-1212? 這裡是不是 555-1212？
A: Yes, we just moved in. 是啊，不過我們才剛搬進來。

# We don't have anyone by that name.
這裡沒有人叫那個名字。

A: We don't have anyone by that name. 這裡沒有人叫那個名字。
B: Are you sure? 你確定嗎？
A: Of course I'm sure. 我當然確定。

# ⑦ Is Shane there?

夏恩在嗎？

09-07.mp3

以前，大家都以為「請問某人在嗎」的英文說法只有 "May I speak to ...?"。其實，在美國還有另一種十分簡單的說法，就是這句 "Is Shane there? "。

A: Is Shane there? 請問夏恩在嗎？
B: Let me check. 我確定一下。
A: Okay. 好的。
B: Yes, he's here. He'll be right with you. 是的，他在。他馬上就來。

## May I talk to Shane, please?
請找夏恩接電話，謝謝。

和 "Is Shane there?" 的意思相同，是更為禮貌的說法。

A: May I talk to Shane, please? 可以請夏恩接電話嗎？
B: He isn't home at the moment. 他現在不在家。
A: Okay, thank you. 這樣啊，謝謝。

## I'd like to speak to Shane, please.
我想和夏恩說話。

A: I'd like to speak to Shane, please. 我想和夏恩說話。
B: He is busy. Can I take a message? 他正在忙，你要留言嗎？
A: Just tell him Frank called. 告訴他法蘭克來過電話就可以了。
B: Sure, Frank. 好的，法蘭克。

# ⑧ Mr. Shelley, please.

09-08.mp3

**請找薛利先生聽電話，謝謝。**

這實在是簡單到不行的句子，看一眼就能馬上記住了。就把它當成是必要時的最後絕招，請各位務必牢牢記住。

A: Mr. Shelley, please. 請找薛利先生聽電話，謝謝。

B: Mr. Shelley is unavailable. May I take a message?
薛利先生不在，請問要留言嗎？

A: No, thank you. I will call again another time. 不用了，我再打來好了。

## Is Shelley in?
**薛利在嗎？**

A: Is Shelley in? 薛利在嗎？

B: He's at a meeting right now. 他正在開會。

A: This is kind of an emergency. 我有急事找他。

B: I see. I'll go get him. 這樣啊，我去找他。

### 活用 365 個單字也能這麼說！

He's an easy-going type. 他人很好相處。

She's not my type. 她不是我中意的類型。

# ❾ Could you tell him Sarah called?

### 可否轉告他莎拉來過電話?

　　請對方轉告時說 "Could you tell him sb called?" 算是很完整的說法了。就算頭腦已經學會了,一開始可能覺得不太順口,多試幾次之後自然就會了,不要害怕,盡量多嘗試。

A: Could you tell him Sarah called? 可否轉告他莎拉來過電話?
B: Yeah. Does he have your number? 可以啊,他知道妳的號碼嗎?
A: It's 7075-3702. 我的號碼是 7075-3702.
B: I'll have him give you a call. 我會請他回電給妳。

## Tell him Mr. Wang called.
### 請轉告他王先生來過電話。

A: Tell him Mr. Wang called. 請轉告他王先生來過電話。
B: I'll be sure to give him the message. 我一定會轉告他的。
A: Thanks a lot. 非常謝謝妳。

## Could you tell him to call me back?
### 請他回電給我好嗎?

A: Could you tell him to call me back? 請他回電給我好嗎?
B: No problem. 沒問題。
A: Thank you. 謝謝你。

＊ call me back 是「回電給我」的意思。

絕對派上用場！
最常用的情境單字！

## The Body 身體各部位名稱 I

09-w2.mp3

| | | |
|---|---|---|
| head [hɛd] | n. | 頭 |
| hair [hɛr] | n. | 頭髮 |
| forehead [ˋfɔrˏhɛd] | n. | 額頭 |
| face [fes] | n. | 臉 |
| eye [aɪ] | n. | 眼睛 |
| eyebrow [ˋaɪˏbraʊ] | n. | 眉毛 |
| ear [ɪr] | n. | 耳朵 |
| earlobe [ˋɪrlob] | n. | 耳垂 |
| nose [noz] | n. | 鼻子 |
| cheek [tʃik] | n. | 臉頰 |
| chin [tʃɪn] | n. | 下巴 |
| mouth [maʊθ] | n. | 嘴巴 |
| lip [lɪp] | n. | 嘴唇 |
| tongue [tʌŋ] | n. | 舌頭 |
| tooth [tuθ] | n. | 牙齒 |
| sideburns [ˋsaɪdˏbɝnz] | n. | 鬢角 |
| mustache [ˋmʌstæʃ] | n. | 鬍子 |
| beard [bɪrd] | n. | 下巴鬍 |
| neck [nɛk] | n. | 脖子 |
| shoulder [ˋʃoldɚ] | n. | 肩膀 |
| chest [tʃɛst] | n. | 胸部 |

# ⑩ When will he be back?

09-10.mp3

### 他何時會回來？

　　用英文打電話時，如果聽到對方不在，會很想問對方一句 "When will he be back?"。當然啦，也可以用 What time 替代 When，換成 "What time will he be back?" 的說法，這兩個句子的意思是類似的。

A: When will he be back? 他什麼時候會回來？
B: He'll be back on Saturday. 他星期六會回來。
A: Is he on vacation? 他是去度假嗎？
B: He's on a business trip. 他去出差。


## Do you know where he is?
你知道他在哪裡嗎？

A: Do you know where he is? 你知道他在哪裡嗎？
B: He went to the restroom, I believe. 我想他去洗手間了。
A: I'll wait for him to return. 我等他回來好了。


## Do you have any idea where he is?
你知道他在哪裡嗎？

A: Do you have any idea where he is? 妳知道他在哪裡嗎？
B: Yes, but I won't tell you. 知道啊，但是我不會告訴你。
A: Please? 拜託妳好不好？
B: No, Goodbye. 不行，再見。

＊回答句的説法有兩種，"Yes." 或是 "I have no idea."。

# ⑪ I'm sorry to call you so late.

09-11.mp3

## 很抱歉這麼晚打電話給你。

　　有時候，難免會在深夜打電話找人，把對方給吵醒了。遇到這種無可奈何的情形，只要誠心地向對方表示歉意，然後長話短說就可以了。這個句型是我們經常用得到的英文說法。

A: I'm sorry to call you so late. 很抱歉這麼晚打電話給妳。

B: What's up? 什麼事？

A: We have an emergency. 我們有件急事。

# Did I wake you up?
## 我吵醒你了嗎？

　　這是日常生活中使用率很頻繁的句型，今晚就立刻打電話給朋友實際演練一下吧。

A: Did I wake you up? 我吵醒你了嗎？

B: No, I was having sex with my wife. 沒有，我剛和我太太在做愛做的事。

A: Oh, I'm sorry! 噢，抱歉！

B: You should be. 妳是該覺得抱歉。

# It's urgent.
## 這件事很急。

A: It's urgent. 這件事很急。

B: Okay, I'll get Mr. Phillips. 好的，我去請菲力普先生過來。

A: Thank you very much. 非常謝謝妳。

＊ urgent 是「緊急的」。相反的說法可用 "It isn't urgent."（這件事不急。）

239

09-12.mp3

# I think I have the wrong number.

### 我想我打錯電話了。

撥錯號碼的人應該跟對方說一句 "I think I have the wrong number."，如果能夠接著說 "Sorry." 就更有禮貌了。另外，接電話的一方則可以簡短地說 "Wrong number." 或者 "You've got the wrong number." 告知對方打錯電話了。

A: I think I have the wrong number. 我想我打錯電話了。
B: Who are you calling? 你要找哪一位？
A: Pete Dawson ... 我要找彼特‧道森…
B: Oh, you've got the wrong number. 噢，你打錯電話了。

## I have the wrong number.
### 我打錯電話了。

A: I'm sorry. I have the wrong number. 抱歉，我打錯電話了。
B: Then quit bothering me! 那就別再煩我了！
A: Sorry. 對不起。

## Is this 323-1212?
### 這裡的電話號碼是 323-1212 嗎？

A: Is this 323-1212? 這裡的電話號碼是 323-1212 嗎？
B: No, this is 323-1213. 不，這裡是 323-1213.
A: My mistake. 抱歉。（是我弄錯了。）

＊各位有沒有發現這是一句很常聽到的說法呢？別在意太多，只管記住就對了，再說就變得囉唆囉唆。

絕對派上用場！
最常用的情境單字！

09-w3.mp3

# The Body  身體各部位名稱 II

| | | |
|---|---|---|
| arm [ɑrm] | n. | 手臂 |
| armpit [ˋɑrmˏpɪt] | n. | 腋下 |
| elbow [ˋɛLˏbo] | n. | 手肘 |
| waist [west] | n. | 腰 |
| hip [hɪp] | n. | 臀部 |
| buttocks [ˋbʌtəks] | n. | 屁股 |
| navel / belly button | n. | 肚臍 |
| leg [lɛg] | n. | 腿 |
| thigh [θaɪ] | n. | 大腿 |
| knee [ni] | n. | 膝蓋 |
| calf [kæf] | n. | 小腿 |
| shin [ʃɪn] | n. | 小腿前側、脛骨 |
| hand [hænd] | n. | 手 |
| finger [ˋfɪŋgɚ] | n. | 手指 |
| fingernail [ˏfɪŋgɚˏnel] | n. | 手指甲 |
| wrist [rɪst] | n. | 手腕 |
| thumb [θʌm] | n. | 拇指 |
| index finger | phr. | 食指 |
| middle finger | phr. | 中指 |
| ring finger | phr. | 無名指 |
| pinky [ˋpɪŋkɪ] | n. | 小指 |
| foot [fʊt] | n. | 腳 |
| toe [to] | n. | 腳趾 |
| toenail [ˋtoˏnel] | n. | 腳趾甲 |
| ankle [ˋæŋkl] | n. | 腳踝 |

09-13.mp3

# ⑬ I guess I've got to go.

### 我想我該掛電話了。

與朋友或是同事講電話的當下，如果突然有事不得不結束通話時，只要簡單地說 "I guess I've got to go." 就行了。這個句型可不能照字面解釋成「到某個地方去」，它正確的意思是「該結束通話了」。

A: I guess I've got to go. 我想我該掛電話了。
B: Call me later. 待會再打給我。
A: I will. 我會的。

## I have to go. Talk to you later.
**我該掛電話了，之後再聊。**

"Talk to you later." 是 "I'll talk to you later." 的簡說。

A: I have to go. Talk to you later. 我該掛電話了，之後再聊。
B: OK, talk to you later. 好吧，之後再聊。
A: Bye. 再見。

## I'm sorry, I have to get back to work.
**抱歉，我得回去工作了。**

A: I'm sorry, I have to get back to work. 抱歉，我得回去工作了。
B: What are you doing? 你在忙什麼呢？
A: Making a table. 做一張桌子。
B: Want some help? 需要幫忙嗎？

＊電信業者會為顧客提供來電插撥服務，所以像 "There's someone on." 或是 "I have a call on the other line."（我有插撥。）這些說法也會用到。

# ⑭ I will call back later.

稍後再打給你。

09-14.mp3

當然，換成 "I'll call you back." 的說法也是可以的。同樣的意思有各種不同的說法，各位就挑一個自己最拿手的盡情發揮吧。

A: I will call back later. 稍後再打給妳。
B: What time? 什麼時候啊？
A: I'll call at about 6. 大概是六點吧。
B: That sounds good. 好。

## I'll get back to you.
我再打給你。

A: I'll get back to you. 我再打給你。
B: You do that. 妳一定要打喔。
A: I will. I promise. 我會的，我答應你。

## May I call you back at a better time?
有空時可以再打給你嗎？

A: May I call you back at a better time? 有空時可以再打給妳嗎？
B: If you want. 你想打就打吧。
A: What's a good time for you? 什麼時間對妳比較方便呢？
B: Sometime next month. 下個月吧。

＊類似的說法有 "Can I call you back?"（可以回電給你嗎？），這個句型也很常用。

# ⑮ I need the number for Pizza Hut.

09-15.mp3

## 請幫我查必勝客的電話號碼。

　　國內的電話號碼查號台是 104、105，而美加等地的查號台則是 411。現在查號台大多採用語音辨識而不是真人服務，所以講得不好也沒什麼丟臉的。讓我們來透過以下的例句，練習一下這個情境的會話。

A: I need the number for Pizza Hut. 請幫我查必勝客的電話。

B: Which Pizza Hut do you want? 你要查哪一家必勝客？

A: There's more than one in town? 鎮上不只一家必勝客嗎？

B: There are three. 有三家。

## Can you give me the number for Mr. Lee on Sunset Street?

### 可以給我日落街李先生的電話嗎？

A: Can you give me the number for Mr. Lee on Sunset Street?
   可以給我日落街李先生的電話嗎？

B: I'm sorry, he is unlisted. 抱歉，他沒有登記喔。

A: That's strange. 奇怪了。

# 16 **Call me at 333-3131.**

09-16.mp3

打 333-3131 這個號碼聯絡我。

要表達打到哪個電話號碼，可以用介系詞 at 表示。

A: Call me at 333-3131. 打 333-3131 這個號碼聯絡我。

B: When should I call? 什麼時候可以打呢？

A: I don't care. Anytime. 任何時候都可以，我無所謂。

# COOL ENGLISH

時下美國年輕人常用的電話用語

09-x1.mp3

## I'll give her a buzz. 我會打電話給她。

buzz 和 call 一樣可以表示「打電話」，意思等於 "I'll give her a call."。

A: Where on earth is Mary? 瑪麗到底在哪裡啊？
B: I'll give her a buzz. 我來打電話給她。

## The telephone is her best friend.
她很愛講電話。

這句話用來形容人超愛講電話。

A: Everytime I call my girlfriend, her phone is always busy.
　　每次我打電話給我的女朋友時，她的電話總是在佔線。
B: It sounds like the telephone is her best friend.
　　聽起來她似乎是個很愛講電話的人呢。

## Don't make love to the phone.
別整天抓著電話不放。

這一句話也是用來形容成天抓著電話不放的人。

A: Don't make love to the phone. 別整天抓著電話不放。
B: I'm not on the phone that much. 我又沒有打多久。

## Just a sec. 請等一下。

"Just a sec." 是 "Just a second." 的簡略說法，意思和 "Hang on."、"Hold on." 一樣。

A: Is Miss Lee there? 李小姐在嗎？
B: Just a sec. 請等一下。

# COOL ENGLISH

時下美國年輕人常用的電話用語

09-x2.mp3

## The phone is dead. 電話不通。

這句話說「電話死了」，其實是指「電話不通」。

A: After that heavy rain last night, the phone is dead.

經過昨晚豪雨的侵襲，電話線路都不通了。

B: The phone company will fix it soon.　電信局很快就會修理了。

## Just tell him Jason called.
## 請轉告他傑森來過電話。

打電話給別人而對方不在，這是最簡便的留言。

A: Can I speak with Mr. Smith? 我可以和史密斯先生說話嗎？

B: He's not in. Can I take a message? 他不在。請問你要留言嗎？

A: Just tell him Jason called. He has the number.

請轉告他傑森來過電話，他知道我的號碼。

## He's really tied up right now.
## 他正忙得不可開交。

某人處在 tied up 的狀態，是指他「忙得走不開」。

A: Is Jason there? 請問傑森在嗎？

B: Sorry, he's really tied up right now. 抱歉，他正忙得不可開交。

A: OK. I'll call later. 好吧，我待會再打來。

## Are you there? 你在聽嗎？

和人講電話，如果對方都不出聲，就可以這樣說。

A: Are you there? 你有在聽嗎？

B: Yes, I'm here. 有啊，我在聽啊。

★請在以下空格中填入適當的單字★

I will __1__ the phone. 我來接電話。

__2__ number. 你撥錯號碼了。

I'm sorry to __3__ you so late. 抱歉這麼晚還打電話給你。

Is __4__ 323-1212? 這裡的電話號碼是 323-1212 嗎？

I need the __5__ for Pizza Hut. 請幫我查必勝客的電話號碼。

What's the __6__ ? 區域號碼是多少？

He has my __7__ number. 他有我的手機號碼。

He'll be __8__ with you. 他馬上就來接電話。

Could you tell him to __9__ me __9__ ? 請他回電給我好嗎？

It's __10__ . 這件事很急。

---

1. get　　　　2. Wrong　　　3. call　　　4. this
5. number　　6. area code　7. cell phone
8. right　　　9. call, back　10. urgent

★請在以下空格中填入適當的單字★

A: __1__ 請問哪裡找？

B: Jacob. 我是雅各。

A: Just a minute. 請等一下。

A: __2__ 傑森在嗎？

B: Hold on, please. He's outside. 請等一下，他正在外面。

A: No, I can leave a message. 沒關係，我留言就好了。

A: I'd like to speak to Shane, please. 我想找夏恩講話，謝謝。

B: He's busy. __3__ 他正在忙，你要留言嗎？

A: Just tell him Frank called. 請轉告他法蘭克來過電話。

B: Sure, Frank. 好的，法蘭克。

A: I think he's out for lunch. 我想他出去吃午餐了。

B: How long is his lunch? 他會吃多久？

A: __4__ 他一點之前會回來。

A: __5__ 這裡沒有人叫那個名字。

B: Are you sure? 你確定嗎？

A: Of course I'm sure. 我當然確定。

> 1. Who's calling, please?　　　　2. Is Jason there?
> 3. Can I take a message?
> 4. He'll be back by 1 o'clock.
> 5. We don't have anyone by that name.

# Chapter 10
# 旅行靠自己，
# 旅遊用語
# 讓你信心倍增

前往國外旅遊，無可避免地必須搭飛機或是租車，所以，一定要懂得用正確的英文詢問正確的資訊。如果對訊息理解錯誤的話，可能發生必須重買機票、找不到行李、違反租車規定而得付罰金等諸如此類的麻煩。

一提到國外旅行，大家應該會想要和異國遇見的人互相交流。因此，充分結合本書一開始介紹過的像是「問候」或「對話」這些章節的情境會話與旅遊用語，才有可能順利達成預期的旅行目標。

本書特別收錄了坊間英語工具書不常介紹的 "I need to reschedule my flight."（我想調換飛機班次。），或是搭機用語 "Beef, please."（請給我牛肉。），"I need a room for two."（我需要一間雙人房。）等最實用的情境用語，希望各位讀者在本文中能夠身歷其境般感受旅行的樂趣。

# ❶ I need a ticket to Chicago.

10-01.mp3

### 請給我一張往芝加哥的機票。

在國內搭機旅行不用擔心語言不通，但是，到了美國如果英文能力不足，個性又膽小，想要順利搭對班機應該不太容易喔！需要買機票時一般用 "I need ..." 來造句就可以了。

A: I need a ticket to Chicago. 請給我一張往芝加哥的機票。

B: What class? 請問要哪一種等級？

A: First class. 頭等艙。

B: We have no more first class tickets available.

我們頭等艙的機票已經賣完了。

## I'd like to book a flight.
**我想訂機票。**

這裡的 book 並不是指書籍，而是用來指「預約」班機的意思。

A: I'd like to book a flight. 我想訂機票。

B: Where to? 要到哪裡呢？

A: Indiana. 印地安那。

B: Which city? 哪一個城市呢？

## I'd like a round-trip ticket to New York, please.
**請給我一張紐約的來回機票。**

A: I'd like a round-trip ticket to New York, please.

請給我一張紐約的來回機票。

B: That will be $650. 一共是 650 塊美金。

A: That's expensive. 好貴啊。

\* round-trip ticket 是指來回票，而 one-way ticket 則是單程票。一般來說，買來回票比單程票便宜多了。

# ❷ I need to leave early in the morning.

10-02.mp3

**我必須一早就出發。**

"The early bird catches the worm.",早出發就早有收穫,這是中外皆然的。

A: I need to leave early in the morning. 我必須一早就出發。
B: We have a flight at 5 am. 我們有上午五點的班機。
A: Perfect. 太好了。
B: I'll book you on it. 我來為您預訂。

## I need to return on Saturday.
**我必須在週六回來。**

A: I need to return on Saturday. 我必須在週六回來。
B: That can be arranged. 能為您安排。
A: Can you arrange it now? 可否請你現在就幫我安排呢?

活用 365 個單字也能這麼說!

I was tied up in traffic. 我被車陣困住了。

# ❸ How much is coach?

經濟艙的價位是多少？

10-03.mp3

coach 指的是三級座位「經濟艙」。頭等艙的價位可以是經濟艙的三倍，商務艙的價位可以是經濟艙的兩倍。因此，各艙所提供的服務水準當然也就有所差別。在商務艙以上的等級座位，用餐時間一到，除了提供點菜單以外，咖啡也會用專用的杯子盛裝，還會把咖啡杯放在杯盤上端給你。

A: How much is coach? 經濟艙的價位是多少？
B: A coach ticket will be $150. 150 塊美金。
A: Okay, I'll take that. 好的，就給我經濟艙吧。

## How much is the flight?

機票要多少錢？

A: How much is the flight? 機票要多少錢？
B: It depends on which class you want. 那要看妳想坐哪個艙等。
A: I don't care. The cheapest. 我不在乎，最便宜的就行了。

## Do you have any cheaper ticket?

你們有更便宜的票嗎？

A: Do you have any cheaper ticket? 你們有更便宜的票嗎？
B: This is the cheapest we have. 這是我們最便宜的票了。
A: Forget it, then. 那算了。
B: Do you want me to cancel the booking? 您要我取消訂票嗎？

＊ cheaper tickets 指的是「比較便宜的票」。

10-04.mp3

# ❹ Can I put it on reserve?

**我可以預約嗎?**

預約的英文名詞是 "reservation",動詞則是 "reserve"。"Can I put it on reserve?" 是「我可以預約嗎」的意思。

A: Can I put it on reserve? 我可以預約嗎?

B: No, we don't do reserve. 抱歉,我們不接受預約。

A: Why not? 為什麼不呢?

## Can I put my name on the waiting list?

**可以將我的名字列入候補名單嗎?**

「登記」姓名的英文可以用 put。

A: Can I put my name on the waiting list? 可以將我的名字列入候補名單嗎?

B: Yes, you can. Please fill out this form. 可以,請填寫這張表格。

A: Okay. 好的。

---

**活用 365 個單字也能這麼說!**

This steak is really A1! 這個牛排實在是美味極了!

# ⑤ I need to cancel my flight.

10-05.mp3

我必須取消班機預約。

cancel 是指「取消某件事情」的意思，所以 cancel my flight 是「取消班機預約」之意。

A: I need to cancel my flight. 我必須取消班機預約。

B: What's your last name, sir? 請問先生貴姓？

A: Norris. 諾里斯。

B: I don't have a Norris registered on the flight.
這班飛機並沒有登記諾里斯這個姓氏。

## I need to reschedule my flight.
我想調換飛機班次。

A: I need to reschedule my flight. 我想調換飛機班次。

B: What's your name? 您的大名是什麼？

A: Frank. 法蘭克。

B: Last name? 姓氏是什麼？

## I'd like to confirm my ticket.
我想確認我的機票。

A: I'd like to confirm my ticket. 我想確認我的機票。

B: This ticket is to Buenos Aires. 這張機票是往布宜諾斯艾利斯的。

A: To where?! 去哪裡啊？

B: Isn't that where you want to go? 那不是您要去的地方嗎？

＊這裡的 confirm 是確認手上已經買好的機票是否和預定內容吻合、行程有無改變等的用語。

絕對派上用場！
最常用的情境單字！

# Airport 機場

| | | |
|---|---|---|
| ticket counter | phr. | 售票櫃台 |
| security guard | phr. | 機場保全人員 |
| check-in counter | phr. | 登機櫃台 |
| boarding pass | phr. | 登機證 |
| gate [get] | n. | 登機門 |
| duty-free shop | phr. | 免稅商店 |
| suitcase [ˋsut͵kes] | n. | 旅行箱 |
| customs [ˋkʌstəmz] | n. | 海關 |
| passport [ˋpæs͵port] | n. | 護照 |
| visa [ˋvizə] | n. | 簽證 |
| passenger [ˋpæsəndʒɚ] | n. | 乘客 |
| flight attendant | phr. | 空服員 |
| overhead compartment | phr. | 置物櫃 |
| window seat | phr. | 靠窗座位 |
| middle seat | phr. | 中間座位 |
| aisle seat | phr. | 走道座位 |
| tray [tre] | n. | 餐盤 |
| seat pocket | phr. | 座位置物袋 |
| life vest | phr. | 救生衣 |

10-w1.mp3

## 6 Can I get an aisle seat?

10-06.mp3

可以給我靠走道的座位嗎？

有些人就算擠破了頭也想坐在靠窗的機位！其實，靠窗的座位既不方便上洗手間，窗外風景更是除了大片雲海之外什麼也沒有，反而是走道旁邊的座位方便多了。

A: Can I get an aisle seat? 可以給我靠走道的座位嗎？

B: No, we only have window seats left. 抱歉，只剩下靠窗的座位了。

A: That will have to do. 那也只能這樣了。

# When is the departure time?
## 起飛時間是什麼時候？

"departure time" 是指「出發的時間」，那麼，到達時間的英文說法是什麼？答案就是 "arrival time"。

A: When is the departure time? 起飛時間是什麼時候？

B: It's scheduled to take off at 7:50 pm. 預定是在晚上 7 點 50 分起飛。

A: That's good enough. 時間還來得及。

# Can I check my baggage through to Hong Kong?
## 我可以把行李託運到香港嗎？

A: Can I check my baggage through to Hong Kong?

　　我可以把行李託運到香港嗎？

B: Sure. 當然可以。

＊將手提包或是行李託運到飛機上，登記時一定要在櫃台確認清楚才好。從美國到台灣，飛機勢必會經過各個不同的城市，此時如果想說「我可以把行李寄到台灣嗎」，英文應該說 "Can I check my baggage through to Taiwan?"。

# Just coffee is fine.

## 我只要咖啡就好。

10-07.mp3

在飛機裡常有機會說到英文，而有幾點可不能馬虎。比方說，想向服務人員要飲料時應該加 please。此外，到了用餐時間通常會有 beef 和 chicken 兩種餐點可以選擇，而大部分的乘客會選擇 beef（可能因為 beef 比較貴吧）。如果 beef 沒了，你可能會聽到 "Sorry, we're out of beef now. Chicken is good, too."。

A: Just coffee is fine. 我只要咖啡就好。
B: You don't want anything to eat? 您不需要吃的嗎？
A: No, thank you. 不要，謝謝。

## Beef, please.
### 請給我牛肉。

A: Beef or chicken? 請問要牛肉還是雞肉？
B: Beef, please. 牛肉，謝謝。
A: Here it is. 請慢用。

## Can you get me a blanket?
### 給我一條毯子好嗎？

A: Can you get me a blanket? 給我一條毯子好嗎？
B: Yes, I can. 好的。
A: My wife needs one, too. 我太太也要一條。
B: I'll get you two. 我拿兩條給你們。

＊坐在飛機裡頭，由於空調設施很完善，所以入睡時會感到涼意。如果遇到這種情況千萬別悶不吭聲，因為不小心可能會感冒了。所以，記得開口向空服員要一條 blanket（毯子），但別把毯子帶回家留作紀念喔！

### 活用 365 個單字也能這麼說！

He has a poker face. 他有一張撲克臉。（他面無表情。）

# ⑧ My luggage is missing.

10-08.mp3

我的行李遺失了。

託運行李一定會碰上一、兩次中途遺失的情形，要是在旅行途中遺失真的會讓人叫苦連天。如果自己的行李真的不見了，必須盡快到負責的航空公司服務櫃台填寫遺失表格，大概經過兩三天那些失物就會直接寄到失主家裡。不過，常見的情況是永遠都找不到行李。所以囉，出外旅行最好隨身攜帶重要物品，而且最好準備一個小型手提包比較方便。

A: My luggage is missing. 我的行李不見了。
B: What did you have? 你有哪些行李呢？
A: I had three suitcases. 我有三個行李箱。

## One of my bags seems to be missing.
我的一個行李好像不見了。

A: One of my bags seems to be missing. 我的一個行李好像不見了。
B: Are you certain? 妳確定嗎？
A: Yes, I'm certain. 是的，我確定。

活用 365 個單字也能這麼說！

Stop being a backseat driver! 別再對我頤指氣使！

絕對派上用場！
最常用的情境單字！

10-w2.mp3

## Outdoor Recreation 戶外休閒

| | | |
|---|---|---|
| tent [tɛnt] | n. | 帳篷 |
| tent stakes | phr. | 帳篷鉚釘 |
| backpack [`bæk͵pæk] | n. | 背包 |
| sleeping bag | phr. | 睡袋 |
| lantern [`læntɚn] | n. | 提燈 |
| camp stove | phr. | 露營暖爐 |
| hiking boots | phr. | 登山鞋 |
| trail map | phr. | 地圖 |
| rope [rop] | n. | 繩索 |
| blanket [`blæŋkɪt] | n. | 毛毯 |
| picnic basket | phr. | 野餐籃 |
| lifeguard [`laɪf͵gɑrd] | n. | 救生員 |
| swimmer [`swɪmɚ] | n. | 游泳者 |
| wave [wev] | n. | 海浪 |
| surfer [`sɝfɚ] | n. | 衝浪者 |
| vendor [`vɛndɚ] | n. | 攤販 |
| sunbather [`sʌn͵beðɚ] | n. | 做日光浴的人 |
| beach umbrella | phr. | 海灘傘 |
| beach towel | phr. | 大浴巾 |
| swimsuit [`swɪm͵sut] | n. | 泳衣 |
| bathing cap | phr. | 泳帽 |
| kite [kaɪt] | n. | 風箏 |
| tube [tjub] | n. | 游泳圈 |
| sunglasses [`sʌn͵glæsɪz] | n. | 太陽眼鏡 |
| beach ball | phr. | 海灘球 |
| cooler [`kʊlɚ] | n. | 冰桶 |

# ⑨ I'm here to rent a car.

10-09.mp3

我要租一輛車。

到美國旅行，自己租一部車到處玩是最經濟的做法，而且和國內的租金比較起來便宜很多。在美國租用車子必須使用信用卡，另外，還有年齡上的限制。所以如果有需要，建議提早打聽相關資訊。

A: I'm here to rent a car. 我要租一輛車。
B: What type of car would you like? 你想租哪一種車呢？
A: The cheapest thing you got. 最便宜的哪種。

## I'd like to rent a car.
**我想租一部車。**

A: I'd like to rent a car. 我想租一部車。
B: I have one here for you. 這裡有一部。
A: Only one? 只有一部啊？
B: Well, you can choose if you want. 嗯，如果妳想要也可以挑選。

## I'd like to reserve a car, please.
**我想預約一部車。**

A: I'd like to reserve a car, please. 我想預約一部車。
B: No need to reserve one. 我們這裡不需要預約。
A: Why not? 為什麼呢？
B: We have plenty here. 我們的出租車很多。

# ⑩ Do you have any convertibles?

10-10.mp3

### 你這裡有敞篷車嗎？

出租的車子種類繁多，最好先比較大小和價格再做決定。美國的 convertibles 光是租金就貴得嚇人了。

A: Do you have any convertibles? 妳這裡有敞篷車嗎？
B: We have two. 有兩部。
A: Are they taken? 別人租走了嗎？
B: Only one of them is taken at the moment. 目前其中一部被訂走了。

## What's the price difference?
**價位差多少？**

A: What's the price difference? 價位差多少？
B: They all cost the same. 價錢全都一樣。
A: That's interesting. 真有意思。

## What's the rate for a compact?
**小型車的租金是多少？**

A: What's the rate for a compact? 小型車的租金是多少？
B: $90 per day. 一天 90 塊美金。
A: That's a good price. 價錢還可以。

# ⑪ I want a compact car.

10-11.mp3

## 我要租一輛小型車。

compact car 是指經濟型的小型房車，如果是短程旅行，小型的房車比較適合；相反地，長途旅行則比較適合開大型的休旅車。

A: I want a compact car. 我想租一輛小型車。

B: We don't have compacts. 我們沒有小型車出租喔。

A: Why not? 為什麼沒有啊？

B: We hate compacts. 我們不喜歡小型車。

# How many miles per day is the limit?
## 一天限跑幾哩呢？

哩程數分為 limited 和 unlimited 兩種。limited 是限制每天的哩程數，價格比較便宜；相反地，unlimited 則是一天內不限哩程數，但是價格會比 limited 昂貴。

A: How many miles per day is the limit? 一天限跑幾哩呢？

B: There's the $50 and $100 miles plan.
   有 50 塊美金的哩程數和 100 塊美金的哩程數兩種。

A: I'll take the $50. 我要 50 塊美金哩程數的。

# I'd like the unlimited miles.
## 我要租不限哩程數的。

A: I'd like the unlimited miles. 我要租不限哩程數的。

B: That will cost $100 extra. 那會貴 100 塊美金喔。

A: I know. 我知道。

絕對派上用場！
最常用的情境單字！

10-w3.mp3

# Hotel 飯店

| bed [bɛd] | n. | 床 |
| pillow [ˈpɪlo] | n. | 枕頭 |
| pillowcase [ˈpɪloˌkes] | n. | 枕頭套 |
| blanket [ˈblæŋkɪt] | n. | 毛毯 |
| blind [blaɪnd] | n. | 窗簾 |
| clock radio | phr. | 自動定時開關收音機 |
| mirror [ˈmɪrɚ] | n. | 鏡子 |
| twin bed | phr. | （成對的）單人床 |
| mattress [ˈmætrɪs] | n. | 床墊 |
| double bed | phr. | 雙人床 |
| queen-size bed | phr. | 加大雙人床 |
| king-size bed | phr. | 特大雙人床 |
| bunk bed | phr. | 雙層床 |
| sofa bed | phr. | 沙發床 |

# ⑫ I'd like to check in.

## 我要登記住房。

10-12.mp3

　　入住飯店和買機票一樣，事先預訂通常會比較便宜。另外，預訂之後一定要透過 fax 或是 e-mail 再次確認比較保險。到了飯店要 check in 時只要簡短地說句 "Check in, please." 就夠了。

A: I'd like to check in. 我要登記住房。
B: Do you have a reservation? 您有訂房嗎？
A: No. 沒有。
B: You need a reservation, ma'am. 女士，您必須事先預訂。

＊結論是沒有房間可以入住。

# Do you have any vacancies?
## 有空房嗎？

　　行駛在美國的高速公路上，可以看見兩旁有許多飯店和汽車旅館的廣告招牌。入夜之後，這些地方的門口會立著 vacancy 或是 no vacancy 等的字樣。vacancy 是指尚有空房，no vacancy 是指客滿的意思。所以，"Do you have any vacancies?" 這整句話的意思是「你這裡有空房嗎」。

A: Do you have any vacancies? 有空房嗎？
B: I'm afraid not. 恐怕沒有了。
A: Okay. 了解。

## 活用 365 個單字也能這麼說！

It was an awesome game. 那真是一場驚人的競賽。

# ⑬ I need a room for two.

10-13.mp3

**我需要一間雙人房。**

在飯店或汽車旅館沒有事先預約但需要入住時，可以用這句話向櫃台人員詢問。

A: I need a room for two. 我需要一間雙人房。
B: How many beds? 要幾張床呢？
A: One bed. 一張床。

## I need a room with a double bed.
**我需要一間雙人床房。**

A: I need a room with a double bed. 我需要一間雙人床房。
B: We have one left. 我們還剩一間空房。
A: What luck! 真幸運！

## I need a room at the front.
**我要一間前排的房間。**

A: I need a room at the front. 我要一間前排的房間。
B: That can be arranged. 可以安排。
A: Good. 太好了。
B: I'll give you room 2. 給您 2 號房。

### 活用 365 個單字也能這麼說！

My girlfriend stood me up last night. 我女朋友昨晚放我鴿子。

# ⑭ Give me a wake-up call at 6 o'clock.

10-14.mp3

## 請在六點叫我起床。

飯店的叫醒服務不是 morning call，而是 wake-up call，wake-up call 不限定是早上打內線電話叫醒房客，隨時有需要都可以用。

A: Give me a wake-up call at 6 o'clock. 請在六點叫我起床。

B: Sure. 好的。

A: Thank you. 謝謝。

## This is room 910. I'd like to order.

**這是 910 號房，我要點餐。**

A: This is room 910. I'd like to order some wine.
這是 910 號房，我想點酒。

B: What wine would you like? 您要什麼酒呢？

A: Send some white wine. 送點白酒過來。

## I have some laundry.

**我有一些衣服要洗。**

A: I have some laundry. 我有一些衣服要洗。

B: We'll send someone up right away. 我們馬上派人上去。

A: Thank you. 謝謝。

＊飯店通常設有洗衣服務，當然是使用者付費囉。要洗的衣物英文叫做 laundry.。

### 活用 365 個單字也能這麼說！

I'm dying to know what her name is. 我好想知道她叫什麼名字。

# **15 I need to check out.**

10-15.mp3

我要退房。

退房的時候建議仔細檢查收費帳單，結算的時候現金支付或是刷卡都可以。

A: I need to check out. 我要退房。

B: It's after noon. You'll have to pay for another day.
已經超過中午 12 點了，您必須多支付一天的費用。

A: But I want to leave now! 但是我現在要離開了耶！

B: I'm sorry, miss. 抱歉，小姐。


## **I'd like to put it on my Visa.**
**我想用 Visa 卡支付。**

A: I'd like to put it on my Visa. 我想用 Visa 卡支付。

B: We don't accept Visa. 我們不收 Visa 卡。

A: Are you serious? 妳是說真的嗎？

B: Yes. We take cash only. 是的，我們只收現金。


## **I'd like to stay a day longer.**
**我要延後一天退房。**

A: I'd like to stay a day longer. 我要延後一天退房。

B: I'm afraid you can't. 抱歉，恐怕不行。

A: You're making me leave? 你是要趕我走囉？

B: Other people have reservations for your room.
其他客人已經預訂了您的房間。

＊如果需要延後退房，一定要提早跟訂房人員說一聲，要不然很可能就得乖乖收拾東西走人了。

# COOL ENGLISH

## 時下美國年輕人常用的旅遊用語

10-x1.mp3

## I just want to get there in one piece.
## 我只希望可以平安到達。

"in one piece" 是祈望不要經歷飛機失事或其他交通事故，能「平安無事」到達目的地的意思。

A: I just want to get there in one piece. 我只希望可以平安到達。
B: Don't worry, man. 不用擔心啦，老兄。

## I'm jet-lagged. 時差讓我頭昏腦脹。

台灣和美國的時差很大，經過長途飛行後，頭幾天由於要適應時差，會過得比較辛苦。"I'm jet-lagged." 是「我還在調時差」的意思。

A: How was your flight? 飛行之旅如何？
B: I'm jet-lagged. 時差讓我頭昏腦脹。

## I took the red-eye. 我搭晚班飛機。

所謂「紅眼班機」就是「夜班飛機」的意思。

A: I took the red-eye. 我搭晚班飛機來的。
B: I think you'd better get some sleep. 我想你最好去睡一下。

## Where can I rent some wheels?
## 哪裡可以租車呢？

wheel 是指汽車的方向盤，這裡用來代指 car。整句話的意思是「我能在哪裡租車呢」。

A: Where can I rent some wheels? 哪裡可以租車呢？
B: I think Enterprise is a good place to rent a car.
　　我想 Enterprise 是不錯的租車公司。

★請在以下空格中填入適當的單字★

How much is ___**1**___ ? 經濟艙的價位是多少？

Can I get an ___**2**___ seat? 可以給我靠走道的座位嗎？

Do you have any ___**3**___ ? 你們有敞篷車嗎？

I ___**4**___ a room for two. 我需要一間雙人房。

___**5**___ out, please. 退房，謝謝。

This is the ___**6**___ we have. 這是我們最便宜的。

Please ___**7**___ this form. 請填寫這張表格。

Can I check my baggage ___**8**___ to Taiwan?
我可以把行李託運到台灣嗎？

Can you get me a ___**9**___ ? 給我一條毯子好嗎？

Do you have any ___**10**___ ? 有空房嗎？

---

1. coach　　2. aisle　　3. convertibles　　4. need
5. Check　　6. cheapest　　7. fill out
8. through　　9. blanket　　10. vacancies

★請在以下空格中填入適當的單字★

A: __1__ 我必須一早就出發。

B: we have a flight at 5 am. 我們有上午五點的班機。

A: Perfect. 太好了。

B: I'll book you on it. 我來為您預訂。

A: __2__ 我必須取消班機預約。

B: What's your last name, sir? 請問先生貴姓？

A: Norris. 諾里斯。

B: I don't have a Norris registered on the flight.
這班飛機並沒有登記諾里斯這個姓氏。

A: __3__ 請在六點叫我起床。

B: Sure. 好的。

A: Thank you. 謝謝你。

A: __4__ 你們有更便宜的票嗎？

B: This is the cheapest we have. 這是我們最便宜的票了。

---

1. I need to leave early in the morning.
2. I need to cancel my flight.
3. Give me a wake-up call at 6.
4. Do you have any cheaper tickets?

# Chapter 11

# 禮尚往來！
# 居家、拜訪
# 用語最感心

接著，我們要來看看居家情境的英文用語。在這一章，我把重點放在家人、鄰居之間互相遵守的「禮儀」。例如，想到朋友家拜訪可不能說去就去，應該事先聯絡詢問對方 "Can I come over?"，如果對方很歡迎，應該禮貌性地問一下 "Can I bring anything?"，然後帶個巧克力或是水果禮盒前往。家裡如果有朋友來訪，也應該友善地詢問對方 "Can I take your coat?"。

此外，像是睡過頭時要說 "I overslept."；見到新生兒時可以說 "He has his mother's eyes."；參加喪禮時會對喪家說 "I'm so sorry for your loss."。這些與我們的生活密切相關且重要的情境英文，都整理在這一章裡，讓各位讀者一目瞭然。

離開了文化，會話便會索然無味。英文，是一種語言，語言則是一種文化。

# ❶ Dinner's ready.

11-01.mp3

**晚飯做好了。**

媽媽在廚房裡準備好了晚餐,打算叫孩子們準備開飯,這時她會怎麼說呢?「孩子們,開飯了。」英文的說法其實大同小異:"Hey, guys. Dinner's ready."。

A: Go sit down, dinner's ready. 坐好,要開飯了。
B: OK. 好。
A: Sarah, would you say grace? 莎拉,妳要祈禱了嗎?

## Time to eat.
**吃飯時間到了。**

A: Time to eat. 吃飯時間到了。
B: Okay. 知道了。
A: Who wants roast? 誰想吃烤肉?

## Would you set the table?
**你可以擺一下餐具嗎?**

A: When do we eat? 我們什麼時候吃飯?
B: It's almost ready. Would you set the table?
   就快好了,妳可以擺一下餐具嗎?
A: Sure. 當然可以。

＊把筷子、湯匙等餐具放到餐桌上準備開飯的英文說法就是 set the table.。

273

## ❷ **What's on TV?**

11-02.mp3

### 電視在播什麼節目？

說明「電視上」正在播映的節目，英文用 on。所以問別人電視播什麼節目該怎麼說？只要說 "What's on TV?" 就搞定了。

A: What's on TV? 電視在播什麼節目？

B: I dunno. 不知道。

A: Give me the remote. 把遙控器給我。

＊ "I dunno." 是 "I don't know." 的口語說法。

## Is there anything good on?
**有什麼好看的節目嗎？**

A: Is there anything good on? 有什麼好看的節目嗎？

B: I dunno. 不知道。

A: Check the TV Guide. 查一下節目表。

＊前面提過「電視上」播某個節目要用 on，還記得嗎？所以在 "Is there anything good on?" 這句話裡同樣也是用 on。

## Stop flipping channels.
**別再轉台了。**

A: Hey, stop flipping channels. 嘿，別再轉台了啦。

B: OK. 好啦。

A: Give me the remote. 把遙控器給我。

B: No way, I had it first. 不行，我先拿到的。

## ③ Would you stop that, please?

11-03.mp3

### 可以請你住手嗎？

有些人遇到頑皮的小孩，處理方式傾向於籐條教育。因為打小孩而被抓去關時有所聞，有些家長一旦發起火來便把小孩打得遍體鱗傷，這是最錯誤的教育方式。下面例句中的 tease 這個字，中文是指「欺負、戲弄、故意激怒」。

A: Teacher. 老師。

B: Yes, Sarah. What is it? 是，莎拉。什麼事？

A: John is teasing me. 約翰一直在鬧我。

B: Excuse me, John.  Would you stop that, please?
　　抱歉，約翰，可以請你住手嗎？

## Stop that.
**別再那樣。**

A: Stop that. Behave yourself. 別再那樣了，規矩一點。

B: I wasn't doing nothing. 我什麼也沒做啊。

A: Stop teasing your little sister. 別再欺負你妹妹了。

## Stop it.
**住手。**

A: Hey, stop it. 嘿，住手。

B: Okay, okay. 好，好。

＊這句話的意思與 "Stop it." 是一樣的。

11-04.mp3

# ④ Are you gonna be home?

**待會兒你會在家嗎？**

在美國，先邀請別人是種禮貌。受到別人的邀請後，花 3 到 5 塊美金買巧克力或是水果禮盒帶過去是另一種禮貌。有趣的是，如果派對 6 點開始，美國人通常會 6 點 10 分左右才到。

A: Are you gonna be home later? 待會兒妳會在家嗎？
B: Sure. 會啊。
A: Great. I might stop by. 好極了，我可能會順便去一趟。

＊ "Are you gonna ..." 是 "Are you going to ..." 的口語說法。stop by 是「短暫拜訪」的意思。

## Are you free later tonight?
**今晚你有空嗎？**

A: Are you free later tonight? 今晚你有空嗎？
B: Why? 有事嗎？
A: Let's have some beer. 我們一起喝杯啤酒吧。

## Can I come over?
**我可以去找你嗎？**

A: Hey, Mike? 嘿，麥克？
B: What? 什麼事？
A: Can I come over to your place tonight? 今晚我可以去你家嗎？
B: Sure. Bring some beer. 好啊，帶些啤酒來喔。

# ⑤ Can I bring anything?

11-05.mp3

### 要不要我帶些東西過去？

邀請老外參加宴會或是餐會時，他們會回應的第一句話常是 "Can I bring anything?"。由此可見，他們也是盡量不欠人情呢。

A: Hello, Jane. 哈囉，珍。

B: Yeah? 嗯？

A: We're having a dinner party. Can you make it?
   我家要辦晚餐餐會，妳能來嗎？

B: I'd love to. Can I bring anything?
   我很樂意參加，要不要我帶些東西過去呢？

## What should I bring?
**我該帶什麼去呢？**

A: What are you doing tonight? 今晚你打算做什麼？

B: I'm free. 我沒有什麼事。

A: You wanna come over to my place for dinner? 要不要來我家吃晚餐？

B: Sure. What should I bring? 當然好啊，我該帶什麼去呢？

A: Nothing. 人來就好。

## Let me bring dessert.
**讓我帶點心過去。**

A: Bring some beer. 帶些啤酒過來。

B: Okay. Let me bring dessert, too. 好啊，我也會帶點心過去。

## ⑥ I was stuck in traffic.

路上塞車。

路上塞車情形很嚴重，英文的說法是 "I was stuck in traffic." 。stuck 是指「進退不得」的狀態。

A: Hey, you made it. 嘿，你來啦。
B: Sorry, I'm so late. I was stuck in traffic. 抱歉我來晚了，路上塞車。
A: No problem. 沒有關係啦。

## I overslept.

我睡過頭了。

A: Where have you been? 妳到哪裡去了啊？
B: Oh, I overslept. Sorry. 噢，我睡過頭了，對不起。
A: It's okay. 沒關係。

## I had to drop someone off.

我（當時必須）順道載人去一個地方。

A: Why are you so late? 你怎麼這麼晚才來？
B: I had to drop someone off. 我順道載人去一個地方。
A: I see. 原來是這樣啊。

＊ drop someone off 是「載某人去某處」的意思。

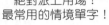

絕對派上用場！
最常用的情境單字！

WORD BOX

# Living Room 客廳

11-w1.mp3

| | | |
|---|---|---|
| coffee table | n. | 咖啡桌 |
| rug [rʌg] | n. | 地毯 |
| floor [flor] | n. | 地板 |
| armchair [`ɑrmˌtʃɛr] | n. | 有扶手的椅子 |
| lamp [læmp] | n. | 燈 |
| window [`wɪndo] | n. | 窗戶 |
| sofa [`sofə] | n. | 沙發 |
| ceiling [`silɪŋ] | n. | 天花板 |
| wall [wɔl] | n. | 牆 |
| television [`tɛləˌvɪʒən] | n. | 電視機 |
| stereo system | phr. | 音響 |
| loveseat [`lʌvˌsit] | n. | 雙人椅 |
| fireplace [`faɪrˌples] | n. | 壁爐 |
| bookcase [`bʊkˌkes] | n. | 書櫃 |
| table [`tebl] | n. | 餐桌 |
| chair [tʃɛr] | n. | 椅子 |
| tablecloth [`teblˌklɔθ] | n. | 桌布 |
| candle [`kændl] | n. | 蠟燭 |
| teapot [`tiˌpɑt] | n. | 茶壺 |

# **7** **Come on in.**

快進來坐。

11-07.mp3

美國老外邀請別人進來坐時普遍會說 "Come on in."，在 "Come in." 中間多加了 on，用以強調「快一點」。

A: Hi! 嗨！
B: Hey, come on in. Have some wine. 嘿，快進來坐坐。喝點酒吧。

## Come in and sit down.
**快進來坐。**

A: Come in and sit down. 快進來坐。
B: Okay, thanks. 好的，謝謝。

## Please come in. Have a seat.
**歡迎，請坐。**

A: Please come in. Have a seat. 歡迎，請坐。
B: Thanks. It's really hot out there. 謝謝，外頭實在很熱啊。
A: Yeah. 是啊。

### 活用 365 個單字也能這麼說！

I work nine-to-five. 我只是個平凡的上班族。

# 8 Can I take your coat?

## 把外套給我吧？

受邀的客人走進玄關時，主人為客人接過外套和帽子是基本的禮儀。此時派上用場的英文就是 "Can I take your coat?"。

A: Hello, come on in. 哈囉，請進。

B: Hi, I'm sorry I'm late. 嗨，抱歉我來晚了。

A: That's OK. Can I take your coat? 沒有關係，把外套交給我吧？

B: Oh, thank you. 噢，謝謝。

# Here, let me take your coat.

**把外套給我吧。**

A: Hey, Jimmy. Let me take your coat. 嘿，吉米。把你的外套給我吧。

B: Thanks. 謝謝。

### 活用 365 個單字也能這麼說！

This is a once-in-a-lifetime opportunity. 這是千載難逢的機會。

# ⑨ Would you like something to drink?

11-09.mp3

喝一點飲料嗎？

這個句型絕對要記起來，因為它很常聽到，也時常有機會說到。當然，也可以用 "Do you want something to drink?" 來代替。不過，使用 "Would ..." 來開頭會比較有禮貌。

A: Would you like something to drink? 喝一點飲料嗎？
B: Sure. I'll have a Coke. 當然，可樂好了。

## Get yourself a drink and something to eat.

請隨意取用飲料和食物。

這個句型對初學者而言可能會有點難度。不過，它可是很實用的一句話喔。照字面的意思是「拿給你自己喝的和吃的」，換句話說，就是要對方隨便自己愛吃什麼就吃什麼。

A: The bar's over there. Get yourself a drink and something to eat.
   吧台在哪裡，請隨意取用飲料和食物。
B: OK. Do you mind if I smoke? 好的，妳介意我抽煙嗎？
A: Not in the house. 在屋子裡不行喔。

## Would you like a taste?

你想嚐一口嗎？

A: Jimmy, Would you like a taste? 吉米，來嚐一口嗎？
B: Sure. 好啊。

＊這不就是老外煮湯時品嚐味道的樣子嗎？這是一句學起來還滿好用的句型。雖然很簡單，不過真正遇到狀況時，很多人還是會腦袋空空，什麼也想不到。

# ⑩ Well, it's getting late.

11-10.mp3

**嗯，時間已經這麼晚了呀。**

　　一群人玩得正高興，常會有人突然緊張地看著時鐘說 "Well, it's getting late."，然後起身要走。該走人的時候毫不遲疑也是老外一貫的作風。

A: Well, it's getting late. We'd better be going.
　　嗯，時間已經這麼晚了呀，我們該走了。
B: So soon? 這麼快就要走了嗎？
A: Yeah. We both have to get up early tomorrow.
　　是啊，我們明天都得早起。
B: Okay. 好吧。

# Time to go.
**我該走了。**

　　"Time to go." 是 "It's time to go." 的簡短說法。

A: Time to go. Nice talking with you. 我該走了，和你聊天很愉快。
B: Okay. See you later. 好的，下次見囉。
A: Bye. 再見。

# I've got to hit the road.
**我該走了。**

A: I've got to hit the road. 我該走了。
B: Okay. See you. 這樣啊，再見。

＊ hit the road 的字面解釋是「打路面」，其實那就是「上路」的意思。

# ⑪ Would you like to stay for dinner?

11-11.mp3

## 要不要留下來吃晚餐？

"stay for dinner" 是「為了晚餐而留下」，也就是「吃了晚餐再走」的意思。以 "Would you like to ..." 開頭就是一句很有英文程度的說法囉。

A: Hey, Bill. What time is it? 嘿，比爾，現在幾點了？
B: It's five. 五點。
A: What? Five o'clock? I have to go. 啊？五點啦？我該走了。
B: Would you like to stay for dinner? 要不要留下來吃晚餐？

## Can you stay for dinner?
### 你可以晚餐之後再走嗎？

A: Tom, can you stay for dinner? 湯姆，你可以晚餐之後再走嗎？
B: Sorry, I can't. I have a lot of things to do.
不好意思，我沒辦法。我有很多事情要做。

## Can you have dinner with me?
### 你可以和我一起吃晚餐嗎？

A: Honey, can you have dinner with me?
親愛的，妳可以和我一起吃晚餐嗎？
B: No, I can't. I'm really busy. 不，沒辦法。我真的很忙。
A: Okay. 好吧。

# ⑫ Thank you for inviting us.

謝謝你邀請我們。

"Thank you for ..." 應該是大家都很熟悉的句型了吧？就算受邀的場合不如想像中有趣，想早一步離開時還是得有禮貌地說聲 "Thank you for inviting us / me."。

A: Are you leaving now? 你們要走了嗎？

B: Yes. Thank you for inviting us. 是啊，謝謝妳邀請我們。

A: Oh, no problem. 噢，別客氣。

# We had a real nice time.

我們玩得很開心。

A: Well, it's getting late. We have to go. 嘿，時間已經晚了，我們該走了。

B: We had a real nice time. 我們玩得很開心。

A: Me too. 我也是。

# Thank you for a lovely evening.

謝謝你帶來很棒的一晚。

A: Thank you for a lovely evening. 謝謝你帶來很棒的一晚。

B: You're welcome. 你客氣了。

11-w2.mp3

# Bathroom 洗手間

| | | |
|---|---|---|
| toilet [ˋtɔɪlɪt] | n. | 馬桶 |
| toilet paper | phr. | 衛生紙 |
| toilet paper holder | phr. | 衛生紙掛勾 |
| toilet brush | phr. | 馬桶刷 |
| hair dryer | phr. | 吹風機 |
| mirror [ˋmɪrɚ] | n. | 鏡子 |
| toothbrush [ˋtuθˏbrʌʃ] | phr. | 牙刷 |
| soap [sop] | n. | 香皂 |
| wastebasket [ˋwestˏbæskɪt] | phr. | 垃圾桶 |
| shower curtain | phr. | 浴簾 |
| bathtub [ˋbæθˏtʌb] | n. | 浴缸 |
| rubber mat | phr. | 橡膠踏墊 |
| comb [kom] | n. | 梳子 |
| shampoo [ʃæmˋpu] | n. | 洗髮精 |
| toothpaste [ˋtuθˏpest] | n. | 牙膏 |
| mouthwash [ˋmaʊθˏwɑʃ] | n. | 漱口水 |
| shaving cream | phr. | 刮鬍膏 |

# ⑬ **Are you all right?**

你還好嗎？

11-13.mp3

同樣的含義還有 "Are you OK?"。

A: Are you all right? You look pale. 妳還好嗎？看起來臉色不太好耶。

B: I'm dizzy. And I think I've got a temperature.

我有一點頭暈，而且我想我發燒了。

A: Lie down. 躺一下吧。

# Are you OK?

你還好嗎？

A: Are you OK? 你還好嗎？

B: No, I'm not okay. I've got a cold. 不，我覺得不好。我感冒了。

A: You'd better take a rest. 你最好休息一下。

# Are you feeling OK?

你（感覺）還好嗎？

A: Hello, Janet. 哈囉，珍妮。

B: Hey, you look tired. Are you feeling OK? 嘿，你看起來很累。還好嗎？

A: Yeah, I'm okay. 嗯，我還可以。

11-14.mp3

# ⑭ You look tired.

**你看起來很累。**

也許有人會說成 "You looks tired."。誠如大家所知的，looks 是 "He looks tired." 或 "She looks tired." 等第三人稱單數主詞的動詞形態。希望各位讀者小心，不要養成錯誤的習慣，因為這是在中文裡見不到，也因此常被忽略的。

A: You look tired. 妳看來很累。
B: Yeah, I just finished my midterm test. 是啊，我剛考完期中考。
A: Take a rest. 休息一下吧。

## You don't look good.
**你的臉色看起來不好。**

A: You don't look good. 你的臉色看起來不好。
B: Thanks. 謝謝關心。
A: No, I'm serious. You should be in bed.
　不，我是説真的。你應該去休息一下。
B: I know. 我知道。

## You look pale.
**你的臉色很蒼白。**

A: Are you OK? 妳還好吧？
B: Yeah, why? 還好，怎麼啦？
A: You look pale. 妳的臉色很蒼白耶。
B: I'm okay. 我還好啦。

# 15 I don't feel good.

11-15.mp3

我不太舒服。

　　身體感覺不舒服的時候，英文可以說 "I don't feel good."，比較嚴重可以說 "I'm sick." 或是 "I feel sick."。

A: Hello, doctor. 哈囉，醫生。
B: What seems to be the problem? 你哪裡不舒服呢？
A: I don't feel good. I've got a cough. 覺得身體不太舒服，還有點咳嗽。

## I'm sick.
我病了。

A: I'm sick. 我病了。
B: Did you take some aspirin? 妳有沒有吃些阿斯匹靈啊？
A: This morning. 今天早上有吃。

## I feel sick.
我感覺不舒服。

A: I feel sick. 我感覺不舒服。
B: Me too. Let's take a break. 我也是耶，我們休息一下吧。
A: OK. Want some aspirin? 好啊，要吃幾顆阿斯匹靈嗎？
B: Sure. 好。

# ⑯ She's pregnant.

**她懷孕了。**

11-16.mp3

「懷孕」的英文叫做 pregnant，但是，美國人比較常用 expect（期待）的進行式 expecting，表示是「期待著孩子誕生」的意思。

A: Sally's pregnant. 莎莉懷孕了。
B: Who's the father? 孩子的爸爸是誰啊？
A: I don't know. 我不知道。

## She's expecting.
**她懷孕了。**

這個句型採用 expecting 的說法。「她的預產期在下個禮拜」的英文是 "She is expecting her baby next week."。

A: Are you expecting? 妳懷孕了嗎？
B: Yes. I'm due in August. 是啊，預產期在 8 月。
A: How nice! I'm so happy for you. 太好了，我真為妳感到高興。

## When are you due?
**妳的預產期是什麼時候？**

A: When are you due? 妳的預產期是什麼時候？
B: Next month. 下個月。

\* due 是「預定…」的意思，除了用在預產期之外，也可以用來說明飛機或火車預定到達的時間。

# ⑰ Oh, isn't she cute?

11-17.mp3

## 噢，她是不是很可愛呀？

見到別人的小孩一定要很用力地誇讚孩子長得很可愛啦、很漂亮之類的，小孩子的父母親才會樂不可支。那麼，有人知道這句話之後該怎麼說嗎？你可以說 "Can I hold her?"（我可以抱抱她嗎？）。

A: Oh, isn't she cute? Can I hold her?

噢，她是不是很可愛呀？我可以抱她嗎？

B: Sure. 當然可以。

A: What's her name? 她叫什麼名字？

B: Anne. 安。

# She's got her father's nose.
### 她的鼻子像她爸爸。

我們在形容某人長得像另一個人時，第一個想到的英文單字可能是 resemble 或是 look like，但是美國人比較常用 get 或是 have, just like 等。

A: Oh, she's beautiful. 噢，她真漂亮。

B: Yeah, I think she's got her father's nose. 是啊，我想她的鼻子像她爸爸。

A: Yes. 是啊。

# He has his mother's eyes.
### 他的眼睛像他媽媽。

A: Look at him! He has his mother's eyes. 看看他！眼睛像他媽媽呢。

B: Yeah! 對啊！

# ⑱ I'm so sorry for your loss.

11-18.mp3

**我（對於你失去親人）感到很遺憾。**

　　我們去別人家裡弔喪時，常會對喪主說「我很遺憾」聊表慰問。美國在這方面的作法和我們差不多，會輕輕地擁抱喪主及其家人，然後說一聲 "I'm sorry."。

A: I'm so sorry for your loss. 我感到很遺憾。

B: Thank you. 謝謝你的安慰。

A: If you need anything at all, just call me. 有什麼需要的就打電話給我。

B: Thanks. 謝謝。


## You're in our prayers.
**我們會為您祈禱的。**

A: I'm sorry. 我感到很遺憾。

B: Thank you. 謝謝妳。

A: You're in our prayers. 我們會為你祈禱的。

# COOL ENGLISH

時下美國年輕人常用的說法

11-x1.mp3

## I feel cooped up. 我快被悶死了。

待在家裡太久開始覺得煩悶，此時說 "I feel cooped up." 是指「我一直悶在家裡」的意思。

A: Why do you want to go out? 你為何想出去？
B: I feel cooped up. 我快被悶死了。

## You're such a couch potato.
## 你真是個電視迷耶。

couch 是指寬大的美式沙發，potato 是指馬鈴薯，由此看來，這是用來形容整天都坐在沙發上啃洋芋片看電視的人。

A: I stayed home all weekend and watched TV.
　　整個週末我都待在家裡看電視。
B: You're such a couch potato. 你真是個電視迷耶。

## I need to get some shut eye.
## 我要去閉目養神一下。

shut 是指「關上、閉起」的意思。

A: Where are you going? 你要去哪裡啊？
B: I need to get some shut eye. 我需要去閉目養神一下。

## I'm really burned out. 我真的快不行了。

burn out 用來形容「體力透支」的狀態。

A: You really look tired. 妳看起來很累。
B: I'm really burned out. I've been studying all night.
　　我真的快不行了，我整晚都在唸書。

★請在以下空格中填入適當的單字★

Are you __1__ later tonight? 今晚你有空嗎？

Can I __2__ your coat? 我來幫你拿外套好嗎？

Would you like to __3__ ? 你要不要留下來吃晚餐？

Thank you for __4__ us. 謝謝你邀請我們。

She's __5__ her father's nose. 她的鼻子像她爸爸。

Can I __6__ to your place tonight? 今晚我可以去你家嗎？

I was __7__ in traffic. 我遇到塞車了。

When are you __8__ ? 妳的預產期是什麼時候？

Would you __9__ the table? 你可以擺一下餐具嗎？

You'd better take a __10__ . 你最好去休息一下。

---

| | | | |
|---|---|---|---|
| 1. free | 2. take | 3. stay for dinner | |
| 4. inviting | 5. got | 6. come over | 7. stuck |
| 8. due | 9. set | 10. rest | |

★請在以下空格中填入適當的單字★

A: Where have you been? 你到哪裡去了啊？

B: Oh, ___1___ Sorry. 噢，我睡過頭了，對不起。

A: It's okay. 沒關係。

A: Hey, Bill. What time is it? 嘿，比爾，現在幾點啦？

B: It's five. 五點。

A: What? Five o'clock? ___2___ 啊？五點？我該走了。

B: Would you like to stay for dinner?
你要不要留下來吃晚餐？

A: ___3___ for your loss. 我感到很遺憾。

B: Thank you. 謝謝你的安慰。

A: If you need anything at all, just call me.
有什麼需要的就打電話給我。

B: Thanks. 謝謝。

A: Please come in. ___4___ 歡迎，請坐。

B: Thanks. It's really hot out there. 謝謝。外頭實在很熱。

A: Yeah. 是啊。

1. I overslept.          2. I have to go.
3. I'm so sorry          4. Have a seat.

# 用 1、2 個單字
# 就能說出好英語！

學習英語的讀者，尤其對於初學者來說，用比較有趣且簡短的方式學習，進而熟稔英文是必要的途徑。捨棄冗長且無趣的英文長句，希望各位讀者都能藉由短短的「三言兩語」體認學英語的樂趣。本章內容嚴選使用機率最高的英語短句，每一句都是時下老外最常採用的說法喔。

# Chapter 12

# 絕對讓老外
# 大吃一驚的
# 22 種最 in 英語

"Deal?" 和 "So what?"，"Try some!" 以及 "How come?"，"It's up to you." …這些是老外彼此交談頻繁使用的短句。但是，像我們這些「外國人」幾乎不太可能會想到這些用語。因為，若非身處其境，其實並不容易具備這種語言的敏感度。

本章彙整了多個時下最常使用的會話短句，能讓老外一聽便感到驚訝：「你竟然知道這些用語？！」希望各位讀者試著將這些英文變成屬於自己的一部分，輕鬆應用在日常生活上。

# ① **Almost.** 幾乎。

12-01.mp3

A: Almost ready? 好了嗎？
B: Almost. 快了。
A: Hurry, please. 快一點，拜託。

A: I'm almost done. 我快做好了。
B: What are you doing? 你在做什麼？
A: School work. 做學校作業。

# ② **It's you!** 原來是你！

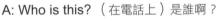

12-02.mp3

A: Who is this? （在電話上）是誰啊？
B: This is Sam. 我是山姆。
A: Oh, it's you! 噢，原來是你啊！

A: Who's the murderer? 誰是兇手？
B: I don't know. 我不知道。
A: It's you, isn't it? 就是你，不是嗎？

＊ 逛街買衣服的時候，店員說「很適合你」的英文也可以用 "It's you!" 來表達。

# ③ **So what?** 那又怎麼樣呢？

12-03.mp3

A: I got a present. 我收到了一件禮物。
B: So what? 那又怎麼樣呢？
A: I love presents! 我喜歡禮物！

A: I have a car. 我有一部車子。
B: So what? 那又怎麼樣呢？
A: Not everybody does. 不是每個人都有耶。

## ④ What? 什麼？

12-04.mp3

A: I ate a pizza. 我吃了比薩。
B: What? 什麼？
A: Didn't you hear me? 你沒聽到我說話嗎？

A: What? 什麼？
B: I said I'll see you later. 我說再見。
A: Oh, okay. 噢，好。

## ⑤ Yourself? 你呢？

12-05.mp3

A: How are you? 妳近來如何？
B: I'm good. Yourself? 我還好，你呢？
A: I'm fine. 我也滿好的。

A: I'm tired. Yourself? 我好累，你呢？
B: Yes, I am, too. 對啊，我也是。
A: Let's rest. 我們休息一下吧。

## ⑥ Relax. 別激動。

12-06.mp3

A: I hate that guy! 我討厭那個人！
B: Relax. 冷靜一點。
A: No, I won't relax! 不行，我沒法冷靜！

A: He hit me! 他打我耶！
B: Take it easy. He didn't mean to. 放輕鬆一點，他不是故意的。
A: How do you know? 你怎麼知道？

# ❼ No way. 不行。

12-07.mp3

A: Feed the bear. 去餵那隻熊吧。

B: No way. 不要。

A: You'll be safe. 你會很安全的。

A: Go to school. 去上學。

B: No way! 不要！

A: Why not? 為什麼不要？

# ❽ Forget it. 休想。

12-08.mp3

A: Give me some money. 給我一些錢。

B: Forget it. 休想。

A: Please? 求求妳好不好？

A: Would you help me? 請妳幫幫我好嗎？

B: Forget it. 休想。

A: Are you still mad? 妳還在生氣啊？

# ❾ Got that. 知道了。

12-09.mp3

A: Do you have milk on the list? 購物清單上有沒有牛奶？

B: Yes, got that. 有。

A: What about bread? 那麵包呢？

A: Clean the house today. 今天要打掃家裡喔。

B: OK, got that. 好，我會的。

A: Thank you. 謝謝。

## ⑩ Deal? （協商條件或約定某事）可以了嗎？

12-10.mp3

A: Deal? 可以了嗎？
B: Sure, it's a deal. 當然，可以了。
A: Good. 太好了。

A: Is it a deal? 我們算是達成共識囉？
B: I don't know. 我不確定。
A: Think about it. 考慮一下嘛。

＊商務會議中彼此確認「達成協議了嗎」，就會說這句話。

## ⑪ Hold on. 等一下。

12-11.mp3

A: Get off the phone. 該掛電話了啦。
B: Hold on. 等一下嘛。
A: I need to use the phone! 我要用電話！

A: Hi, is James home? 嗨，詹姆斯在家嗎？
B: Hold on. I'll check. 請等一下，我去看一下。
A: Okay. 好的。

## ⑫ Take care. 保重。

12-12.mp3

A: It was nice seeing you. 很高興見到你。
B: Take care. 保重喔。
A: You too. 你也是。

A: Take care of yourself. 好好照顧自己。
B: I will. 我會的。
A: I'll see you later. 再見。

# ⑬ Like what? 比如說？

12-13.mp3

A: Do you want to do something? 你想做什麼嗎？
B: Like what? 比如說？
A: Go golfing? 去打高爾夫球？

A: Do you like movies? 你喜歡看電影嗎？
B: Like what? 比如說？
A: I don't know. Any movies. 我不知道，隨便哪一部囉。

# ⑭ Guess what? 猜猜看？

12-14.mp3

A: Guess what? 猜猜看？
B: What? 什麼？
A: I'm pregnant. 我懷孕了。

A: Guess what? 猜猜看？
B: What? 什麼
A: I have a job. 我找到工作了。

# ⑮ How come? 為什麼呢？

12-15.mp3

A: I have to go. 我得走了。
B: How come? 為什麼呢？
A: It's late. 很晚了。

A: I can't eat. 我吃不下了。
B: How come? 為什麼呢？
A: I ate earlier. 稍早我吃過了。

## ⑯ Just checking.

只是問問罷了。

12-16.mp3

A: How tall are you? 妳有多高？
B: 5' 11". Why? 五呎十一吋，做什麼？
A: Just checking. 只是問問罷了。

A: Are you done? 妳做完了嗎？
B: No, not yet. 沒有，還沒。
A: Okay. Just checking. 好吧，我只是隨口問問。

## ⑰ It's up to you. 隨你囉。

12-17.mp3

A: What should I do? 我該做什麼呢？
B: It's up to you. 隨你囉。
A: I know. 我知道了。

A: What college should I go to? 我該上哪一所大學呢？
B: It's up to you. 隨你囉。
A: This college sounds good. 這間學校聽起來不錯。

## ⑱ You're kidding.

你在開玩笑吧。

12-18.mp3

A: I won the lottery! 我中樂透了！
B: You're kidding. 妳在開玩笑吧。
A: No, I'm not! 不，我是說真的！

A: He asked me out. 他約我出去耶。
B: You're kidding. 妳在開玩笑吧。
A: No, I'm not! 不，我不是在開玩笑！

## ⑲ Give me a break.

你得了吧。

12-19.mp3

A: I went on a date with him. 我和他去約會了。
B: Give me a break. 妳得了吧。
A: I'm serious! 我是認真的啦！

A: I'm a good singer. 我很會唱歌。
B: Give me a break. 妳得了吧。
A: I am! 我真的會！

## ⑳ Try some. 嚐一些看看。

12-20.mp3

A: Try some beer. 嚐一些啤酒。
B: I don't drink beer. 我不喝啤酒。
A: Try it anyway. 喝一點試試看嘛。

A: Try some of this drink. 喝喝看這個飲料。
B: Is it good? 好喝嗎？
A: It will surprise you. 會讓你驚喜喔。

## ㉑ I don't care. 我無所謂。

12-21.mp3

A: It's Sunday. 今天是星期天。
B: I don't care. 我無所謂。
A: You have to go to church! 你得去教會！

A: You hurt me. 你傷了我。
B: I don't care. 我不在乎。
A: You don't care about me? 你不在乎我嗎？

## 22 And stuff like that.

類似那些東西。

12-22.mp3

A: We need some fruit. 我們需要一些水果。

B: What fruit? 哪些水果？

A: Apples, oranges, and stuff like that. 蘋果、柳橙，類似那些東西。


A: He has lots of toys. 他有很多玩具。

B: What kind of toys? 什麼樣的玩具？

A: Balls, little toys, and stuff like that. 球、小玩具，類似那些東西。

＊此句經常放在舉例的末尾。

# Chapter 13

# 住過美國才知道的
# 22 種道地說法

　　各位有沒有聽過 "awesome" 這個字？有人覺得是「可怕」的意思嗎？以往的字典可能只有這個解釋。其實，老外說這個字時並不是指這個意思，他們會用它來表示「了不起到可怕的程度」。

　　如果聽到老外高喊 "Awesome!"，表示他們很高興，是對於很棒的事物發出的讚嘆。如果想說「可怕的」，則經常會用 awful 這個形態相似但含義卻相去甚遠的字。

　　接下來，我們就一起來了解像 "Awesome!" 這種美國的道地用語吧。

# ① Whatever. 什麼都可以。

13-01.mp3

A: What do you want to do? 你想做什麼事呢？
B: Whatever you want. 只要妳想的，什麼都可以。
A: Well, I don't know what I want to do. 嗯，我不知道我想做什麼耶。

A: You're stupid! 你真是個笨蛋！
B: Whatever. 管妳怎麼說。
A: Don't say that to me! 別那樣回應我。

# ② Ditto. 我也是。

13-02.mp3

A: I love you. 我愛妳。
B: Ditto. 我也是。
A: Can't you say it? 妳就不能說出來嗎？

A: I like popcorn. 我喜歡爆米花。
B: Ditto. 我也是。
A: It's the best. 爆米花最好吃了。

＊也可以說 "Me too."。

# ③ Exactly. 的確。

13-03.mp3

A: What time is it? 現在幾點了？
B: It's exactly 3:05. 精確來說是三點五分。
A: Thanks. 謝謝。

A: How many cups are there? 有幾個杯子？
B: Ten. 十個。
A: Exactly? 正好十個嗎？

## ④ **Well.** 這個嘛。

13-04.mp3

A: Do you have a boyfriend? 妳有男朋友嗎？
B: Well, not really. 這個嘛，不算有。
A: What does that mean? 那是什麼意思？

A: Well, I'll see you later. 這個嘛，再見囉。
B: Okay. 好吧。
A: Bye. 拜。

## ⑤ **Incredible!** 真不可思議！

13-05.mp3

A: I climbed a mountain. 我去爬山了。
B: Incredible! 真不敢相信！
A: Yes, it was a big mountain. 是啊，那是一座高山呢。

A: Look at my house. 看看我的房子。
B: Incredible. It's huge. 真不可思議，它好大。
A: Thank you. 謝謝。

## ⑥ **Awesome!** 真有趣！（了不起！）

13-06.mp3

A: How do you like the game? 妳覺得這遊戲怎麼樣？
B: It's awesome! 真有趣！
A: I think so, too. 我也這麼覺得。

A: Awesome! I like your bike! 真了不起！我喜歡你的單車！
B: Thanks. 謝謝。
A: Is it new? 是新的嗎？

* awesome 的相反詞是 awful。

## ⑦ Time's up. 時間到了。

13-07.mp3

A: Time's up. Hand in your papers. 時間到，交出妳的考卷。

B: I'm not finished yet. 我還沒寫完耶。

A: Too bad. Time's up. 太可惜了，時間到了。


A: Time's up. 時間到。

B: I just finished. 我剛好寫完。

A: Give me your paper. 把妳的考卷給我。


## ⑧ Why not? 為什麼不行？

13-08.mp3

A: Can you come? 你可以來嗎？

B: No. 不行。

A: Why not? 為什麼不行？


A: You can't come with me. 妳不能跟我一起來。

B: Why not? 為什麼不行？

A: Because I said so. 因為我說不行。


## ⑨ Can't complain.
### 好得沒話說。

13-09.mp3

A: How was your new house? 你的新家怎麼樣？

B: Can't complain. 好得沒話說。

A: It's okay, then? 那麼，都還好囉？


A: You have a great wife. 你有個好老婆。

B: I can't complain. 好得沒話說。

A: I want a good husbund, too. 我也想有個好老公。

# ❿ **Kind of.** 有一點。

13-10.mp3

A: Are you busy? 你在忙嗎？
B: Kind of. Can you call later? 有一點，妳可以晚一點再打來嗎？
A: Okay. 好。

A: Do you like me? 你喜歡我嗎？
B: Kind of. 一點點啦。
A: Well, I like you. 嗯，我喜歡你。

# ⓫ **Not really.** 並不全然是。

13-11.mp3

A: Did you have fun? 妳玩得開心嗎？
B: Not really. 並不全然是。
A: Why not? 為什麼不呢？

A: Can you see? 妳看到了嗎？
B: Not really. 看不太清楚。
A: Try these glasses on. 戴這副眼鏡試看看。

＊通常用來表達否定的意味。

# ⓬ **Good job.** 做得好。

13-12.mp3

A: Good job. 做得好。
B: Thanks. 謝謝。
A: Will you work for me again? 可以請妳再幫我一次嗎？

A: I'm finished. 我完成了。
B: Good job. 做得好。
A: I'm glad to be done. 我很高興做完了。

## ⑬ Same here. 我也是。

13-13.mp3

A: I didn't eat breakfast. 我沒有吃早餐。
B: Same here. 我也是。
A: Why didn't you? 你為什麼沒有吃啊？

A: I love women. 我喜歡女人。
B: Same here. 我也是。
A: What do you like best about them? 你最喜歡她們的什麼地方？

＊這裡的 here 是指「我」的意思。

## ⑭ That's it. 就是那樣。

13-14.mp3

A: Is this high enough? 這樣夠高了嗎？
B: That's it. Stay still. 就是那樣，不要動喔。
A: Okay. 好。

A: Should I park the car here? 我該把車子停在這裡嗎？
B: That's it. Thanks. 就是那裡，謝謝。
A: No problem. 別客氣。

## ⑮ You doing okay?
你還好吧？

13-15.mp3

A: I don't feel like playing. 我不想玩。
B: Are you doing okay? 妳還好吧？
A: Yes, I'm fine. 嗯，我還好。

A: You doing okay? 妳還好吧？
B: Of course. You? 當然，你呢？
A: I'm fine. 我還不錯。

**16 Who cares?** 誰在乎？

13-16.mp3

A: I'm the president! 我是會長耶！
B: Who cares? 誰在乎？
A: I do. 我在乎。

A: I found a neat rock. 我找到了一顆漂亮的石頭。
B: Who cares? 誰在乎？
A: Do you want to see it? 你想不想看一下？

**17 It's about time.**
該是時候了。

13-17.mp3

A: I'm here. 我來了。
B: It's about time. 也該是時候了。
A: Did you miss me? 妳想我嗎？

A: It's about time you got here. 你早該到這裡了。
B: Sorry I'm late. 對不起，我遲到了。
A: Where were you? 你到哪裡去了？

**18 Is that clear?**
（我的意思）懂了嗎？

13-18.mp3

A: Is that clear? 懂了嗎？
B: I think so. 應該是吧。
A: Do you understand? 妳到底懂不懂啊？

A: Is that clear? 妳懂我的意思嗎？
B: I'm not sure. 我不確定。
A: What don't you understand? 哪一點還不懂？

＊相似的説法還有我們熟悉的 "Do you understand?"。

# ⑲ Listen up! 聽好！

13-19.mp3

A: Listen up! 聽好！

B: We're listening. 我們在聽。

A: I have some new rules for you. 我有些新規定要告訴你們。

A: Listen up, everybody! 大家聽好！

B: We're listening. 我們在聽。

A: I need to tell you something. 我要告訴你們一些事情。

# ⑳ No kidding. 是真的。

13-20.mp3

A: Are you serious? 妳是說真的嗎？

B: Yes, no kidding. 是啊，是真的。

A: I don't believe you. 我不相信妳。

A: She asked me out. 她約我出去呢。

B: No kidding? 真的嗎？

A: Yes, no kidding. 是啊，是真的。

# ㉑ I appreciate it. 感謝你。

13-21.mp3

A: Thanks for the help. 謝謝妳的幫忙。

B: No problem. 不客氣。

A: I appreciate it. 我很感謝妳。

A: You helped a lot. 妳幫了我很多忙。

B: I guess I did. 我想也是。

A: I appreciate it. 我很感謝妳。

## ㉒ I swear. 我發誓。

A: That isn't my gun. I swear! 那不是我的槍，我發誓！

B: I don't believe you. 我不相信你。

A: I'm telling the truth! 我說的是事實啊！

A: I swear I didn't do it! 我發誓我沒有做！

B: Prove it. 證明給我看啊。

A: I can't. 我不能。

# Chapter 14

# 每天一定會說到的
# 25 種原味英語

在這一章裡，我們來看看每天一定會用到的一些基本短句，像是 "Nothing."、"Never?"、 "Anytime."、"Say again?"、"No problem." 等等。透過這些我們熟悉而且每天都用得到的基本句型，我們能夠更貼近英語會話。

此外，如果發現自己原先所知的並不是正確的說法，或者沒有正確了解意義，請藉由這一次的學習糾正自己。來吧，讓自己的英文更道地！

# ① Fine. 好。

A: How are you? 你過得怎麼樣？
B: I'm fine. 我過得很好。
A: Good. 那就好。

A: I don't want to listen to you. 我不想聽你說。
B: Fine. 好吧。
A: Good-bye. 再見。

＊雖然是表示「過得好」、「好」的意思，但並非是 100% 正面的回答。

# ② Okay. 好的。

A: Are you okay? 妳還好嗎？
B: Yes, okay. 嗯，滿好的。
A: I'm worried about you. 我很擔心妳耶。

A: Go to school. 該上學了。
B: Okay. 好。
A: Hurry. 快點。

# ③ Nothing. 沒什麼。

A: What's wrong? 有什麼不對嗎？
B: Nothing. 沒什麼啦。
A: Are you sure? 是嗎？

A: What are you doing? 你在做什麼？
B: Nothing. 沒什麼。
A: Want to do something? 想不想找些事情做？

# ❹ Never? 從來都沒有？

14-04.mp3

A: I've never done this before. 我以前從來沒做過。
B: Never? 從來都沒有？
A: Like I said, never. 像我剛才講的，從來都沒有。

A: I'll never go out with you. 我絕對不會跟妳出去約會。
B: Are you sure? 你確定？
A: Yes, I'm sure! 是啊，我確定！

# ❺ Great! 太好了！

14-05.mp3

A: I'm having fun, are you? 我玩得很開心，你呢？
B: Sure. 我也這麼覺得。
A: That's great! 太棒了！

A: I'll be at the party. 我會出席派對。
B: Great! 太好了！
A: Okay, I'll see you there. 好，派對上見囉。

# ❻ Sure. 好啊。

14-06.mp3

A: Would you like to come with me? 你想跟我去嗎？
B: Sure. 好啊。
A: Let's go. 那我們走吧。

A: Do you want some coffee? 你想喝點咖啡嗎？
B: Sure. 好啊。
A: I'll buy you some. 我請你。

# ❼ Anytime. 任何時候。

14-07.mp3

A: Thanks for helping. 謝謝你的幫忙。
B: Anytime. 任何時候需要幫忙都可以找我。
A: You're a good friend. 你真是個不錯的朋友。

A: Come to my house anytime. 任何時候都可以來我家。
B: Okay, I will. 好，我會的。
A: I'll see you later. 再見。

# ❽ Thanks. 謝謝。

14-08.mp3

A: Thanks for being a friend. 謝謝你做我的朋友。
B: No problem. 別客氣。
A: You're a good friend. 你真是個不錯的朋友。

A: Thanks for helping. 謝謝你的幫忙。
B: It was my pleasure. 那是我的榮幸。
A: I'm glad you helped. 很高興你幫了我。

# ❾ Please. 拜託。

14-09.mp3

A: I can't help you. 我無法幫你。
B: Please. 拜託。
A: I'm busy. 我很忙啊。

A: Help me. 幫幫我吧。
B: I can't. 我沒有辦法。
A: Please. 求求妳。

## ❿ Say again?
### 你說什麼？（再說一次？）

14-10.mp3

A: I'm dead. 我死了。
B: Say again? 妳說什麼？
A: I'm in big trouble. 我有大麻煩了。

A: I ate fish. 我吃了魚。
B: Say again? 再說一次？
A: You know, fish. 你知道的嘛，魚啊。

## ⓫ Right? 對嗎？

14-11.mp3

A: It's seven miles to the city, right?
　　到那座城市還有七英哩，對嗎？
B: Yes, you're correct. 是的，沒有錯。
A: I thought so. 我想應該是。

A: She's cute. 她好可愛喔。
B: She's your sister, right? 她是你妹妹，對嗎？
A: Yes, but she's still cute. 是啊，不過，就算是我妹妹也實在太可愛了。

## ⓬ That's right. 是的。

14-12.mp3

A: Did you earn some money? 你有賺到一些錢嗎？
B: That's right. 是啊。
A: How much? 賺了多少？

A: I turn left here, right? 我應該在這裡左轉，對嗎？
B: That's right. 是的。
A: Okay. 知道了。

## ⑬ No problem. 沒問題。

14-13.mp3

A: Can I stay at your house? 我可以待在你家嗎？
B: No problem. 沒問題啊。
A: I'm glad it's no problem. 幸好沒有問題。

A: I can't come to the party. 我不能去派對了。
B: No problem. 不要緊。
A: You aren't upset? 你不生氣嗎？

## ⑭ Not bad. 還不錯。

14-14.mp3

A: How are you? 妳好嗎？
B: Not bad. You? 還不錯，你呢？
A: I'm good. 我還好。

A: She's pretty. 她滿漂亮的喔。
B: Yeah, not bad. 是啊，還不錯。
A: Just not bad? I think she's beautiful.
還不錯而已嗎？我覺得她滿美的耶。

## ⑮ Of course. 當然。

14-15.mp3

A: Are you married? 你結婚了嗎？
B: Of course. 當然。
A: I see. 喔。

A: Is this your dog? 這是你的狗嗎？
B: Of course. 是啊。
A: I should have known. 我早該知道的。

## ⑯ Me too. 我也是。

14-16.mp3

A: I like country music. 我喜歡鄉村音樂。
B: Me too. 我也是。
A: It's the best. 鄉村音樂最棒了。

A: I need to take a shower. 我得去洗個澡了。
B: Me too. 我也是。
A: Okay. 那就這樣了。

## ⑰ Come on. 走吧。

14-17.mp3

A: We're leaving now. 我們該離開囉。
B: I'm not ready. 我還沒有準備好。
A: Yes you are. Come on. 可以了啦，走吧。

A: I'm your real father. 我是你的親生父親。
B: Come on. No you aren't. 別說笑了，你才不是呢。
A: I was just kidding. 我只是開個玩笑。

## ⑱ Any questions?
有任何問題嗎？

14-18.mp3

A: Any questions? 有任何問題嗎？
B: Yes. 有。
A: What's your question? 妳有什麼問題？

A: Any questions? 有任何問題嗎？
B: No. 沒有。
A: Okay, get to work then. 好的，那開始工作吧。

# ⑲ Are you sure? 你確定？

14-19.mp3

A: Are you ready? 準備好了嗎？
B: Yes. 是啊。
A: Are you sure? 妳確定？

A: That's him! 就是他！
B: Are you sure? 妳確定？
A: I think so. 我想是吧。

# ⑳ I don't think so.
## 我不認為。

14-20.mp3

A: Do you want to go golfing? 妳想不想去打高爾夫球？
B: I don't think so. 我不想去。
A: Why not? 為什麼不想？

A: Is that her? 那是她嗎？
B: I don't think so. 我不認為是她。
A: Is she taller? 她長高了嗎？

# ㉑ Let's go. 走吧。

14-21.mp3

A: Are you ready? 妳準備好了嗎？
B: Yes. 好了。
A: Let's go. 我們走吧。

A: Let's go. 走吧。
B: I'm not ready. 我還沒準備好耶。
A: Hurry up. 快一點啦。

## ㉒ I'm sorry. 我很抱歉。

14-22.mp3

A: You lied to me. 你騙我。
B: I'm sorry. 我很抱歉。
A: Why did you do it? 你為什麼要那麼做？

A: I'm sorry I hurt you. 我很抱歉我傷了妳。
B: Don't do it again. 別再那樣。
A: I won't. 我不會了。

## ㉓ Don't worry. 別擔心。

14-23.mp3

A: I'm sorry. 我很抱歉。
B: Don't worry about it. 別在意。
A: Okay. 好的。

A: I'm late for work. 我上班遲到了。
B: Don't worry about it. 別擔心。
A: The boss hates it when I'm late. 老闆最討厭我遲到了。

## ㉔ I didn't mean it.
我不是那個意思。

14-24.mp3

A: You insulted me. 你侮辱我。
B: I didn't mean it. 我不是那個意思。
A: Yes, you did. 你明明就是。

A: I didn't mean it. 我不是那個意思。
B: Then don't say it. 那就不要那樣說。
A: I'm sorry. 我很抱歉。

# 25 **Really?** 真的嗎？

14-25.mp3

A: I bought a new CD. 我買了一張新的 CD。
B: Really? 真的嗎？
A: Yes. Want to see it? 是啊，你要看嗎？

A: A war started. 戰爭爆發了。
B: Really? 真的嗎？
A: Yes, I saw it on the news. 是啊，我看到新聞了。

# Chapter 15

# 讓英語表達更生動的
# 22 個私房句大公開

　　就算只是短短的幾句話，如果能運用得當，也有可能讓平凡的對話生

動起來。即使是很普通的對話，只要用帶有情感的「一、兩個單字」，就

能搖身一變成為生動活潑的表達方式。

　　接下來，我們會透過 That's true.（那是真的。）、After you.（你

先。）、It takes time.（需要一點時間。）、Time to go.（該走了。）之

類的短句，就像會話中的潤滑劑一樣，能為你的英文能力錦上添花。希望

各位都能仔細閱讀，並且在生活中加以善用。

# ❶ So-so. 還可以。

15-01.mp3

A: How are you? 你好嗎？
B: So-so. 還可以。
A: Is everything okay? 過得還順利嗎？

A: How is your brother? 你的弟弟還好嗎？
B: So-so. 還可以。
A: I heard he's in the hospital. 我聽說他住院了。

# ❷ Terrible. 糟糕透了。

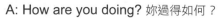

15-02.mp3

A: How are you doing? 妳過得如何？
B: Terrible. 很糟。
A: What's wrong? 怎麼了？

A: That movie was terrible. 那部電影好爛。
B: Yes, it was a bad one. 是啊，是一部差勁的電影。
A: It's the worst I've ever seen. 是我看過最爛的電影。

# ❸ So? 所以呢？

15-03.mp3

A: I don't feel good. 我覺得不舒服。
B: So? 所以呢？
A: I can't work when I'm sick. 我沒辦法在生病時工作。

A: Tomorrow is Sunday. 明天是星期天。
B: So? 所以呢？
A: I'm going to church. 我要去教會。

## ④ That's impossible.
### 難以置信。（那是不可能的。）

15-04.mp3

A: I won a million dollars! 我贏了一百萬美金！
B: That's impossible. 不可能的。
A: It really does happen! 它真的發生了！

A: I found money. 我撿到錢了。
B: That's impossible. 不可能的。
A: Why is it so impossible? 為什麼會不可能？

## ⑤ That's true. 那是真的。

15-05.mp3

A: Men are pigs. 男人都是沙豬。
B: So are women. 女人也一樣。
A: That's true. 那是事實。

A: You don't have to work tomorrow. 明天你不必上班。
B: Yes, but I like my work. 是啊，但我喜歡我的工作。
A: That's true. 那是真的。

## ⑥ What else? 還有其他的嗎？

15-06.mp3

A: Get me some milk. 拿一些牛奶給我。
B: What else? 還要其他的嗎？
A: Some eggs, too. 順便給我幾顆雞蛋。

A: What is on the table? 桌上有什麼東西？
B: A pen. 一枝筆。
A: What else? 還有其他的嗎？

# ⑦ Not me. 不是我。

15-07.mp3

A: Who broke my mirror? 誰弄破了我的鏡子？

B: Not me. 不是我。

A: Who did, then? 那會是誰？

A: Who stole my car? 誰偷了我的車子？

B: Not me. 不是我。

A: I know that. 我知道。

＊練習時若能再加上否認的手勢會更逼真。

# ⑧ Nothing much.
## 還不是老樣子。

15-08.mp3

A: What's up? 最近過得怎麼樣？

B: Nothing much. You? 還不是老樣子，你呢？

A: Nothing much here either. 我也差不多。

A: What do you see? 妳看到什麼？

B: Nothing much. 沒什麼不一樣啊。

A: Okay. 是喔。

# ⑨ Got it. 知道了。

15-09.mp3

A: Do you understand? 懂了嗎？

B: Yes. Got it. 嗯，懂了。

A: Good. 很好。

A: Get it? 懂了沒？

B: Got it. 懂。

A: Good. 很好。

## ⑩ After you. 你先。

15-10.mp3

A: Are you entering the building? 妳要進去大樓嗎？
B: After you. 你先。
A: Oh, thank you. 噢，謝謝妳。

A: After you. 你先。
B: No, ladies first. 不，女士優先
A: You're such a gentleman. 你真是位紳士。

## ⑪ Think twice. 再考慮一下。

15-11.mp3

A: Think twice about your decision. 再考慮一下你的決定。
B: Did I make the right choice? 我的決定是正確的嗎？
A: Perhaps. 或許吧。

A: I don't like her. 我不喜歡她。
B: Think twice before you tell her that. 在你告訴她之前再考慮一下。
A: Yes, I will. 嗯，我會的。

## ⑫ What for? 為什麼？

15-12.mp3

A: Give her this note. 把這張紙條拿給她。
B: What for? 為什麼？
A: Please just do it. 拿給她就對了。

A: Mow my lawn, please. 麻煩幫我家的草地割草。
B: What for? 為什麼？
A: The grass is high. 草長長了嘛。

## ⓭ Anything new?
有什麼新鮮事嗎？

15-13.mp3

A: Hey, Todd. 嘿，陶德。
B: Hey. Anything new? 嘿，有什麼新鮮事嗎？
A: No, nothing new. 沒有，沒什麼新鮮事。

A: Anything new? 有什麼新鮮事嗎？
B: Not much. You? 沒有，你呢？
A: Nothing. 我也沒有。

## ⓮ What's up? 過得好嗎？

15-14.mp3

A: What's up? 過得好嗎？
B: Not much. 還可以。
A: Not much here either. 我也是。

A: What's up? 近來如何？
B: Well, I got a job. 嗯，我找到工作了。
A: Cool! 酷喔！

＊這句話是 "What have you been up to?" 的簡短說法。

## ⓯ It takes time. 需要一點時間。

15-15.mp3

A: When will the flowers grow? 什麼時候才會開花？
B: It takes time. 需要一點時間。
A: How much time? 要多久？

A: When will I learn how to do this? 我學做這件事要學多久？
B: It takes time. 需要一點時間。
A: I'm so frustrated. 我覺得好灰心。

# 16 **Ready to go?**

## 準備好要走了嗎？

15-16.mp3

A: Ready to go? 準備好要走了嗎？
B: Not yet. 還沒。
A: Tell me when you are. 準備好了再告訴我。

A: Ready to go? 準備好要走了嗎？
B: Yes. 好了。
A: Let's go. 我們走吧。

＊ 這是從 "Are you ready to go?" 中省略 Are you 的說法。

# 17 **Got a minute?** 有空嗎？

15-17.mp3

A: Got a minute? 有空嗎？
B: No, I'm sorry. 沒有，不好意思。
A: That's okay. 沒關係。

A: Got a minute? 有空嗎？
B: Yes. 有啊。
A: I need help with something. 我有事需要幫忙。

# 18 **My mistake.** 是我弄錯了。

15-18.mp3

A: Are you my teacher? 你是我的老師嗎？
B: No, I'm not. 不，我不是。
A: My mistake. 是我弄錯了。

A: Are you Jack? 你是傑克嗎？
B: No, you have the wrong guy. 不，你認錯人了。
A: My mistake. 是我弄錯了。

## ⑲ It's okay. 沒有關係。

15-19.mp3

A: I'm very sorry, I'm late. 非常抱歉，我遲到了。
B: It's okay. 沒有關係。
A: No, it's not. I'm sorry. 不，我很抱歉。

A: I'm sorry. 我很抱歉。
B: It's okay. 沒有關係。
A: You're very forgiving. 你真寬容。

## ⑳ Bingo! 正確！

15-20.mp3

A: Is that his house? 那是他家嗎？
B: Bingo! 正確！
A: We found it! 我們找到了！

A: Are you Ted? 你是泰德嗎？
B: Bingo! 正確！
A: So you're Ted! 所以你就是泰德囉！

## ㉑ Time to go. 該走了。

15-21.mp3

A: Time to go. 該走了。
B: Do we have to go now? 我們一定得現在走嗎？
A: Yes, we do. 是啊，一定要。

A: Time to go. 該走了。
B: I'm busy. 我在忙耶。
A: No, we have to go. 不行，我們得走了。

# 22 Trust me. 相信我。

15-22.mp3

A: Trust me. 相信我吧。

B: Why should I trust you? 我為什麼要相信你？

A: Because I'm telling the truth. 因為我說的是事實。


A: Grab my hand. 抓緊我的手。

B: You'll drop me. 你會把我丟下去。

A: No, I won't. Trust me. 不，我不會的。相信我。

# COOL ENGLISH

## 時下美國年輕人常用的口語英文

15-x1.mp3

## You bet. 當然。（不客氣。）

"You bet." 可以用來表示兩種含義，一個是指 "Sure."，另一個是指 "You're welcome."。

A: Hey! You want some pizza? 嘿！你要不要吃點比薩？

B: You bet.（= Sure.）當然要。

A: Well, you'd better hurry. It's almost gone.
　　嗯，最好快點喔，快被吃光了。

A: Here's your receipt. 這是妳的收據。

B: Thank you. 謝謝。

A: You bet.（= You're welcome.）不客氣。

## Life sucks. 人生爛透了。

suck 有「吸吮、爛透」的意思。

A: What's wrong? 發生了什麼事？

B: Life sucks. 人生爛透了。

A: Any problem? 出了什麼問題嗎？

B: Yeah. I lost my job. 是啊，我失業了。

## Two thumbs up. 太棒了。

遇到令人讚賞的事，我們會豎起大姆指，老外也會。不過，老外習慣同時豎起兩隻姆指，所以才會說 "Two thumbs up."。

A: What do you think of the movie? 你覺得那部電影怎麼樣？

B: Two thumbs up. How about you? 太棒了，妳覺得呢？

A: It was really great. 真的很棒。

# 台灣廣廈 國際出版集團
Taiwan Mansion International Group

國家圖書館出版品預行編目（CIP）資料

用365個單字讓英文會話變簡單/白善燁著；徐若英譯. -- 初版.
-- 新北市：語研學院出版社, 2021.02
　　面；　公分
ISBN 978-986-99644-3-2（平裝）
1.英語　2.會話
805.188　　　　　　　　　　　　　　110000248

## LA PRESS 語研學院
Language Academy Press

# 用365個單字讓英文會話變簡單
## 超好學！不再害怕開口說英語！第一次面對老外就能輕鬆溝通

作　　　者／白善燁　　　　編輯中心編輯長／伍峻宏・編輯／賴敬宗
翻　　　譯／徐若英　　　　封面設計／張家綺・內頁排版／東豪
　　　　　　　　　　　　　製版・印刷・裝訂／東豪・紘億・秉成

行企研發中心總監／陳冠蒨　　媒體公關組／陳柔彣
　　　　　　　　　　　　　　綜合業務組／何欣穎

發　行　人／江媛珍
法律顧問／第一國際法律事務所 余淑杏律師・北辰著作權事務所 蕭雄淋律師
出　　版／國際學村
發　　行／台灣廣廈有聲圖書有限公司
　　　　　地址：新北市235中和區中山路二段359巷7號2樓
　　　　　電話：（886）2-2225-5777・傳真：（886）2-2225-8052

代理印務・全球總經銷／知遠文化事業有限公司
　　　　　地址：新北市222深坑區北深路三段155巷25號5樓
　　　　　電話：（886）2-2664-8800・傳真：（886）2-2664-8801
郵政劃撥／劃撥帳號：18836722
　　　　　劃撥戶名：知遠文化事業有限公司（※單次購書金額未滿1000元需另付郵資70元。）

■出版日期：2021年2月
ISBN：978-986-99644-3-2　　版權所有，未經同意不得重製、轉載、翻印。

영어회화 365 단어로 코쟁이 기죽이기 ©1999 by Baek, Seon Yeob
All rights reserved.
Original Korean edition published by Baek, Seon Yeob
Chinese Translation rights arranged with Baek, Seon Yeob
Chinese Translation Copyright ©2021 by Taiwan Mansion Publishing Co., Ltd.
Through M.J. Agency, in Taipei.